Drama in the Church

a novel by
Dynah Zale

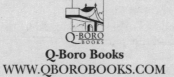
Q-Boro Books
WWW.QBOROBOOKS.COM

An Urban Entertainment Company

Published by Q-Boro Books
Copyright © 2005 by Dynah Zale

ISBN-13: 978-1-933967-58-5
ISBN-10: 1-933967-58-7
First Printing September 2006
Mass Market Edition October 2008

10   9   8   7   6   5   4   3   2   1

This is a work of fiction. It is not meant to depict, portray or represent any particular real persons. All the characters, incidents and dialogues are the products of the author's imagination and are not to be construed as real. Any references or similarities to actual events, entities, real people, living or dead, or to real locales are intended to give the novel a sense of reality. Any similarity in other names, characters, entities, places and incidents is entirely coincidental.

Cover Copyright © 2005 by Q-BORO BOOKS all rights reserved
Cover Layout & Design—Candace K. Cottrell
Cover photo by Ted Mebane
Editors—Melissa Forbes, Candace K. Cottrell
Proofreader—Tee C. Royal

Q-BORO BOOKS
Jamaica, Queens NY 11431
WWW.QBOROBOOKS.COM

Dedication

To my mother, Lorraine Evans.
Your support of my dreams has shown
me just how blessed I am.
You've been more than a mother, but my best
friend.
You encourage me, stand by me, and love me.
I thank God for you every day.
Love, your daughter.

Acknowledgments

To my loving Father in Heaven, Your word has been a lifeline for me throughout the conception of this book, and I pray that every person who reads this will recognize that **ALL THINGS** come from you.

To my BIG brother, Michael Holmes, you have exceeded my expectations of what a big brother is supposed to represent. I love you, not because of what you do, but because of who you are. Your kindness, compassion, and generosity is what places you above all the rest.

To my FIRST brother, Kalee Evans, biology tells us that we're only cousins, but because of our close relationship, you feel more like a brother. We fight and argue like siblings, but I'm glad to say you are one person I can count on. You are there when I call for help and ready to lend a helping hand. You never forget about me, and for that, I love you.

Roxanne Evans, you have been a shining example to me of what a prayer-driven life looks like. You have passed your Godly wisdom down to me and now I'm trying to share that with the world. Thanks for caring, thanks for driving me to all those church conference meetings, and, most of all, thanks for praying for me.

Shantece, Courtney, and Michael Jr., you three are all a part of me. Your spirit and words are kept in my heart and that pushes me to succeed. Auntie loves you XOXO.

I have to shout out my Philly connection. Special thanks go out to Shelly, Gwen, Kathy, and Dana for being true friends. You ladies don't realize how much a simple phone call or letter from each one of you has meant to me. You have kept my spirits up with your words of encouragement, and I truly appreciate every single word.

Macdonald Taylor, you should be a motivational speaker because I can't count the number of times you've called at just the right time to remind me that I CAN DO ALL THINGS THROUGH CHRIST.

A special shout out to my friends down in the ATL: LeKisa Blackmon, Dajuan Boyd, Kimberly Flagg, Alfred Giavance, and Tamiko Young/Miller. Holla at your girl. DramaInTheChurch@hotmail.com. Lil Little, I am thankful to have you as a friend, confidant, and sister in Christ.

Special recognition goes to Tatiana Cody, Monica Fauntleroy, Maurice Lomax, and the entire Evans family. Tatiana's lighthearted wit and humorous critique of the book cover was priceless advice that I couldn't do without. Maurice and Monica, I appreciate your invaluable time that you disposed to me at my convenience. Thanks to my entire family for your support and encouragement. (Janae Gilbert thanks for being my little helper) Hugs and kisses go out to my cousin Leah Long for reading the first three chapters of the book and wanting to read more. I guess I need to put an APB out on Margo Lane Muse because that will be the only way I can get the girl to get in touch with a sistah. (You know I love you from the bottom of my heart.)

To Deborah Mathis, a special friend who extended her help, advice, and expertise. Thank you so much and I hope to work with you again one day.

To Mr. Kenny Johnson, a solider who is overseas defending this country. Stay in prayer, read your bible, and have faith, and before you know it God will be sending you back home to all those who care and love you. You are in my prayers. Love ya.

I need to thank the entire Q-Boro family; from each and every single individual who has read, edited, and touched my book. To those individuals I will be working with in the future. Thanks.

Candace, I once heard a pastor say that angels come to earth as friends and they will bless you at a time when no one else can. I see you as being one of those angels. . . . I'm a firm believer that everything happens for a reason. Our connection was not a chance meeting, but definitely a well-orchestrated plan. Without you, none of this would have been possible. Thanks again.

Last, but definitely not least, Mr. Mark Anthony. You have blessed me with an opportunity that most people only dream of. Thanks for recognizing my talent and being such a versatile visionary that you saw a place for Christian fiction at Q-Boro.

CHAPTER 1

JUNE 2003

Valencia Benson, a twenty-year-old, mocha-brown knockout—which was how most guys referred to her—stood five feet, three inches tall with a small body frame and ample 38D breasts. Her large bust size drew a lot of attention, which at times could be a problem. Guys would approach her just to stare at her chest. She had seriously considered undergoing a breast reduction, but when it came time for her to meet with the doctor, she lost the nerve. Her bust was probably the only part of her body she wanted to change. Val's body closely resembled an Olympic athlete's; her stomach was tight, her thighs were strong, and her booty was firm. She worked out often and drank plenty of water to keep her body fit.

Val tossed her shoulder-length weave over her

shoulder and gazed up at the wooden cross illuminated by light hanging above the pulpit and whispered a silent prayer. *That cross held so much power*, she thought to herself. She had knelt in front of it a zillion times since she was old enough to walk. The cross was a reminder to her that God was her foundation and nothing would break the promise He made to walk with her through life. She often looked to the cross when she was going through bad times, but she was glad to know that God was also there during the good times.

"Here you go, dear. Enjoy the service," came a soft voice.

A startled Val looked up to see Ms. Young handing her a Sunday program. Ms. Young was a member of the prestigious Seniors Club. There were only a few senior members left in the church. All of the others had gone on to see the Savior, but Ms. Young was still biding her time here on Earth. She was a dedicated member who walked a mile to church every Sunday. She never allowed a foot of snow or a deadly hurricane stand in her way of serving the Lord. Val admired Ms. Young's commitment and love for Jesus.

Val loved being a member of First Nazareth A.M.E. Church, where the congregation felt like family. Every Sunday she was always welcomed with a huge smile and a warm hello. Once she entered the church, the Spirit took over and all she could do was sit back and enjoy the ride. The choir shouted praises to the Lord and Reverend Simms jumped for joy at the teachings of God's word.

Although First Nazareth was a small church with

less than seventy-five members listed on its church roster, it still ranked high on the list of lying, scheming, backstabbing, and deception that played out among its members.

Mrs. Simms, the pastor's wife, interrupted Val's thoughts when she began to speak before the congregation. "The time has come for us to bring our burdens to the Lord," she said. "We use this time to tell God what's in our hearts and minds. It's also a time for us to repent to the Lord for the wrong things we've done by thought, word, or deed." She motioned for Olivia to come to the front of the church.

"Church, our dear, sweet Olivia has an announcement to make." Mrs. Simms held Olivia's shaking hand tightly. Silence filled the church. All eyes settled on Olivia, waiting on her to speak. Finally, words began to drift from Olivia's mouth.

"Church, I'm a s-s-sinner," she stammered. "I'm pregnant."

The announcement stunned Val. She stared at her cousin and tried to understand what she was doing. Val thought everyone in the church was a sinner, so for Olivia to make a public announcement was extreme. The congregation replied with disapproving stares and whispers.

The women in the church ran to her, poured oil over her head, and began to speak in tongues. Others caught the Holy Spirit and ran around the church. The remaining members formed a circle around her and held hands while they prayed. They acted as if they were performing an exorcism on her. Val wanted to console her very passive cousin, but Mrs. Simms lovingly placed her arms around Olivia's shoulders.

"I've spoken to Reverend and Mrs. Simms, and they have shown me the error of my ways," Olivia continued. "I have repented to the Lord, and I want to apologize to the church for any shame or embarrassment I may have caused." Olivia wiped her eyes as tears fell down her face.

"Church," Mrs. Simms yelled above the commotion. "I have assured Olivia that the Lord loves her and no one here would ever judge her. Isn't that right, church?" she asked. Suddenly, amens and hallelujahs exploded throughout the sanctuary. Olivia's announcement had really moved the congregation. The pianist began to play, and members stomped their feet.

Val felt like the church was treating Olivia's confession as a black stain on a pure white wedding dress—like it was something she was supposed to hide or be ashamed of. When Val looked at Olivia she saw that innocence she had possessed since they were kids. Her light brown hair was pulled back in a ponytail that cascaded down her back. Most people would describe Olivia as plain looking, if not homely. She never wore make-up or any type of revealing clothing that showed off her curves. The only distinctive features she had were her light, hazel eyes and round, full lips.

Val was older than Olivia by seven months, and it was still hard for Val to accept that Olivia was no longer her little cousin. Val remembered the many times she had to fight girls on the playground because Olivia wouldn't stick up for herself. She was always very quiet and kept to herself.

Bryant, whom Val had met a few times, was Olivia's very first boyfriend. Olivia never dated much, so when Olivia began often talking about the things she and Bryant had done together, Val knew he must have been something special. Val was eager to get to know him better, but every time she suggested they go out together, Bryant was always working out of town. It was a surprise for Val to find out that Olivia was having sex. She had always assumed that she would be the first one to have a baby.

The church settled down and refocused its attention on Mrs. Simms and Olivia.

"Olivia has decided to keep the baby," Mrs. Simms announced. "And the church is going to support her in any way we can."

Another series of amens and hallelujahs stirred the church. Mrs. Simms hugged Olivia one more time before Olivia returned to her seat next to Val.

Val immediately pounced on her. "Olivia!"

"Val, don't say anything to me. You're going to make me cry." Olivia took a tissue out of her purse and wiped her eyes.

"Olivia, how could you not share this kind of information with me?" Val whispered.

"I was going to tell you. I could never find the right time."

"But you found the time to tell the entire church?" Val asked, astonished by her cousin's last comment.

"Val, can we discuss this later?"

"Hell no!"

"Val, we're in church!" Olivia said. She looked over her shoulder to make sure no one had heard her cousin's foul mouth.

"How could you let them coax you into doing that?"

"What . . . what did they do?"

Val hated it when Olivia acted so naïve. She was always trying to please somebody instead of doing what was right for her. Val knew that Olivia was blind to many things that went on around her, but she thought the girl would know when someone was trying to manipulate her.

"They had you crucify yourself as the sacrificial lamb. You put your flaws on public display, when not one of them is any better than you. They ain't nothin' but a bunch of hypocrites."

"Val, stop it! I won't have you speaking against the church."

"Olivia, you know I'm telling the truth. Remember how Desiree Carter stole the Sunday School Superintendent position from you?"

"She didn't steal it! The elders appointed her to the position."

"Yeah, right. She played you for months, stealing all your ideas for the Sunday School." Val laid her hand down on the Bible. "You told her all the plans you had, and she pretended to be your friend, telling you that you would be perfect as Sunday School Superintendent. Then when the announcement was made, Desiree acted surprised when her name was called.

"Her husband made a three thousand dollar donation to help the church get a new roof," Val continued. "Then the following week an announcement was made that she had accepted the position of Sunday School Superintendent. They never even held the required elections like they were supposed to."

Olivia tried to ignore Val by opening her Bible.

"Val, what does that have to do with anything?" she asked anxiously.

"It bothers me that you told the entire congregation personal information, when you couldn't even tell me, and we're cousins."

"Val, I needed to talk to someone. I spoke with Mrs. Simms about it and she suggested I tell the church. She said I would feel a lot better if I confessed my sins."

"Yeah, confess your sins to the Lord, not to the whole damn church!"

"Val, stop cursing in church!"

"I can't help it. I'm so mad. I don't believe they did this." Val tried to calm down.

Focusing back on the service, the pastor asked everyone to open their Bibles to John 8:7. "My sermon this morning is entitled, 'Let thee without sin, cast the first stone.'"

"What a coincidence," Val sarcastically mumbled.

Elise, Val's Bible Study facilitator and mentor, walked through the church gathering Bibles. Val followed behind her ranting and raving about what had happened to Olivia on Sunday. Elise believed in giving direction and spiritual guidance to each one of the young adults in her Bible Study class. She listened to their problems and gave advice on how to lead a righteous life, but it wasn't always easy trying to nurture a young adult's mind.

"Elise, are you listening to me?"

"Val, I'm listening to you. I was there."

"I know. That's why I don't understand why you didn't do anything." Val took the Bibles out of her hand.

"What was I supposed to do?" Elise ran her fingers through her Halle Berry haircut.

"They used her!" Val said boldly.

"Are you cold?" Elise asked, trying to change the subject. She walked over to the thermostat. "They didn't use her. They just helped her realize the wrong she had done," Elise finally commented.

"So, you agree with what they did?"

"Val, Olivia committed a major sin. This sin is going to follow her for the rest of her life. Perhaps Mrs. Simms thought that if Olivia acknowledged her sin then others wouldn't make the same mistake. The pastor's wife did say that the church was going to support her in any way they could."

"Elise, you were the one who taught us that a sin is a sin, that it doesn't matter how big or small you may think it is. It's all sin," Val said.

Again, Val stared at the wooden cross that hung in the front of the church. She was determined to get her point across. "Listen to this." She sat in one of the pews. "Olivia never actually admitted to doing anything wrong. She just announced she was pregnant."

"The last time I checked, sex outside of marriage was a sin," Elise replied.

"Yeah, but pregnancy outside of marriage isn't."

Elise looked at her strangely. "Val, what are you talking about?"

"The Virgin Mary wasn't married when she got pregnant with Jesus. She wasn't considered a sinner, so why should Olivia?" Val replied with a smirk on her face.

"You always have to have the last word, don't you?"

Val smiled brighter.

Suddenly, the church doors swung open and Julian Pennington, Val's boyfriend, strolled down the church aisle flashing his pearly whites.

Val and Julian had been together since their freshman year in high school. They had endured their share of ups and downs like every couple, but their love for one another always pulled them through.

Most of the girls at Philly High School described Julian as a pretty boy with a baby face. He was often told he resembled the R&B singer, Usher. Julian was considered a good catch, not just because of his handsome good looks, but also because of his determination to be successful.

Obsessed with the dream of one day becoming a basketball star, Julian perfected his basketball skills by spending all his spare time in the gym. Ultimately, it paid off, securing him a spot on the varsity team. The coach recognized his talent and appointed him co-captain of the team his freshman year.

Despite Julian's arrogant attitude and boastful behavior, Val's love for Julian was rare. He was her first love and she dedicated her life to making him happy. She would do just about anything he asked. Whether she had to stay up all night writing a paper for him or finishing his homework before her next class, Val was the kind of woman who stood by her man through the good and the bad.

Julian's feelings were mutual for her. He knew how lucky he was to have Val in his life. The love they shared was special and hard to describe. Their bond was strong and they refused to let outsiders interfere with their love. Their decision to wait until after marriage to have sex seemed to strengthen their relationship.

Julian finished his sophomore year at the University of Kentucky, and after several debates with his parents, he decided to forfeit the remaining two years of his scholarship and enter the National Basketball Association.

With his six feet, two inch, 210-pound frame, Julian bent down to kiss Val on her lips. "Valencia, I hope I wasn't interrupting anything." Julian always used Val's full name. He loved the way her name rolled off his lips.

Elise shot Val a look that asked the question, "Were we finished?"

"No, honey you didn't interrupt anything," Val responded. "Where have you been?"

"I went to get a haircut and then I went to the gym." He thrust his arms into the air and bulged his biceps, mimicking Popeye. "I'm trying to get in shape. Is it working?"

"Yeah, baby, it's working," Val replied sarcastically.

The next person to arrive for Bible Study was Montrese Cox, whom they called Tressie.

"Hey, Tressie." Elise greeted her with open arms. "We missed you in church on Sunday. Where were you?"

"I overslept," Tressie responded. She took a seat in the pew directly in front of Val and Julian.

Elise stood up. "While we wait on Danyelle and Olivia, I thought maybe—"

"Danyelle is outside," Tressie said, interrupting Elise mid-sentence. "She's outside smoking a joint." Tressie made a loud cracking sound with her gum.

Elise walked to the church doors and stuck her head outside. "Danyelle, what did I tell you about smoking marijuana in front of the church? If the police catch you they're going to arrest you."

Danyelle took one long last drag of her joint and threw it on the ground. She walked up the church steps. "I'll just tell them that it's a European cigarette."

"I'm sure they can tell the difference," Elise said.

"Jesus loves me," Danyelle sang as she entered the church. Her high-pitched voice went to a screeching high that made everyone in the church stop and look at her.

"Yes, Jesus loves me," she sang out again. She laughed because she was used to getting strange looks because of her odd behavior at times.

Danyelle was a hefty girl and nobody would ever make the mistake of calling her petite. Her body had lots of curves. Her hips were wide and her huge bust size was a genetic trait that had been passed down in her family from generation to generation.

Danyelle smoked morning, noon, and night. She claimed that marijuana was her motivation to get out of bed in the morning. Before inhaling her first puff, she would always kiss it up to God first and say a silent prayer. She prayed that the Lord would bless her experience, so she would get the most out of her high. She believed that God made weed as a natural herb, and it was there for everyone to enjoy.

"For the Bible tells me so." Danyelle finished her song. Julian laughed at her.

Elise walked in after picking up the joint Danyelle threw on the ground. "Danyelle, why must you do that every time you enter the church?"

Danyelle knew she was referring to her singing, "I'm just letting the Lord know that I've arrived."

"I'm sure the Lord could never miss you. Where's Olivia?" Elise asked Danyelle.

"She said she wasn't feeling well and decided to stay home."

Val gently cleared her throat to signal to Elise that Olivia was embarrassed by what happened on Sunday.

Elise spoke up. "Today, I would like to talk about the power of prayer. It is so important for us to maintain a close and intimate relationship with the Father." She clasped her hands. "The only way to do that is through prayer. God wants us to tell Him about any burdens that we are carrying. He also wants us to tell Him about the amazingly good things that happen in our lives. We can only do that by going to Him in prayer. I challenge everyone in here to double the amount of time they spend in prayer. If you pray for five minutes a day, double it to ten minutes. If you pray for an hour a day, double it to two hours a day. Prayer is going to be our focal point for the next few weeks. We will have a more in-depth conversation on prayer next week. Does anyone have any questions?"

Julian raised his hand. "Is it all right that I pray about which team I prefer to get drafted to?"

Elise laughed at his question. "Yes, Julian, if you want something specific, you need to be specific in your prayer. If you desire something and it's in God's plan for you to have it, you will receive it. God wants to bless you. All you have to do is ask."

"Can I pray for a man?" Tressie asked.

"Sure."

"Can I pray that the Lord send me Nasir Jones?"

"Who is Nasir Jones?" Elise asked.

"Nasir Jones is this rapper who's already engaged to Kelis," Val spoke up.

"Tressie, I'm pretty sure God isn't going to give you someone else's fiancé, so you need to change your prayer request."

Elise fielded the other attendees' questions and they all sang a few hymns.

Elise concluded her lesson by saying, "For the first week everyone should pray for one thing. Next week, when we gather again, we'll discuss whether or not God answered your prayer. Is that all right with everyone?"

Everyone in the room nodded.

"I'll close out in prayer."

Everyone held hands while Elise prayed.

"Heavenly Father, I want to thank you for once again bringing us safely together. I ask that you bless each and every heart here, and that they increase their prayer life to get closer to you. Through prayer they will realize and experience that you have control over all things great and small. Amen."

In unison everyone responded, "Amen."

CHAPTER 2

The following day, Olivia walked into the apartment she shared with her sister, Danyelle, and was welcomed by a cloud of smoke. She waved her hand in front of her face to see what was causing the entire apartment to be engulfed in smoke. She found Bryant and Danyelle sitting in the living room with what appeared to be a pound of marijuana lying on the coffee table.

"Why can't you two smoke outside?" Olivia asked, annoyed. This was not the first time she had asked them not to smoke in the house.

"Hey Livie," Bryant said. "How was your doctor's appointment?"

Olivia looked at him, surprised that he had even asked. After her first doctor's appointment, weeks had passed before he asked her how it went. Lately, he had lost interest in the baby, which concerned her because when she first told him, he was

so excited. Olivia badly wanted Bryant to participate more in her pregnancy.

Ever since Olivia was a little girl she had wanted
to be a mother, and the idea of her soon becoming
one bought joy to her heart. She looked forward
to the monthly doctor visits and midnight food
cravings.

Her only regret was that she and Bryant weren't
married. She never thought she would be having a
baby out of wedlock, but she knew there wasn't too
much she could do about it now. Bryant had made
it clear that he was not going to marry her just because she had gotten pregnant.

"Well the doctor said that . . ." Olivia began.

"Hold up, baby." Bryant held up his finger. He
turned toward Danyelle. "Yo, where you going with
that?" Danyelle had gotten up from the couch and
started to retreat to her bedroom, taking the
smoking joint and the ashtray with her.

"Oh!" She looked back at Olivia. "I was going to
my room. I wanted to give you and Livie some privacy."

"Yeah right, you were trying to smoke the whole
joint by yourself."

Danyelle pointed back at Bryant. "Negro, you've
got five joints rolled up in front of you that we
haven't even touched." Then she pointed over in
the corner. "Not to mention the bundle we haven't
even opened."

Olivia looked over at the cube of marijuana se-
curely wrapped in clear plastic wrap lying on the
floor.

"No need to get hostile. I forgot. My fault!" He

turned back to Olivia. "Sorry, honey. Now what did the doctor say?"

"Forget it!" Annoyed, Olivia stormed toward her bedroom. She was tired of Bryant putting his marijuana habit before their baby.

"Where are you going?" Bryant yelled out.

Olivia closed the door and cried. She felt like her life was falling apart. She wanted the baby to come into the world feeling that it was loved by both its parents, but Bryant acted so selfish at times she wondered if that was possible.

She wished her mother were there to fix the problems in her life. She remembered the last conversation she had with her. Olivia was in her bedroom getting ready for bed when her mother walked in.

"Livie, can I speak with you for a minute?"

"Sure, Mommy." Olivia jumped into bed and pulled the comforter over her legs.

Her mother smiled and took a deep breath. "Olivia, I don't like to ask you to promise me anything because I know you're only nine years old and you have a lot of growing up to do, but I have to ask that you make me this one promise."

Olivia's soft eyes asked, *What is it, Mommy?*

"Promise me that no matter what happens in life, you will always keep the word of God close to your heart. Being obedient to God will carry you through the roughest times in your life. Trust him. He will never leave you."

Olivia held her mother's final words close to her heart. Later that night her mother had a heart attack in her sleep and died instantly.

Since then Olivia had kept her promise to her mother and was a devoted Christian who read her Bible regularly. She tried to live the life of a right-eous woman, but lately she struggled in her Christian walk. It all started with Bryant.

From the beginning, Olivia was very up front with Bryant. She told him she was a virgin and explained how important it was for her to remain one until her wedding day. Olivia knew how most men felt about being in a celibate relationship, and she had prepared herself for the possibility of him walking out of her life forever. Surprisingly, he wasn't angry nor did he walk out on her. In fact, he told her that he respected her values and her desire to wait.

Three months later, he suddenly had a change of heart and started pressing her to have sex with him. Every time they went out he would beg her to make love to him, but Olivia was strong and held on to her vow. Before long, arguments arose and he threatened to end their relationship. Olivia panicked. She didn't want to lose him. He was her first boyfriend and the only man she ever cared about besides her father. She felt cornered, and after careful consideration, she gave in to his demands, but only under one condition: that they always use a condom.

The first time they made love Bryant made her feel like he was the one she had been saving herself for. He was gentle and compassionate. She couldn't help but fall in love with him. Being in his arms and sharing her body made her happy. There was nothing she wanted more than to be with him. After they made love, they realized the condom had broken. She missed her period, and then the morning sickness began. She bought a home pregnancy test and that's when her greatest fears were confirmed. She was pregnant.

Depression set in fast and Olivia isolated herself from friends and family. Val often questioned Olivia's strange behavior. Olivia reassured her that the stress from working long hours at the bank was making her tired, but Val wasn't buying it. Bryant was also concerned about her. Unsure of what to do, he asked her if she wanted to have an abortion. *An abortion?* The baby growing inside of her was so unexpected. And then to suddenly get rid of it? Would that be another sin? She needed somebody to talk to. She usually confided her problems to Val, but this was different. Val and Olivia had made a pact to remain virgins until marriage, and now Olivia was embarrassed to admit she had broken their vow to one another. For weeks Olivia prayed that the whole situation would just go away. Finally, the burden of hiding her secret became unbearable. That's when she went to see the pastor's wife.

Mrs. Simms always encouraged members of her husband's congregation to come and pray with her if they had problems that were too much for them to bear alone. Mrs. Simms and Olivia prayed for over an hour. Afterwards they discussed the pros and cons of her pregnancy. Mrs. Simms pointed out that terminating her pregnancy wouldn't erase the sin that had already been committed, but ultimately Olivia would have final say on the fate of her baby. Olivia pushed her fears aside and decided to give her baby a chance at life.

Mrs. Simms asked a lot of questions about

Bryant. Where was he from? Did he have any ties to the community? What did his parents do?

Olivia couldn't answer any of her questions. She didn't know too much about Bryant's background because he never talked about family or friends. One time he did tell her that he was raised by an elderly aunt in North Carolina. He described himself as a drifter who never stayed in one place for too long. Bryant worked for Amtrak as a conductor, which required him to travel a lot. That was how they met.

Anxious to get back to Philly after a long, uneventful visit with her Aunt Gretchen in Chicago, Olivia ran through the train station trying not to miss her train. She was already late because her aunt tried to get her to stay another week, but one week of playing bridge with the old woman in her retirement community and watching reruns of *The Golden Girls* was more than Olivia could bear.

She couldn't figure out why her aunt never invited Val or Danyelle to come visit her. Olivia had been branded with the term 'Favorite Niece'. Olivia hated going out to visit her aunt every year, but because her aunt didn't have any of her own children and she was Olivia's mother's only sister, she felt she couldn't refuse her offer.

She looked at her watch as the whistle blew, giving the signal for the final call. People ran past and around her. Olivia made it just in time. She lifted her foot to climb on board when her foot missed the first step. Just before she hit the ground, Bryant came out of nowhere and caught her mid-air.

"You have to be careful. These steps are tricky," he told her.

"Thank you." Olivia was embarrassed by her clumsiness, but she was more embarrassed that the handsome conductor witnessed it firsthand. Olivia gathered her things and occupied the first empty seat she could find. Soon after, the same handsome conductor who broke her fall walked through the train collecting tickets. When he approached her aisle he asked her again, "Are you sure you're all right?"

Olivia wished he would forget her small but humiliating accident. "I'm fine," she replied.

"Good. Now that I know you're all right, would you mind going to dinner with me?"

Excited by his invitation, she gladly accepted. Over time they began to spend more time together and eventually their friendship developed into a relationship. When Olivia found out she was pregnant, Bryant asked if he could move in with her so they could be a real family.

Olivia looked at her growing belly in the mirror. The baby was getting bigger every day and her clothes were getting tighter around the waist. It wouldn't be long before she would have to start shopping for maternity clothes. Olivia grabbed her baby book and plunged into the first chapter when the phone rang.

"Hey mommy-to-be! What's up with you?" Val screamed into Olivia's ear.

"Nothing much. I just came from the doctor's office."

"How's the baby?" Val asked.

"The doctor said the baby is fine. I should have a healthy baby in six more months," Olivia nonchalantly responded.

"Why do you sound so down? This should be one of the happiest times in your life."

"I *am* happy," Olivia unconvincingly replied.

Val heard concern in Olivia's voice and she wondered what was bothering her, but instead of asking, Val decided on a different approach.

"Why don't you come to the mall with me? I need to pick up some things for Julian's party tonight."

"I don't know. I'm really tired."

Val acted like she didn't hear her cousin's response. "I'll be there to pick you up in ten minutes."

"I would like to see those three rings," Val pointed to three platinum diamond rings displayed in the glass showcase. The saleswoman laid them before Val and Olivia on a black velvet cloth. Val slipped a ring on her finger. "What do you think?" she asked, holding up the ring for Olivia to see.

"Nice," Olivia replied

"But do you think it's me? I don't want something too big, but it has to be classy."

Olivia looked at the rings more closely. "They're all nice."

"I think I like that one." Val looked at a fourth ring sitting inside the display case. The saleswoman retrieved the ring and handed it to Val. "Yes, I really do like this ring." Val stared at the large marquise diamond.

"I thought you said you didn't want anything too big," Olivia said.

"I don't, but this ring is beautiful. This is the one I want!"

The sales lady beamed. Val could see her brain

calculate how much her commission would be on such an expensive purchase.

"Thank you." Val handed the ring back to the saleswoman, and the pleasant expression on her face turned sour.

"She thought she was getting that sale," Olivia whispered.

"She should have known better than that. What woman purchases her own engagement ring, except for Britney Spears?"

Olivia chuckled at the thought. They strolled through the mall and window-shopped.

"So, you and Julian are really going to get married?" Olivia asked.

"Yes. We've been talking about it more and more now that the draft is here. I think he's going to propose any day now. He doesn't want to get married his first year in the league because he wants to concentrate on the team and the role he's going to play with that team. He's really worried about his performance and how well he'll compete against different players. Playing in the NBA is so different from playing at the collegiate level. He wants to be able to go in and defend Kobe Bryant or block Kevin Garnett's shots. I keep telling him not to worry so much about proving himself to the other players. If he concentrates on his game, the respect he wants will follow."

Olivia pretended she was interested in what Val was saying, but she couldn't help thinking about Bryant and the baby.

"Do you want to eat here?" Val asked. They stopped in front of a small lunch café called Kaffe Crossing.

"Sure. I am hungry."

They entered the café and squeezed through the crowd of patrons to grab an empty table in the corner. Val and Olivia were regulars there. They loved the quiet, serene atmosphere that was provided by the dim lights and burning incense, in addition to the great food.

"What would you ladies like?"

Val heard a male voice behind her that was laced with the softness that accompanied a woman's voice. She turned and looked into the eyes of man built like a sculpture. He wore a black tee shirt that outlined his well-defined pecs and revealed the bulging muscles in his arms.

"I'll have a glass of lemonade and a chicken Caesar salad," Val told the waiter. "What about you, Livie?"

"I'm starving. Can I get the Angus cheeseburger with cheese fries, and a pickle? I'll also have a lemonade."

"Darn Livie, you really are pregnant. I've never seen you eat so much food."

The waiter scribbled their orders down on his pad and switched away.

"Do you believe that?" Olivia pointed to the waiter. "He is fine. He should be a model."

"A lot of male models are gay. They just don't advertise it. He apparently does," Val responded.

"Whoever his man is, he's lucky." Olivia stared in his direction.

"Livie, you could try to change him." Val laughed. "Seduce him back over to the loving arms of a woman."

The waiter walked back over to the table and

placed their food and drinks in front of them. Before he had a chance to walk away, Val stopped him. "Excuse me."

He paused, turned, put his hands on his hips and looked at Val with attitude.

"Can I have some French salad dressing?" she asked.

Being overly theatrical, he acted as if Val's request was a nuisance. He snatched a bottle of salad dressing from the table next to theirs and slammed it down on their table.

"Is that all?" he asked.

"No," she replied. "What's your name?"

"Derrick!" he replied.

"Derrick, I love that name," Val said. Derrick responded with a blank stare.

Val continued. "Derrick, when did you start here? I come here often and this is my first time seeing you."

His body language expressed how unhappy he was with Val's question. "Well, Lois Lane, if you must know, I don't work here. I'm friends with the owner and his waitress called out, so I'm helping him for the day."

"Oh, okay. I was just wondering. I didn't mean to upset you."

He sucked his teeth and switched away.

"He acts just like I do when I'm on my period," Olivia said.

"Forget him. Back to what I was saying. I've been thinking about the wedding. I decided that I want something intimate. No press and no media. Also, I've decided not to hold the ceremony at the church."

"Well, where else would you get married?" Olivia asked.

"I have been thinking about getting married atop the Bellevue Tower. Julian and I went to visit their ballroom the other day and the place is exquisite. It would be romantic to get married by candlelight."

"That sounds beautiful."

"I want a six o'clock wedding." Val paused. "Livie, will you be my maid of honor?"

Olivia's heart was softened by Val's request. "I would love to be your maid of honor."

"Great, so you're going to help me with everything?"

"Yes, I'll help with whatever you need."

Olivia was happy about Val's pending nuptials, but she couldn't help but feel a little jealous. Val had a great boyfriend who not only loved her, but showed her how much he loved her. He always bought her little presents or would leave small notes reminding her of how much he loved her. She wished Bryant could be more like Julian.

Val knew there was something on Olivia's mind, and she was dying to find out what was bothering her. She hoped that if she kept talking, Olivia would eventually open up.

"Julian went to training camp with a lot of different teams, but he thinks that the teams most interested in him were the Miami Heat, Seattle Supersonics, and Milwaukee Bucks. I hope he doesn't get picked by Milwaukee. Girl, I can't imagine myself living in Wisconsin. There isn't anything there but cheese. I would go crazy."

"Val, you'll adjust."

"What school would I transfer to, the University of Wisconsin? Wouldn't it be exciting if he went to Miami with the warm sunshine, celebrities, and the parties? I heard that they party in Miami twenty-four hours a day. It would be great, but I'm not going to complain. Wherever my man goes, I will follow."

They sat for a brief moment not saying a word before Val finally broke the silence.

"Livie, what's up? You've been blue all day long. Is everything all right?"

Olivia flashed Val a phony smile, scared that if she said too much she would burst into tears.

"Is the baby all right?"

"The baby is fine."

"It's the church, isn't it?" Val concluded with a hint of menace in her voice.

Unable to hold back the tears any longer, the burdens and concerns Olivia had held in for so long poured forth.

"I knew it was the church," Val said, her teeth clenched. "I am so mad at what they did to you, Livie. But don't worry, I will handle everything. I will give them a piece of my mind. They will be sorry they ever messed with you."

"No, don't do that, Val!"

"Girl, I'm so sick of that church taking advantage of you. I think it's disgraceful how those members sit in church every Sunday and call themselves children of God when they treat people so badly."

Val paused to take a forkful of her salad. "The church is where people go for acceptance and church people are the most judgmental. I attend

First Nazareth because Pastor Simms knows his Bible and he preaches the word, but outside of that I can't support that church."

"Don't condemn the church like that, Val. They're not bad people."

"No, they're not bad people, but they are not without sin either. So who are they to point out someone else's faults when they have their own?"

Olivia thought for a moment. Val did have a point, but she didn't want to talk about the church. "Val, it's not the church. It's Bryant and the baby."

"Oh, honey, I'm sorry." Val didn't know what to say. "What's wrong with you and Bryant?"

Val never thought to think that Olivia might be having problems with her boyfriend. Since Olivia barely spoke about him, Val often forgot he even existed.

Olivia told Val about how Bryant and Danyelle smoked marijuana in the apartment, even after she had asked both of them not to. She was concerned about how the smoke could affect the baby's health. She also described Bryant's distant behavior toward the baby.

"Olivia, you know that you have got to be positive and stress-free," Val said, stroking her cousin's arm. "Don't worry about tomorrow, for tomorrow will worry about itself. You and the baby are going to be perfectly fine. Bryant will come around. Maybe it just hasn't hit him yet. You really aren't showing yet, but as you get bigger and he realizes that there is a part of him inside of you, he'll be just as excited as you are. So just enjoy the time you have now, because once that baby gets here, you'll have no time for yourself."

Olivia smiled a genuine smile for the first time that day. She was glad Val was not only her cousin, but also her best friend.

"Are you coming to the party tonight?" Val asked.

"I don't know. I've been really tired lately."

Julian's mother was throwing a draft party that night in honor of her son. She had invited all of Julian's friends and family. Julian opted not to go to New York for the draft ceremonies because he preferred to watch it from home.

"Please come. It's going to be such a big night for Julian. And I would like for you to bring Bryant. I really don't know Bryant that well, but tonight would be the perfect time for me to get to know him better."

"All right. We'll be there."

When Olivia and Bryant walked into Julian's mother's house, it was crowded with people. Olivia recognized a few of Julian's family members and a couple of his teammates from Kentucky. She waved hello to Tressie who was standing in the corner talking to a very tall basketball player.

Julian's mother walked by carrying a tray of hot wings. Olivia thought Mrs. McCormick looked stunning every time she saw her. She had her hair pulled up into a ponytail and wore a thin layer of golden-brown gloss on her lips. Her low-rise jeans flattered her petite figure. Mrs. McCormick was often mistaken for a college student. Julian's mother looked much younger than her thirty-seven years. She gave birth to Julian when she was seventeen. Julian never knew his biological father; he was killed in a car accident two days before Julian's birth.

"Hello, Mrs. McCormick."

"Hello, Olivia." She reached over and gave Olivia a hug. "Congratulations. I heard about the baby."

"Thanks," Olivia responded, a little embarrassed that Julian's mother knew about her pregnancy.

"This must be the baby's father," Mrs. McCormick commented while looking in Bryant's direction.

"Yes. Mrs. McCormick, this is Bryant." They exchanged greetings as Bryant reached to shake her hand.

"Val told me you two were coming tonight. Bryant, why don't you come with me? I'll take you in the living room with the rest of the guys. Olivia, you can go see Val. She's in the kitchen."

"Val's in the kitchen?" Olivia asked, not sure if she heard the woman correctly.

"Yes, that child is in my kitchen. Please check in on her before she burns something."

Olivia walked into the kitchen to find Val walking around with an apron on. "Hey cuz, whatcha doin'?" Olivia asked.

Val pulled a tray out of the oven and almost dropped a pan of honey-roasted wings on the floor. "Girl, you scared me. If I had dropped these wings Mrs. McCormick would have my head."

"I was surprised to hear that you were in the kitchen. Of all the rooms in the house, the kitchen is the last place I would expect to find you."

"Yes, I know, but I felt bad. Mrs. McCormick cooked all the food for the party by herself, so I offered to help. I only offered because I thought she was going to turn me down. She hates for me to be in her kitchen."

Olivia laughed so hard she had to hold her stomach. It was weird seeing Val wearing an apron. Olivia pulled out a stool to sit on.

"No girl, don't sit down. Come into the living room with the rest of us. The guys have turned on the draft and my kitchen duty is over." Val took off her apron and threw it on the counter.

"Where's Bryant?" Val asked, looking around the living room.

"I'm not sure. He was supposed to be in here with Julian and his friends."

Val pushed her way to a seat next to Julian, and Olivia sat in a chair not too far away from her cousin. Olivia wondered where Bryant was. *Maybe he went to the bathroom.*

Julian was mesmerized by the pre-draft commentaries being aired by ESPN. A few analysts were sharing their opinions of where various draft hopefuls would wind up by the end of the night. His face was expressionless and his mind was preoccupied with his future.

"Honey," she called out to him. His eyes stayed glued to the television.

"Julian." She pulled his face toward hers and away from the television. "No matter what happens tonight, everything is going to be all right because we'll still be together."

Julian smiled and kissed her lightly on the lips.

"That's why I love you, because you're always by my side."

NBA Commissioner David Stern began the opening ceremony for the NBA Draft by making a short speech about the history of the NBA and the high standards the league holds each one of its players to.

The room fell silent as the celebrants waited to hear the first name called from Mr. Stern's mouth.

"With the first pick for the 2003 NBA Draft, the Cleveland Cavaliers select LeBron James." Julian's head dropped. *The wait and anticipation were taking a toll on him,* Val thought. She massaged the back of his neck to help relieve the pressure. Val watched LeBron hug his mother and walk across the stage to shake the commissioner's hand. They showed a quick interview with LeBron before they moved on to the next draft pick.

"With the second pick for the 2003 NBA draft, the Detroit Pistons select Darko Milicic."

The commissioner repeated his routine until he finally called Julian's name. All of the guests were gathered in the living room listening to every word the commissioner said, "The Seattle SuperSonics select Julian Pennington."

The whole house erupted into a roar. Val jumped up and hugged Julian. His mother pushed through the crowd to congratulate her son. Soon Julian was surrounded by well wishers.

After the commotion settled down, Julian yelled through the crowd, "Valencia! Where is Valencia?"

Val emerged from the crowd and stood beside her man.

"I want to make an announcement while everyone is here," Julian screamed over the crowd of people.

"First, I want to thank everyone for coming tonight. I appreciate all the love my family and friends have shown me, not just today, but throughout the years." He looked toward his mom and stepfather, Jerald. "Thanks for all your love and support, Mom and Dad. Through the years both of you have struggled to provide the best for me, and I appreciate all the things you've done for me." Julian walked over and gave his mom and stepfather a hug. The crowd applauded Julian's kind words.

He walked back to Val and grabbed her hand. "Now, I would like to thank my queen." He looked deep into her eyes. "You have stood by me since the ninth grade. You cheered me on at every high school game. You encouraged me when I lost faith in myself, and I know you will continue to support me in Seattle." Val blushed. "That's why I want to ask you . . ." He bent down on one knee. "Will you be my wife?" Julian pulled a small, burgundy velvet box from his pocket. Inside was a three-carat, pear-shaped solitaire diamond engagement ring.

The surprised expression on Val's face showed that the proposal was totally unexpected. She hugged him and tried to hide her tears from the host of people watching them. Julian pulled her back from out of his arms and looked into her face. "Should I assume that your answer is yes?" he asked her.

"Yes," she replied and again the house erupted into a thunderous roar.

Olivia watched her cousin accept Julian's marriage proposal. She thought it was so romantic how Julian surprised Val. She knew that Val's lifelong dream was coming true. Once again she wished Bryant looked at her the same way Julian looked at Val. Olivia looked around the room for Bryant, but did not see him. She walked into the kitchen, but he wasn't there either. She walked to the back door and found him talking on his cell phone.

"I'll guarantee delivery by the end of the year. Trust me, you'll have your package," Bryant said into the phone. Bryant had his back toward the door, not realizing that Olivia was standing behind him.

Olivia never heard him talk like that before. She wondered what he was talking about and whom he was talking to. *Was Bryant dealing drugs?*

"Bryant!" Olivia opened the door and walked onto the back patio.

Bryant turned around. "I'll have to call you back," he said into the phone.

He walked over to her with his arms wide open. "Hey, baby, did I miss anything? Did Julian get picked yet?"

"Yeah, he was just selected by Seattle."

"That's great. I can't wait to congratulate him. Come on, let's go back inside."

"Wait a minute. Who were you talking to on the phone?"

"Oh, that was nobody. It was an old friend from down south. He wanted to know if I could get him a few cases of shrimp. I work with a guy from Baltimore who can get cases of shrimp at a cheap price."

Olivia looked at him, unsure if she should believe his story.

He noticed the worried look on her face. He gave her hug and said, "Don't worry, it was nothing."

CHAPTER 3

E lise stumbled into the house with a purse, briefcase, and a Bible all in one hand. She planted
her feet firmly on the ground and tried to regain
her balance. She laid her Bible down on the small
vestibule table and walked across the marble floor
that expanded throughout the front foyer. The
clickity-clack of her high heel shoes echoed throughout the empty room. She walked into the kitchen,
expecting to find her husband slaving over the stove,
but to her surprise, he wasn't there. She walked
over and opened the oven door. Inside was a pot
roast with potatoes. The aroma drifted past her nose,
provoking her stomach to growl. From the den,
Elise heard the sound of clacking computer keys.
She followed the sound and there was her husband, with his eyes glued to the computer screen.

"Hey, baby!" Elise said in an attempt to grab her
husband's attention.

Preoccupied with the article he was reading online, he lifted his hand and casually waved to his wife. She walked across the room, sat on his lap, and peered at the screen to see what had him so absorbed. The title of the article was, "Is Impotency Hereditary?"

Elise's temperature immediately rose. Unable to control her anger, she jumped off his lap and stormed into the kitchen. Miles could sense an impending argument. He got up and followed her.

"Elise, I'm trying to find answers to what's wrong with me."

"Miles, you've been tested and your results came back fine. Why do you insist there's something medically wrong with you? The doctor told you to relax."

Uncontrollably, Miles's ears began to twitch, a sure sign that he was frustrated over a situation he couldn't control. She walked over and held his ears in her hands. She looked into her husband's eyes through his glasses. Her husband was not the best looking man, but his ordinary looks were appealing to her. He wasn't stylish nor was he athletic, but he was a man who loved the Lord, and that was so much more attractive than a man who worshipped himself or the material things around him.

"I've been relaxing. I took a month off from work and I haven't done anything, but . . ."

"Sit at the computer and search for medical reasons why you can't keep an erection," Elise said, finishing his sentence for him.

He looked at her strangely. This was the first time they had acknowledged his problem out loud.

"We've been married for six years, and I never had a problem until we decided to have a family."

Elise pulled two plates down from the top cabinet. "Well, you've been seeing a therapist. What does she say?"

"I told Dr. Johnson how I witnessed my father rape and beat my mother repeatedly. She thought my sexual deficiencies had something to do with what I saw as a child. She said that I might be suppressing my feelings of how scared I am of becoming a parent. That traumatic experience could be causing my body to react in a negative way, subconsciously, resulting in my inability to . . . you know."

"I didn't realize that experience affected you so deeply."

"Neither did I. Now I just have to find a way to live with it, because no matter what happens, I can't erase my past. I'm more concerned about the children we were planning. I know how excited you are to start a family."

"We just have to be patient. One day the Lord is going to bless us with a house full of kids. If we continue to pray, God will answer our prayers."

"I've been praying and he hasn't answered them yet."

"He will. Just remember, it's all in his time, not ours."

Elise fixed their plates to eat. They sat down at the dining room table in silence until Miles couldn't suppress his feelings any longer. "Elise, what are we going to do if my condition becomes permanent?" Miles blurted out. "I've been having problems for the past three months. How long can I expect you to wait for me?"

Elise never thought about what would happen if Miles's condition never improved. She realized that sex was a very important part of any marriage. She thought for a moment, *I can do without sex for a while.* But what would she do if he never got better? She looked over at her husband and saw the worried look on his face.

"Elise, I have a responsibility as a man to satisfy you. What's going to happen to our marriage if I can't please you? I can't expect you to live the rest of your life celibate because I have a sexual affliction."

He pulled his chair closer to her and grabbed her hand. "Maybe we should start thinking about what we're going to do if this condition persists."

"I haven't really thought that far ahead," Elise replied.

"First, I need you to know that my number one aspiration in life is to make you happy. You should never be sad, mad, or lonely." He held his head not sure if he should tell her what he had been thinking. "What would you think if I suggested that we explore an open marriage?"

"Open marriage! What is that?"

"It's kind of like having an affair, except you have your spouse's permission to see other people."

"Miles, you can't be serious!" she yelled.

"Hear me out. I know it sounds unorthodox, but it can work. I wouldn't ask you any questions about where you've been or who you've been with.

The only thing I would ask is that you choose
someone I didn't know."

Elise got up and walked over to the refrigerator.
She filled her glass with ice. "Miles, a marriage is
not based on sex. It's based on our commitment to
one another. This is a battle we have to fight together. I love you and only you." She walked over
and kissed him on the lips. "'Til death do us part."

He smiled, relieved that she wanted to fight for
their marriage. He pulled Elise down on his lap
and wrapped his arms around her.

"I love you," Elise said. "Sex is about sharing
yourself with someone you love. I love the way you
wrap your arms around me at night. I love the way
our bodies come together as one. If I have to wait
a lifetime, that's what I'll do. I'll wait out this impotency thing, and God will fix everything."

She took a deep breath before finishing her
thoughts. "If our situation doesn't change by the
end of the year, we can begin to think about getting a surrogate or possibly doing in vitro. Whatever it takes, we will have a baby together."

Miles kissed Elise passionately on the lips.

"Elise, I hate going to these conference meetings."

"Tressie, yesterday you said you were looking
forward to going," Elise shot back.

Elise and Tressie were on their way to Harrisburg,
Pennsylvania. The youth of the A.M.E. Church were
holding their quarterly meeting, where they col-
lectively discussed ways to promote Christ and reach

out to the community. In the past they had food drives, charity events, and church carnivals.

This year the conference president, Payne Boyd, said he wanted the church to "take things to the next level." Tressie wasn't exactly sure what that meant, but she did know from past experience that when Payne had a vision he would drive himself and those around him insane until he achieved his desired goal.

His last project, "Renaissance Children," focused on getting children reacquainted with Christ. He was determined to increase Sunday School attendance across the state of Pennsylvania by at least fifty percent. The project required that Tressie, as the conference secretary, travel with Payne to different churches to promote his campaign. Having to deal with Payne's bossy, pushy, and rude attitude was torture for Tressie. They argued all the time and never agreed on anything.

They arrived at the A.M.E. District Diamond Center just in time for the start of morning church services. Tressie took her place behind the podium as the morning emcee. A lot of different A.M.E. churches throughout the state attended the conference meeting, so the huge sanctuary was crowded and allowed for standing room only.

"I would like to welcome everyone here this morning and thank you for attending the third quarter conference meeting." The congregation applauded. "First, I would like to introduce our conference president, Payne Boyd. He is going to deliver the official welcome."

Tressie stepped down as Payne stood up and

straightened his suit. On his way to the podium he gave Tressie a snide grin. As Payne addressed the congregation, Tressie had thoughts of pushing him out of the pulpit and into the audience. She mouthed a silent prayer: "Lord, forgive me for the mischievous things that just ran through my head."

After the morning service concluded, Payne called a meeting with all cabinet members. Tressie followed Payne into the back office, took a seat, and pulled out a pen and a pad of paper to take notes.

"First, I would like to address the attendance issue. I need for all members who hold office positions to be present at all quarterly meetings. If there is an . . ."

"Excuse me," Tressie interrupted. "Wouldn't it be wise if we opened with prayer first?"

"Of course. I was going to say a prayer after I addressed the attendance issue, but if you'd like for us to pray first, we will."

After prayer he again addressed the issue of attendance. During his speech there was a knock at the door.

"Come in," Payne commanded.

When the door opened Tressie looked up and locked eyes with the man of her dreams. The handsome stranger stared back at her. An electric current drew them both into a trance that neither could break.

"Payce, you wanted something?" Payne asked his twin brother.

"Um, yeah. I came in here to tell you that Daddy has made arrangements for you to catch a ride home with Deacon Law."

"All right, thanks," Payne replied.

Before Payce closed the door behind him, he winked at Tressie, planting a smile on her face that lasted for the remainder of the meeting.

After the meeting concluded, Mariah, the treasurer, walked over to speak with Tressie. "Hey, girl!"

"Hey, Mariah. What's up with you?"

"Nothing much. What about you?" Mariah grinned. "I saw you checking out Payne's brother."

The smile dropped from Tressie's face. "Payne's brother? Where?"

"The guy who interrupted our meeting, Payne's twin."

"Twin!"

"Yes. You didn't notice?" Mariah asked.

"No!"

"That's probably because he had a wave cap on his head. They look exactly alike. He's been locked up for the past year for selling drugs. Since his release, I heard he has been trying to get his life together."

"I bet that's really hard with a brother like Payne."

They laughed together and walked out of the office.

"Girl, give me a call. Maybe we can hang out sometime." Tressie waved good-bye to Mariah and went to track down Elise.

On the ride home Tressie was so excited about her brief encounter with Payce. She couldn't wait to fill Elise in. "Elise, we had a connection. He looked deep into my eyes and I looked into his. That is going to be my new man. I've got to find him."

"Tressie, slow down. You just met the guy."

"Elise, he is what I've been praying for. I prayed for a thug. He is the man I'm supposed to marry."

"Tressie, you didn't even speak to him."

"I didn't have to. We spoke through our eyes," she explained.

Elise laughed, thinking Tressie really had lost it.

"Listen, I prayed to the Lord for a thug. You should have seen him." She began counting off her fingers. "He had a wave cap on his head, a white T-shirt, a pair of baggy shorts, and Timberland boots."

"Well, for someone who only saw him for less than a minute, you sure did get a good look at his wardrobe."

"I know." She rattled on. "I was so mesmerized by his eyes that I didn't even notice that he resembled Payne. I didn't even notice they were twins until Mariah told me. Imagine me having to spend my entire life looking into Payne's face—the person I despise the most."

Elise laughed.

The following morning Elise decided to go for an early morning jog. Running was a stress reliever for her. It helped to clear her mind of the most recent burdens that were testing her faith. Her biggest concern was Miles and the sex that hadn't existed in their marriage for months. She had to admit, it was hard for her to go from having sex just about every day to three months of consecutive celibacy. She was frustrated and unsure of what to do.

Elise stretched her legs in preparation for her

run. Each time she ran the three-mile perimeter around the park, she compared it to running the race of life. She believed that Christians who crossed life's finish line by enduring trials and tribulations would receive an abundance of blessings at the end. But not everyone will finish the race. Some people choose to spend their lives taking shortcuts and following their own plans that lead them off God's desired course. Over time, they get tired of trying to make it to the finish line and quit the race. Unfortunately, a lot of people miss out on what God has to offer them.

Elise took a deep breath and started around the park. The intake of fresh air into her lungs invigorated her. Jogging along the path, she tried to think of alternative ways she could satisfy her sexual desires without committing adultery. *I should invest in a vibrator*, she thought. Although she had never used one before, she had heard they could be quite helpful. She knew that they came in different sizes, but she didn't know what size she would need. She hoped they came with a user's manual. She didn't want to injure herself.

She was quickly approaching the end of the trail. Determined to finish the three-mile trail, she picked up her pace and circled the lake at high speed. Her legs were shaky and her joints ached. Ahead of her, she could see the marker where she started. Two steps from crossing the finish line, she was knocked to the ground with an intense pain that paralyzed her leg. She held her leg while a stream of blood flowed from the gash.

A strange man came and rushed to her side. "I am so sorry, ma'am." She looked up into the stranger's handsome face and was stunned by how handsome he was. His lips caught her attention first. He had a perfect set of full lips with a small mustache above his upper lip. Her sudden fascination with his lips scared her.

He asked her a series of questions, but Elise could not respond. Her sudden attraction to him left her speechless. Without warning, another shot of pain went up her leg.

"Ma'am, are you all right?" the stranger asked.

Elise nodded her head yes.

"I am so sorry."

Elise found the strength to utter the words, "I'm okay."

"I'm so sorry. You came from out of nowhere. I should have been more careful riding my bike."

"No, I should have been looking at where I was going."

"Can I take a look at that?" he asked, pointing to her leg. She slowly moved her hand so he could look at her wound more closely.

"That cut looks pretty deep. You may need stitches."

"You think so?" Elise had a tremendous fear of hospitals. Her Nana died during surgery when she was eleven, and the mere sight of a hospital gave her the chills.

"Can you stand up?" He helped her to her feet, but she couldn't put pressure on her leg. He made a suggestion. "How about you stay here and I'll go get my car? Then I'll take you to the hospital."

"No, you don't have to do that." She looked at her leg. "I don't think it's that bad. I don't need to go to the hospital."

"Let's just get a doctor's opinion." He knelt down and looked at her nasty wound.

Elise became hysterical. Her hands began to sweat and a look of horror came over her face. "No, please. I'm terrified of hospitals. I don't want to go. Please don't ask me to go." Elise grabbed hold of his hand and tried to keep him from going to his car.

He knew she needed medical attention. "Relax; I'm not going to leave you. I promise. You're going to be all right, but you need to have a doctor look at your leg."

"I don't want to go!" she screamed.

Surprised by her outburst, he tried to calm her. "Everything is going to be all right. You have to trust me. I'm going to pull my car around to the trail so you won't have to walk far. Stay right here. I'll be right back. Okay?" he asked.

Elise looked at him and nodded. The stranger ran away and Elise leaned back against a nearby tree. She hoped she wouldn't regret agreeing to go to the hospital.

Sheridan sat in the hospital waiting room watching reruns of *Three's Company* and looking at the hands on the clock move slowly around the dial. He was angry with himself for being so negligent. *How could I have hit someone with my bike? Please, God, let her be alright.* He was tired of waiting. They had been there for hours and the nurses wouldn't give him an update about her condition. When they arrived at the hospital he had attempted to go into the emergency room with her, but the hospital staff stopped him. They said that if he was needed, they would call him. He held her hand the entire ride to the hospital, but when he had to let go, she looked terrified. She even cried out for him. He felt bad. He had broken his promise not to leave her side.

Sheridan's intention that morning was to get in a little exercise by riding his bicycle through the park before he went to his friend Kyle's barbecue. He had been looking forward to the get-together all year long. He and a few of his buddies played cards, drank beer, and ate crabs—a party strictly for the guys.

He looked at the clock again. He had already missed the first three hours and he still needed to go home, shower, and change clothes. He decided to stop a nurse and try again to get some information. "Excuse me, could you give me an update on the woman I brought in?"

"I can't tell you anything, but I'll have a doctor come talk with you," the nurse replied.

Sheridan sat back down. He hoped he wouldn't have to wait much longer. All he wanted to do was get her stitched up and back to her car, and be on his way to the barbecue.

"Mr. Reed." A doctor invited him to walk down the hospital corridor. "Mr. Reed, your wife is ready to go. She just needed a few stitches. She did get a little hysterical when she saw the needle we used to give her a tetanus shot. I guess she's a little scared of hospitals, huh?"

Sheridan looked at the doctor strangely when he referred to Elise as his wife. He guessed the nurses had assumed she was his wife when he informed them that he would be paying for her hospital bill. After all, he was the reason she was in the hospital.

"Oh, yeah! She hates hospitals." Sheridan remembered how she reacted in the park when he suggested that she go to the hospital.

"I gave her a light sedative. She'll sleep 'til morning. You can take her home now."

The doctor pulled the curtain that surrounded the emergency cubicle. Elise lay on the bed sleeping soundly. Sheridan had to admit, she was a very attractive woman. Her slightly tousled hair lay over her left eye. Her beauty branded his heart, leaving a lasting impression.

"Here's a prescription for the pain." The physician handed Sheridan a piece of paper. "The nurse will bring you her discharge papers."

What am I going to do with her now that she is asleep? Sheridan wondered. "Damn, I'm going to miss that barbecue," he said out loud.

Elise focused her eyes on a photograph that hung against the wall across from her. The photo captured the innocence of a twelve-year-old boy dribbling a basketball. The photo and the boy were both unfamiliar to her, so she closed her eyes again, thinking it was all a dream. She turned over and pulled the covers over her head. *This bed seems awfully hard,* she thought. *It's usually much softer.* She smelled the scent of the sheets and that too was unfamiliar. These sheets didn't smell like Gain laundry detergent. She lifted her head and stared around the room. This wasn't her bedroom. The

walls were a dull blue color. The far wall was devoted to baseball caps of various shapes and sizes,
and trophies were crammed onto a small shelf in
the corner.

Not exactly sure where she was, she listened to
the noise coming from the other room. She could
hear someone cooking in the kitchen. Elise attempted to swing her legs off the side of the bed,
but a surge of pain shot up her leg. She grabbed
her leg, hoping to stop the burning sensation.

She looked up and the stranger from the park
was watching her. He stood in the doorway holding a bowl. He wore a Dajuan Wagner basketball
jersey with a pair of black, oversized basketball
shorts. His muscular, tattooed arms exposed the
fact that he worked out daily.

"Good morning. Are you hungry?" he asked.
Elise watched the words slide off his lips. His lips invited her to come closer. For a split second she
wondered what it would feel like to have those lips
pressed against her lips, neck, and breasts.

"Do you remember what happened yesterday?"
he asked.

The last thing she remembered was being in the
hospital and being poked with a needle.

"You may still be a little incoherent from yesterday. The hospital gave you a sedative. They said
you were pretty upset about getting a needle." He
flashed a devilish smile that looked like Denzel
Washington's.

The throbbing pain from her leg was becoming
a little too much for her to bear. The stranger noticed her holding her leg. "Your prescription pain
pills are sitting on the nightstand next to you."

She turned and grabbed the bottle of pills. "Thanks," she replied.

"I'm making breakfast. Would you like something to eat?"

She glanced over at the clock sitting on the nightstand. "Oh my goodness! It's eight o'clock in the morning? I spent the night here?" Elise thought about how worried Miles would be. "I have got to get out of here!" She jumped off the bed and the immediate pressure she applied to her leg caused her to stumble. Sheridan ran over to catch her before she fell to the floor. They looked into each other eyes and the attraction between them multiplied by ten. Elise pulled away from him.

"Where's my cell phone? I can't believe my phone didn't ring all night."

"Ma'am, you didn't have a cell phone on you," Sheridan informed her.

"I must have left it in my car. You kept me here all night? I don't even know you. Did you ever think I could be married? What am I going to tell my husband? He has probably called the police and reported me missing." Elise yelled a series of questions at him. She pushed his hand away from her and leaned against the wall to regain her balance.

"I'm really sorry. I didn't mean to cause you any problems. When I took you to the hospital, they assumed I was your husband. You didn't have any identification on you or a cell phone, so I had no choice but to bring you to my house. The sedative they gave you put you in a deep sleep. I couldn't ask you where you lived." Sheridan's voice got higher and higher. He tried to defend his actions to her.

Elise felt bad for lashing out at him the way she did. "I'm sorry. It's not your fault. You don't know my husband. If I'm ten minutes late coming back from the supermarket, he gets worried. Can you take me back to my car?"

He walked out of the room upset by her accusations. *How dare she get mad at me for helping her out? I could have left her at the hospital and they would have labeled her a Jane Doe. I messed up my plans trying to be a Good Samaritan.* He grabbed his keys from the key holder hanging by the front door. He looked at her, rolled his eyes, and walked out, leaving the front door wide open. She followed behind him, limping.

Sheridan hated for a woman to be upset with him. Although he knew that he had done no wrong, he didn't want her to leave upset. "I really didn't expect for you to sleep through the night. I thought you were going to wake up in an hour or two and go home. Is everything going to be all right at home?" he asked.

"Everything will be fine," she replied.

He pulled up next to her car.

"Do you have a pen and a piece of paper?" she asked.

"In the glove compartment."

Elise pulled out a small notepad and pen. She scribbled her name and address on the sheet of paper, tore it off, and handed it to him. "I assume the hospital is going to send my hospital bill to your address."

"Yeah, I did give them my address."

"When you get the bill, can you send it to me?"

"No." He pushed the paper away. "I'll take care of the bill. I am the one responsible for your accident."

"No, I insist. Please send me the bill and I will have my insurance company take care of it."

"Okay," he replied reluctantly, taking the slip of paper.

Thirty minutes later, Elise opened her front door and came face to face with Miles. He sat on the bottom step of their winding staircase with his head in his hands. He lifted his head and Elise saw the worry in his eyes.

He saw the bandage wrapped around her leg and he ran over to her. He lightly brushed his hand over the gauze covering her leg. "Elise, what happened? I was so worried about you! I've been calling you all night. Where have you been?"

"I got in a minor accident in the park."

"In a car accident? Are you all right?" he asked and pulled her over to sit on the steps.

"No, not in a car accident." She carefully sat down on the steps, trying her hardest not to move her leg any more than she had to. "Some guy ran into me on his bike in the park yesterday. I was bleeding badly, so he took me to the hospital and they gave me stitches."

"You went to the hospital?" he asked, surprised.

"They gave me a tetanus shot. I completely lost it when I saw the needle. They had to give me a sedative to calm me down. So I spent the night at the hospital." This was the first time she had ever lied to her husband. She felt it would be best if she spared him the truth. The truth would only add to the problems they already had.

"The hospital! I didn't even think to call there."

"I left my identification and cell phone in the car, and the man who took me to the hospital didn't know my name. So they had no idea how to contact my family."

"Who is the guy who took you to the hospital?"

"I'm not sure. I didn't get his name."

"You never saw him before at the park?"

"No!" She wondered if he believed her story. "I caught a cab from the hospital back to my car this morning."

"Honey, I was so worried about you. I had so many terrible thoughts running through my mind. I wasn't sure if I should call the police. I thought . . ." He stopped mid sentence.

"You thought what?"

"I thought you left me. Maybe the problems we've been having was too much for you to bear." Her heart crumpled. She hated to hear him talk like that.

"You have no reason to think that way. I told you I'd never leave you."

"I panicked. I couldn't reach you and I thought the worst."

"I love you!" She leaned over and kissed her husband on the lips. "Can you help me up the stairs? I need to take a shower."

CHAPTER 4

The hands on the clock approached the eleven o'clock hour. Sunday school teachers were bringing their lessons to a close while members of the congregation arrived for Sunday morning service.

"Can someone volunteer to close us out in prayer?" Tressie asked her Sunday school class.

A group of seven-year-olds waved their hands, begging to be picked. Tressie looked out among them and chose Dontonio, who was hiding behind his sister. "Dontonio, why don't you close us out in prayer?" she asked.

"Awwwww man, why you pick me?"

" 'Cause you were trying to hide from me, that's why. I'm sure the Lord would love to hear from you. Please close us out in prayer." The children gathered around, held hands, and formed a circle.

"Dear Lord, I want to thank you for waking me

up this morning," the boy said. "Bless my mother, my father, and my sister. Amen. Oh! And bless Ms. Tressie, too."

Tressie looked up and smiled at Dontonio. "Thank you for including me. I'll see you next week, all right?"

"Yes, Ms. Tressie."

Tressie straightened up the church pews as the children gathered their things to go home. She grabbed a stack of Bibles and returned them to their place on the back of the church pews.

"Ms. Tressie?" Ta'Lena, one of her Sunday School students, called out her name. "This man was outside looking for you." Ta'Lena pulled a man by his hand into the sanctuary.

Tressie turned around and looked straight into those eyes. Those captivating eyes that held her completely hypnotized before; long, perfectly curled eyelashes above almond-shaped eyes. It was him. He was here. A wave of heat suddenly passed through her body like a storm. Except this storm held her like a hurricane that kept circling around inside of her.

"Hello," Tressie greeted him.

"Hi," Payce responded. Ta'Lena instinctively let go of his hand and ran back outside with the other children.

"Nice to see you again. What brings you here this morning?" Tressie asked.

"I came here to see you," Payce answered.

Before she could respond, Reverend Kane, the associate pastor, came up to her with the morning service program. "Tressie, I need for you make a few announcements at the start of the morning service, and I want to change the scripture reading."

Tressie stood and listened to the adjustments Reverend Kane wanted for the program. Before the pastor had a chance to walk away, Tressie stopped her.

"Reverend Kane, this is a friend of mine, Payce."

The minister turned and reached for Payce's hand. "Hello, Payce." She greeted him with a huge smile and shook his hand. "I'm glad you came to worship with us this morning." She turned back to Tressie. "Thanks again for those changes, Tressie."

The organist began to play the opening hymn, giving the signal that service was about to begin. Tressie excused herself and took her seat in the pulpit next to Reverend Simms, the senior pastor. After the opening hymn concluded, Tressie led the church in prayer. As she bowed her head, she glanced over in Payce's direction. He winked his eye at her and she replied with a smile. *He is so cute*, she thought to herself.

Reverend Simms stood before the congregation and delivered a soul-wrenching sermon. "Church!" Reverend Simms screamed. "Beware of wolves that disguise themselves in sheep's clothing. Everything ain't what it seems. I Peter 5:8 tells us to be careful and watch out for attacks from the devil; for the devil prowls around like a roaring lion looking for victims to devour." Tressie absorbed the words of wisdom spoken by Reverend Simms.

After church, Payce waited around to speak with Tressie.

"I was so surprised to see you today," she said to him.

"I remember seeing you in Harrisburg, and my brother mentioned that you lived in Philly. Finally, after a lot of harassment and putting myself in debt by promising to get his car washed every week for the next three months, he told me your name and what church you attended."

"I'm flattered that you went through so much trouble."

"On my way over here I hoped that you would be worth all this fuss. Now that I'm here, I can see that you are."

Payce's compliments left Tressie speechless. She silently thanked the Lord for answering her prayers. He was what she had prayed for. She asked the Lord to send her a man who knew the Lord, but also knew the streets. She didn't want an up-tight church boy who always followed the rules. She needed a man who broke at least some of the rules and created his own. It looked like Payce was that man.

"Would you like to go get something to eat?" he asked.

"Sure. There's a diner around the corner we could walk to."

They arrived at the diner and were immediately seated. Tressie had been to the diner at least one hundred times before, so she already knew what she wanted to order.

"Pastor Kane looks very familiar to me. Has she been with your church very long?" Payce asked.

"She's been a part of our church for probably five or six years now."

"She looks so familiar. I've probably seen her at one of the conferences or meetings that my father has, but I don't want to talk about the church. I want to find out more about Montrese Cox."

Tressie looked over at him. He was casually dressed in a blue-striped button up Sean John shirt with a pair of matching blue khakis. She loved his style. She could definitely fall for him.

"There's not much to tell. I'm a full time student at Temple University. I'm majoring in psychology. I lead a boring life."

"Well, it can't be that boring if they voted you in to hold a position with the church state conference, along with my brother."

"Oh yes, your brother. I had no idea your brother had a twin."

"Well, he wouldn't tell anybody. I'm the bad boy of the family."

Luckily I like bad boys, Tressie thought.

"I heard that you were away for a little while," she replied.

"Yeah, I did some stupid things that got me locked up, but I'm home now and I'm determined to do better. I just need a good woman by my side to keep me out of trouble."

"I'll say a prayer that you'll find that woman."

He looked into her eyes. "I think I already have."

"I did it! I prayed without ceasing! I took my troubles to the Lord and he answered my prayers!" Tressie screamed as she danced her way into the church.

Everyone was gathered together going over their current Bible Study lesson when Tressie burst in with her testimony.

"Did everyone see my man in church Sunday?" Tressie asked.

Olivia was glad to see Tressie so happy. It had been a long time since she had smiled so much. She had seen Tressie and Payce together in church and thought they looked like a cute couple.

"I was surprised to see him here!" Elise replied.

"So was I, but he tracked me down and he came there specifically to see me," Tressie rejoiced. She sat down in the pew smiling. She was obviously in a cheerful mood.

"I just want to testify that God does answer prayer. When Elise told us to increase our prayer time, I did. I began praying in the morning before my first class and in the afternoon. Plus, I prayed on the train after my final class ended. Elise said that we could pray for anything we wanted, so I prayed for a man, and I was very specific about the man I prayed for. I did ask God not to send me anyone who would remind me of Payne Boyd."

"But, isn't that exactly what he sent you?" Elise asked.

Tressie started laughing. "Yes. Payne's twin brother, but he is the total opposite of his brother. They may look alike, but that is where the similarities end."

"Wait a minute, you're dating Bishop Boyd's son?" Olivia asked.

Tressie nodded. "Let me finish telling you about my blessing. I began praying to the Lord telling him I wanted a man who believed in God, but I didn't want a corny church guy. I told God that I wanted him to be fine and respect me, and Payce is all those things. He's different from the kinds of guys I've dated in the past, I wanted a change."

Tressie's past boyfriends were at one time all residents of the county jail. Everyone attracted to her had a criminal record, cornrows in their hair, and Timberlands on their feet. It was hard not to confuse them with one another because their matching tan khaki outfits made them look like they were still imprisoned in the penitentiary prison yard. This stereotype included her former, long-time boyfriend, Jabril. Jabril was currently serving a fifteen-year sentence for drug trafficking.

Tressie had plenty of life-threatening stories involving Jabril. They had been stuck up, shot at, and even car-jacked together, but none of this stopped her from standing by her man.

Jabril was a big time drug dealer from Camden, New Jersey who made a lot of money and bought Tressie whatever she wanted. A drug deal gone bad made him a fugitive. He was apprehended by the police on Christmas Day, and his arrest was televised on the eleven o'clock nightly news. Before he was transported to the county jail from the police station, he stopped to give a statement to the press.

"I'd like to thank each and every one of you for coming here tonight to report on my arrest and the pending charges against me. First I want to declare my innocence. I have done nothing wrong. Secondly, I'd like to give a message to my girlfriend, Tressie." Jabril abruptly snatched the microphone from the reporter. "Tressie, I love you, and if you ever leave me or if I catch you with another nigga, I'll kill you."

The police pushed him into the waiting police transport and closed the door. Tressie watched the local affiliate stations air that statement for two days straight. Tressie feared for her life. She knew what Jabril could do to her, even from behind prison walls. During his trial, television stations replayed the threat against her life. Jabril was found guilty and sentenced to fifteen years, plus an additional eighteen months was added to his time for the televised threat he made on Tressie's life. Some time had passed before Tressie felt safe enough to date again.

"When I first laid eyes on Payce, I knew he was the one," Tressie continued. "I just wanted to share my story with everyone here so that you would continue to pray."

"Thank you," Elise said to Tressie. "It is important to pray without ceasing. Pray to the Lord about the things you want and continue to pray for them until he answers your prayer. But keep in mind that the things you pray for must be in accordance with the will of God. Don't ask the Lord to give you someone else's husband because that is not going to happen. Don't ask the Lord to successfully see you through on robbing a bank because it's not going to happen. God is not going to give you or put things in your life that are going to harm you, so if you're praying about something, and he doesn't answer, then perhaps the Lord doesn't want you to have it. Some things were not meant to be."

Olivia thought about herself and Bryant. She had prayed to the Lord every day about them getting married, but she was beginning to think it was useless. She had brought up the subject of marriage to him the other day, and he quickly changed the subject. Perhaps Elise was right. Maybe some things were not meant to be.

MID OCTOBER 2003

Val hung up the telephone as Julian walked into the kitchen.

"Olivia said to tell you hello."

"How is she doing?" he asked.

"She's doing well. She said she's getting bigger and bigger every day."

"I bet she looks funny with her big belly and skinny body," Julian replied.

Val smiled at the thought of her cousin being pregnant. "Julian, where are you going?" Val asked as he kissed her and grabbed his keys.

"Oh, I have a meeting with the general manager."

"What time will you be back?" she asked.

"I'm not sure, but don't wait up."

"Julian, you have gone out every night this week. You said you were going to take me out last night and you couldn't because practice ran late. When are you going to be able to spend some time with me? I sit in this house night after night, alone."

"Valencia, please don't complain. I try the best I can to get home to you at a decent hour. I'm sorry I couldn't take you out last night, but you know how important it is for me to grow with this team. I have to learn everything I can in order to adapt to this new environment. I have to learn new plays, get accustomed to how the other players make advances on the court, and on top of all that, the general manager has asked me to attend a few important meetings concerning the team's future. That's a lot of responsibility for the rookie of the team." Julian took her hand in his. "I promise you that when things settle down I'll spend all my extra time with you. All right?"

Val watched through the living room window as Julian pulled out of their driveway. She was not looking forward to sitting in that big house by herself, again. Is this what she had to look forward to once they got married? Val and Julian had moved to Seattle the first week in September. Julian bought a large house in an exclusive section of suburban Seattle. The five-bedroom house had everything: a swimming pool, two car garage, home theater room, and state-of-the-art kitchen, but even with all those luxuries, she was still lonely.

Before their move out west, Val had been accepted to the University of Washington. She planned on continuing her education so she could graduate on time, but Julian suggested she take a year off. He thought it would be good for her to begin their wedding plans. She reluctantly agreed, but lately every time she mentioned the wedding to Julian, he changed the subject or insisted that they talk about it later.

Val had only been in Seattle a short time, but she already missed the familiar sounds of Philadelphia. She missed the cheese steaks sold at Jim's on South Street, the familiar sound of Carter n' Sanborn on the radio, and the unity of brotherly love that the city represented. She especially missed Olivia. Olivia was going to have her first child in a couple of months and it hurt Val, because she knew she wouldn't be around to watch the baby grow. Val had thought about going for a visit, but she couldn't leave now. The season home opener was next week and she had to be there, plus she was looking forward to attending a party that the owner of the SuperSonics was throwing. The party would give her the opportunity to get better acquainted with the other players' wives and possibly make some new friends.

NOVEMBER 2003

Olivia and Bryant lay in her bedroom watching a Bruce Lee movie. Bryant had rented six of them and they were only on the third one. Tired from reading subtitles, Olivia turned over. The baby kept moving and she couldn't find a comfortable position. Bryant noticed her restless behavior and snuggled in closer to her. Olivia enjoyed her time alone with Bryant. He seemed to change into a different person when they were by themselves—more kind and considerate. For the past few months Bryant had been traveling out of town a lot, working in different cities, but now that her due date was quickly approaching, he had promised to stay close to home.

She lay against his chest as he rubbed her stomach. He pulled up her shirt to glorify the roundness of her belly. "Look at all this baby," he said proudly.

The extra weight was beginning to wear her down. "The baby is getting so big. I wish he would hurry up and come."

The soft kisses Bryant planted on her neck suggested he wanted more than a simple kiss. His hands gradually moved down around her hips and slid off her panties. Olivia sat up and straddled him, allowing the baby to rest on him.

"By the size of your stomach, he should be a ten-pounder," Bryant said.

Bryant slid out of his boxers and into her. Olivia frowned as he entered her.

"Are you all right?" He asked.

"Yeah, I'm all right. Just a little uncomfortable."

"Am I hurting you?"

"No, I'm okay."

Bryant grabbed her hips and took things really slowly. He didn't want to hurt her or the baby. He looked up into her face and her frown had been replaced with a smile.

He was glad she was enjoying herself. It was the first time in a long time Olivia had allowed Bryant to touch her. Any attempts he made to initiate sex were refused. She always claimed she wasn't feeling well. But just because she refused to give him any, didn't mean he went without. When working out of town, Bryant always managed to meet female companions who were willing to share their love with him.

Over the past year Bryant had enjoyed spending time with Olivia. There was definitely something special about her. Usually, Bryant wasn't attracted to churchgoing women. The women he usually dated drank all day and had sex all night. He was used to the fast, ghetto girls, but Olivia possessed a soft, quiet demeanor and beautiful, subtle looks that could easily be overlooked if one didn't pay close attention. Those qualities were probably what attracted him to her, but what made him continue dating her was her kind, compassionate, and unselfish nature. She was the first girl he had ever met who cared about him unconditionally. Bryant was used to girls trying to use him to pay their rent or pay for daycare. Not Olivia. She asked him how his day was and was sincerely interested in his job and the work he did. He loved those attributes and if he ever decided to settle down he wanted to find a girl just like her. Unfortunately, now was a bad time. There was no place in his world for Olivia. He refused to allow his feelings to interfere with business. Like his uncle always said, "Money first, pussy second."

It felt so good being inside of her that Bryant couldn't hold back any longer. He exploded inside of her. Exhausted and tired, he still wanted more, but Olivia had other things in mind. She immediately climbed off him and fell fast asleep. He knew that if he attempted to wake her up, it would be in vain, but maybe later he would be able to entice her into a second round.

Bryant turned over and tried to get some sleep. He tossed in bed until the clock read five a.m. Not able to endure any more restless sleep, he surrendered to his insomnia and got up to cook breakfast.

He walked down the hall into the kitchen and looked in the refrigerator. Inside was a carton of eggs, bacon, and orange juice. Placing them on the kitchen table, Bryant looked around for a frying pan. He opened one cabinet and found drinking glasses. He pulled one out to pour himself a glass of orange juice. After making several more attempts, he finally found a frying pan.

He threw some bacon into the pan. He watched the bacon slowly turn brown and the sizzling sound drew him into a trance. Getting hot from the stove, Bryant walked over and opened the sliding glass door allowing the autumn breeze to cool off the apartment. He looked out into the forest of trees that expanded across the back of their apartment complex. Thoughts of Daneesha drifted through his mind. She had been calling him, leaving several messages on his voice mail. He knew he needed to go see her soon, but he couldn't leave Olivia right now. She was so close to her due date.

"A penny for your thoughts," came a voice from behind him.

Bryant turned around. Olivia was standing in the doorway holding her stomach.

"Are you feeling okay?" he asked.

"I think I'm having contractions. About twenty minutes ago I had a sharp pain go up my back."

Suddenly she grabbed her belly and motioned for the chair. "Bryant, these pains are getting more intense."

"Do you want to go to the hospital?"

"No, my doctor said that I should try to hold out for as long as possible. Lots of new mothers are sent home from the hospital several times before they are actually admitted."

"Maybe we shouldn't have made love last night."

She responded with a look that said *maybe you're right.* She sat in the chair, breathing heavily as if it took all her strength to walk over to that chair.

"Can I get you a glass of orange juice?" he asked.

She nodded. He poured her a glass and placed it in front of her.

"It sure smells good in here. I'm surprised Danyelle hasn't rushed out here yet. Let me go ask her if she's hungry."

As she attempted to get up from the table, she let out a piercing scream. Bryant turned around. Olivia was frozen with fear. She stared down at the kitchen floor. Her water had broken.

Bryant rushed to her side. "Livie, everything is going to be all right. Do you have a hospital bag ready?"

"It's behind my bedroom door," she answered breathlessly.

He ran into the bedroom and grabbed the small yellow suitcase. He raced back to her side. "Come on, I'll help you to the car."

As they were leaving, Danyelle came out of her room. "What's going on? I heard someone scream."

"Olivia's water broke and I'm taking her to the hospital." Bryant said. "Danyelle, call the doctor and tell him to meet us at the hospital. His number is next to the telephone in the living room."

*   *   *

"Bryant, watch out for the—" Bryant came to a screeching halt just before hitting the back of a trash truck. Olivia held one hand to her heart and the other on the dashboard. She felt another contraction. "Oh no! Here comes another one." Olivia reached out for Bryant's hand.

"Breathe," Bryant instructed her. "Breathe out through your mouth."

"Bryant, this hurts." She gripped his hand a little tighter. "Can you get me to the hospital—now?" Olivia demanded through clinched teeth.

Bryant put the car in reverse, pulled around the trash truck, and sped off toward the hospital. Ten minutes later they arrived. A nurse wheeled Olivia away in a wheelchair while Bryant was left with the admitting clerk, providing Olivia's information.

Bryant eventually tracked Olivia down in the maternity ward. Her belly was hooked up to a monitor. She was immersed in an episode of Maury Povich. Bryant looked up at the television screen. The caption read, "I'm a man trapped in a woman's body."

"You appear to be doing better," Bryant commented.

"I do feel a little better, but I'm still in pain. They gave me some ice chips to chew on." Olivia pointed to the bowl sitting beside her. "I'd rather have a cheese steak."

He laughed. "Sweetheart, I'll be right back. I'm going to give Danyelle a call. I want to keep her updated on your progress." Bryant walked toward the door.

"Hurry back," she cried out.

Bryant walked out of her room and down the hall to the waiting area. He pulled out his cell phone and dialed her number.

"Hello."

"Hello, beautiful," Bryant said into the phone.

"Bryant, where have you been? I have been calling you leaving messages and you haven't returned any of my phone calls."

"Daneesha, I've been busy. I told you I had a lot of business to attend to."

"Yeah, well while you've been out there taking care of business, I got Marquise and Marquita's fathers to relinquish their parental rights. Now, all you have to do is come and sign these papers and you can adopt my kids."

"That's great. I should be there in two weeks to come sign the papers."

"Two weeks? I thought we were supposed to be getting married? I haven't spoken to you once to discuss one detail about our nuptials. "

"I thought we decided to wait until after the baby was born. That would give me some time to make some money to support my new family."

"Well, what about the children? You're the one who said you wanted to adopt my kids, but you're never here to spend any time with them. You act just like their real daddies."

"Daneesha, I'll be there in two weeks."

"Marquise, stop hitting your sister!" Daneesha screamed at the children.

Bryant looked up to see Olivia's doctor walking in his direction.

"Listen baby, I have to go, but I'll call you later, I

promise." He hung up before she had a chance to protest.

"Hello, I'm Doctor Purtell. Are you the father of Ms. Benson's baby?"

"Yes, I am. Is everything all right?"

"Yes, everything is fine. Olivia is coming along beautifully. I just examined her and she is dilating quickly. You should have a new baby within a couple of hours. I just wanted to keep you informed of what was going on."

"Thanks a lot, Doc."

Bryant turned and pulled out his cell phone again. "Unc, I'm at University of Penn. I just finished talking with the doctor. He said the baby should be born within the next few hours. Can you get that business together? I want to hurry up and deliver that package and get this over with. Thanks a lot. Call me back when you get a chance."

Bryant hung up the phone and rushed back to Olivia.

"Push, Push!" Bryant yelled.

"Olivia, give me one big push and I promise you we'll be done," the doctor pleaded from between her legs.

They had been in the labor room for over an hour. Olivia was pushing and pushing to birth her son, and finally one more push delivered him.

"Here he is," Dr. Purtell announced. The doctor cleared the baby's nasal passages and passed him to his parents.

"Hello, Bryce Robert Winters," Olivia cooed as she was handed the baby. She held him as he stretched and squirmed. "Look at our son. Isn't he beautiful?"

Bryant smiled at his son. "He came into the world screaming; yelling just like his momma." Olivia looked at Bryant and smiled.

CHAPTER 5

DECEMBER 2003

"... and Lord I ask that you watch out for my cousin Val and Julian while they make crazy dollars out in Seattle. Amen."

"Amen," everyone said in unison.

"Thank you, Danyelle, for opening the meeting in prayer," Elise said, then directed her attention toward the remaining members of their Bible Study group. "Can I get a show of hands of individuals who doubled their prayer time since the last time we met?"

No one raised their hands.

"Okay, who has increased their prayer time by at least twenty-five percent?" Elise asked.

Again, no one raised their hands.

"No one here has increased their prayer time?" Elise asked, astonished.

Olivia spoke up first. "Elise, I've been so busy

with the baby. I haven't had time to sit down and pray."

"Olivia, since you brought it up, let's discuss 'not having enough time to pray.' I realize that everyone here has a life outside of church. Olivia, you're a new mother. Danyelle, you work. And Tressie, you attend college. All of you have very busy schedules, which can leave you with little time to pray."

"Elise, I always plan on saying a prayer in the morning or right before I go to bed, but the baby wakes me up at four thirty every morning. That's the start of my day. I feed him and get him washed and dressed. Then I try to clean the house, and by noon, I'm tired. All I want to do is sleep."

"Olivia, I understand that your days are long. I'm sure everyone here wishes there were more hours in each day to carry out all their responsibilities."

"I sure do," Tressie commented.

"Time management is essential to having a successful relationship with God. Designate private time to commune with God. Keep in mind that you don't have to kneel down to pray. You can talk to God anywhere—in your car, on the train, or at your desk before the workday begins. The important thing is that you take the time to speak with God. Thank him for the things he has done for you and tell him about the different things going on in your life. He loves to hear from his children," Elise pointed out.

"I have set up my cell phone to remind me to pray, but I've found that life is too unexpected to stick to a daily schedule," Danyelle responded.

"I'm constantly being interrupted with different things which make it hard to maintain a constant prayer life. To pray every day is a lot. Isn't it enough to just pray at Bible Study and church? Do we have to pray every day?"

"Danyelle, what if God said 'I'm only accepting prayer requests on Sundays and Wednesdays?' Do you realize how chaotic the world would be? Prayers from parents with sick children and people starving in third world countries—their prayers would go unheard. God wants to hear from us every day."

"I agree with Danyelle," Olivia commented. "Too many unexpected things can happen during a day to throw you off track."

"What about you, Tressie? Do you feel the same as Olivia and Danyelle?" Elise asked.

"I did increase my prayer time when you first asked us to. But since then I have slacked off. With school and spending so much time with Payce, I find it difficult to stay committed to my prayer time. It's been a few days since the last time I prayed," Tressie admitted.

"Ladies, I know it's hard. Satan will do what he has to do to prevent you from speaking with God. His job is to put distance between you and the Lord. If he manages to squeeze a wedge between you and God, things will start happening in your life that will force you to pray. Just keep that in mind."

A chauffeured limousine pulled up in front of their house at precisely six thirty. Val and Julian were attending a party hosted by the owners of the

Seattle SuperSonics. The entire Sonics organization would be in attendance that night—the owner, the general manager, the president, all the players, and their spouses.

Since the season began, Val had only been able to attend one game, and that was the season opener. She was excited to see Julian play in his first professional game. The entire Sonics team ran out onto the court in single file. Julian wore the number three proudly pasted across his back. He stretched with the team at half court. He didn't start the game, but the coach did put him in at the start of the second quarter. He was only in the game for ten minutes, but he scored nine points by making three three-pointers. Val could see the excitement in his face over his spectacular performance. The SuperSonics won the game ninety-nine to ninety-seven.

During the game Val realized how lonely she really was. In Philly, Olivia had always attended Julian's games with her, but in Seattle she was alone. She had been looking forward to attending that night's game, not just to see Julian play, but to possibly make some new friends.

When Val arrived at the Key Arena, an usher escorted her to Julian's reserved seats. Val was well aware of the fact that the women who had seats around hers were either married or dating some of the other players, so she wanted to take the opportunity to get more acquainted with those women. When Val sat down in her seat she flashed a friendly smile to the two women sitting to the right of her, but both responded by rolling their eyes and turning their heads. Surprised by their response, she introduced herself to the women sitting to her left and they too turned their noses up at her. Val was disappointed, but she wasn't going to allow their cold attitude to discourage her from wanting to make friends. She would think of a different way to make friends with them.

They pulled up in front of the Hotel Monaco. The parking lot attendant opened Val's door and helped her step out into the brisk Seattle night air. Julian came up behind her and placed his hand on the small of her back. He led her up the front steps and into the lobby.

Once they were in the elevator the attendant asked, "What floor, sir?"

"We're attending the Sonics party," Julian replied.

The attendant punched the seventy-sixth floor. Val looked stunning in a gold Cynthia Rowley strapless dress, while her fiancé redefined the term debonair in a black suit made by Marc Jacobs.

Julian pulled at his collar. "I wish we didn't have to dress up."

"It doesn't hurt to wear a suit every once in a while," Val responded.

The elevator attendant announced, "Penthouse floor." The elevator doors opened and they stepped into the breathtaking entrance of the banquet hall.

Val was speechless. Her wide eyes studied the unforgettable Seattle skyline from two walls made entirely of glass. A staircase that resembled the one in *Gone With The Wind* led to an outside balcony.

The room was full of people, leading Val to think she and Julian were the last ones to arrive. The first person to greet them was Mr. Hass, the

owner of the team. "Hello, Julian. I've been looking for you all night."

"Hello, Mr. Haas," Julian replied, shaking his
boss's hand. "How are you doing?"

"I'm doing so much better now that you're here,
our star player. There are a dozen people I want to
introduce you to." He noticed Val standing next to
Julian. "Oh, I'm sorry. Where are my manners?
This must be the beautiful bride-to-be, Valencia."

Val reached out to shake his hand.

"You look lovely," Mr. Hass said to Val. He
wrapped Val's arm around his. "Please follow me?"
For the next two hours Theodore Haas introduced
Val and Julian to every employee of the basketball
organization. They met everyone from the president to the towel boys. By the middle of the night
Val was tired.

Val and Julian had stopped mingling to speak
with Carlos and Pilar Torres. Carlos Torres was the
only Latino player on the team, and also one of
the few Latino players in the entire league. Julian
and Carlos entered an intense debate over the future of the team, while Pilar initiated a conversation with Val. "I remember seeing you at the
season home opener on Tuesday."

"Yes, I was there. I don't remember seeing you."

"Oh no, I don't sit in the players' reserved seats.
I usually watch the game from the luxury suites."

Pilar was a beautiful twenty-eight-year-old mother
of three. That did not include the one she was so
elegantly carrying in her womb. Her long, black
hair was pulled back in a classic 1930s style bun.
She wore a form-fitting maroon dress by Nicole
Miller that flowed nicely over her growing belly.

Val swallowed the last of her glass of wine. "Could you walk me over to the bar?" Val asked Pilar. "Do you fellas want another drink? I'm heading over to the bar," Val said.

"No, we're okay," Julian replied.

The two women walked over to the bar where Val ordered herself another glass of wine.

"Carlos is so excited about Julian joining the team. He really thinks they have a chance at winning the championship this year." Pilar enunciated her words as slowly as possible. Her thick Spanish accent was hard to understand at times.

"Well, they are off to a good start. If they continue to play like they did on Tuesday, they have a good chance of bringing the trophy to Seattle," Val said.

"Are you from Seattle?" Pilar asked.

"No, we're both from Philadelphia."

"So you're not familiar with Seattle at all?"

"No, not really."

"How about one day next week we have lunch together? We can go shopping and I'll show you around the city."

"I would really like that. Since I've been here I haven't really had a chance to get out and meet anyone yet."

"So you've been sitting in the house by yourself while Julian goes to team meetings and practice," Pilar guessed.

Val nodded her head yes and took a sip from her glass.

"Yes, it was that way for me too when Carlos and I first moved here. But after a while I got accustomed to him not being home. It gets kind of lonely, so I occupy my time with our children." She leaned her arm against the bar. "Sometimes I have to be both parents to our children. A lot of the time he's on the road, at practice, or out with the fellows."

"Yes, Julian has not spent a lot of time with me. But I have tried to be understanding. I realize that he's just entering the league and it's going to take him a while to get accustomed to handling the responsibilities of work and home. Once his rookie year is over, we'll get married and things will get better."

"You don't think that the money and fame will change him? He signed an awfully large contract."

"I know Julian. Money will never change him."

"Can I offer you some advice?" Pilar asked while gently placing her hand on Val's arm. Val looked at her suspiciously, waiting on her to continue. "If you want to keep Julian, make him realize that home is with you."

"What do you mean by that?" Val asked.

"What I mean is that Julian's financial situation has probably multiplied ten times since he's entered the league and the money only gets better each year. A lot of people, namely home wreckers, will be jealous of what you and him have. They will try their hardest to take what's yours. I suggest you do whatever you think is necessary to keep him from leaving you."

"Oh, I'm not worried. Julian loves me," Val said with a spark of innocence in her eyes.

"Love doesn't have anything to do with sex," Pilar replied.

Val glanced over in Julian's direction. She saw a

woman across the room licking her lips at him. Julian smiled back at the woman and continued his conversation with Carlos.

Pilar watched the scene unfold between Julian and the stranger. "Just keep in mind, the Sonics organization keeps plenty of women available for the players to play with in their spare time."

"Tressie, I promise you I'll call you when I get in." Payce unlocked the passenger side door for his friend, Darshon. "Tressie, I don't know what time I'm going to get in. We're just going out to the club. I have to go. I'll call you later." He hung up his phone.

"What's going on, player?" Darshon yelled out. Payce held out his fist and Darshon responded back with a pound.

"I was on the phone with my girl. She's asking me a million questions. Where am I going? Who am I going with? When will I be home? You would think we were married."

"She acts like that because that's what she wants. That's what they all want. They want the man to willingly put on the handcuffs and walk down the aisle of matrimony."

Payce laughed at his friend.

"Is that the girl you met at your father's church conference?"

Payce nodded his head.

"You've been seeing her for a while. Be careful, man. Church women are the worst. Women already think they're right about everything, but a

church woman will pull out her Bible and recite
scripture to prove she's right."

Payce laughed at Darshon. For once he did have
a point. "Man, why did you have me pick you up at
the corner? Is there something wrong at home?"

"I was looking out for you," Darshon replied.

"Why? What's up?"

"Lisa heard you were home."

"Ah, man. That girl. Is she still up to the same
ole thing?"

"Yeah, she hasn't changed a bit. She kept asking
me, 'Where's Payce? When is Payce coming around?'
I told her you don't roll with her kind, but she swears
she can turn you out."

Payce laughed at the thought of her trying to
track him down. "She thought I was joking when I
told her that if we were to get busy, I'd have to play
the part of the man. She's not strapping nothing
on and doing me."

Darshon laughed. "Man, I don't know. Lisa
must have something lethal. She has all these girls
calling my mom's house for her. They buy her
clothes and jewelry. One even offered to buy her a
car. She makes me wonder what she's doing that
I'm not."

"She must be digging those girls out."

"Man, I'm about to pay her to give me some
lessons. If I had women catering to me the way she
has all those chicken heads, I wouldn't have any
problems."

Payce drove to Center City, Philadelphia where
Darshon directed him to a small street off Market
Street.

"Man, pull into this parking lot," Darshon directed.

"Give these to the attendant." Darshon pulled out two small metal squares that closely resembled a pair of cuff links and gave them to Payce. The attendant took the pieces of metal, walked over to the garage door, and inserted them into the wall. The huge metal garage door that faced them rose up and a ramp platform was lowered to the ground. Payce stared at the ultramodern device.

"Go ahead, man. Enter," Darshon urged him.

"Darshon, where are you taking me?"

"I told you—someplace we haven't been before."

"Yeah, but this seems like some underground shit. Something where you have to have a membership to get in."

"Relax, you're going to enjoy yourself," Darshon reassured him.

They parked the car, walked to the elevator, and rode to the top floor in silence. Payce was skeptical of what Darshon was up to. They had been best friends since the fifth grade, and since then, Darshon always found the freakiest places for them to hang out. For Payce's eighteenth birthday, Darshon told him that they were going to an exclusive resort in Florida. It was a nudist colony. Payce could never forget the time Darshon got them on a cruise ship that was filming the sequel to the *Girls Gone Wild* movie. *Nothing could top that weekend*, Payce thought.

The elevator stopped and the doors opened. Payce followed Darshon down a long hallway until they stopped in front of a pair of glass doors. Payce read the words printed on the door. "The Doll-house Spa."

"A spa?" Payce stopped in his tracks. "Man, I'm not going into a woman's spa. Are you crazy? What happened to you while I was locked up? You've been hanging around your sister too much."

Darshon pulled him to the side. "Man, I promise you, this is not what you think. Would I ever steer you wrong?"

"Yes, everything you do is wrong."

"I'm the one who took you to your first strip club, I'm the one who got you your first three-some, and I'm the one who has always had your back. Now trust me on this one. It's all right!"

Everything he said was true. Payce reluctantly let his defenses down and walked into the spa with him.

A girl with long, sandy blond hair greeted them at the door. She wore a T-shirt three sizes too small. On it were the words "sugar and spice."

"Hi, remember me? I'm Darshon."

The girl looked at him closely. "Oh yeah, I re-member you. The last time you were here you came with your sister," she replied.

"Your sister." Payce chuckled.

Darshon hit him to shut up. "Yeah, that's right. This time I brought my friend with me. This is Payce. This is his first time here and he is also a very good friend of my sister's. So can you make sure he receives the VIP treatment?"

"Of course," she replied. "Any friend of Lisa's is a friend of ours."

She grabbed Payce's hand and led him down the hall. Darshon followed them to a small white room with no furniture. A robe hanging from a hook on the wall was the only thing in the room.

"Take off all your clothes and change into the robe. I'll be back to get you," she instructed Payce.

"Payce, I'll meet you in the massage room," Darshon yelled out before the receptionist closed the door.

"Darshon better not be playing games," Payce said.

After he changed into the robe, the receptionist led him to a room where Darshon was getting a massage by two Japanese women. Payce was surprised to see the women massaging him in the nude.

Darshon lay there as if he were a king. "It's about time you made it."

One of the Japanese women gestured for Payce to lie down on the table next to Darshon.

"Man, what is this place and how did you find out about it?" Payce asked.

"My sister turned me on to this place."

"Oh, now I understand. This is one of her lesbian hangouts."

"Yeah, but not only lesbians work here. So do bisexuals. Man, just lay down and enjoy your massage. The night has just begun," Darshon told him.

They enjoyed the soothing massage with oils being rubbed into their backs and therapeutic candles burning around them.

Darshon ordered them each a shot of Hennessy and a Corona. "Payce, everything here is free—the drinks, the massages."

"How did you manage to work that out?"

"I told you Lisa hangs out here all the time. She is a really good customer, so she gets a lot of fringe benefits."

Darshon held up his glass of Hennessy. "Man, welcome home."

"Thanks. Glad to be home. I'm never going back to jail."

They tapped their glasses together. The sound from their glasses caused a curtain in the room to draw open. A large glass window revealed three women engaging in a threesome.

Darshon smiled at the performance as Payce watched in amazement. Payce was jealous. He wished he could join them.

"Man, you knew this was going to happen?" Payce asked.

"I had it all planned. And you were ready to fight me outside." He pointed to the window. "This is what they do here. They provide you with enjoyment and entertainment."

Payce was amazed. He studied the expressions on their faces. He could tell each one of the ladies was enjoying their time together.

The two Asian women masseuses turned Payce and Darshon over onto their backs and gave them each a full body massage. The feel of the women's hands allowed a low moan to escape from Payce; acknowledging how good it felt.

After the women were done Darshon sat up and wrapped a towel around his waist. "Come on, player. I have another surprise for you."

They walked down the hall together and stopped in front of a white door.

"This is where we part ways. I'll meet you back in the massage room later." He patted Payce on the back and walked down the hall to enter through another white door.

Payce slowly opened the door and three Amazon women attacked him. They pushed him down onto an air mattress and wouldn't allow him to move. Fortunately, this was one time he didn't mind being vulnerable to a group of women. They tossed his towel to the side and gave him a time he would never forget. Payce felt like he was the star of his own porn video. He was used to watching porn, but he had never acted it out.

One woman kissed him passionately and spoke to him in French. He thought this was very sexy as she said things to him he couldn't understand. Each woman kept grabbing at him.

One woman pointed her long finger at him, beckoning him to sit up. Payce was mesmerized by her wild make-up and big hair. The woman's eyes were painted with lots of green and pink paint. She wore a green mini skirt with a matching green halter.

He sat up and the woman went to him; satisfying Payce's sexual desires.

After she was done, each woman wanted a turn, and Payce turned no one away. Two hours later, Payce lay on his back, exhausted. A soft bell rang and instantly the girls untangled themselves from their twist around him and quietly left the room. That was the end of their night together.

"I never thought this night would end like this," he whispered.

After he had a chance to catch his breath, he retreated back to the massage room. He found his clothes lying on the table. As he was buttoning his shirt, he heard a knock at the door.

"Come in," he called.

Darshon entered, smiling like the cat that ate the canary. "How you feel, player?"

"I'm tired."

"I bet you are. Did they work you over?"

Payce smiled as he tied up his boots and looked for his coat. The curtain that covered the huge window was pulled back. Inside, two women were having sex.

"This is a night I will never forget," Payce said out loud.

They watched for a second as the two women pleased one another.

"Man, let's go. I've got to go home and get some sleep. I have to be to work later on tonight," Payce told him.

As they prepared to walk out the door, Darshon yelled, "Hold up man. Let's watch this real quick."

The door inside the window opened and another woman entered. She wore a black leather cat suit with a matching facemask. She held a whip in her hand that she repeatedly swung around. She moved around like she was a cat on the prowl. They watched her gracefully dance around the room. She plotted out a strategy as to which woman she would overcome first. Payce watched as the cat woman pushed one girl to the floor, spread her legs, and before she buried her head down to taste the nectar of the woman, she removed her mask.

At that moment she looked directly into Payce's eyes.

"Oh shit." Payce recognized the woman.

"What?" Darshon asked.

"That's Reverend Kane."

CHAPTER 6

Elise slammed her office door shut, leaving behind the chaos of yelling clients, tight deadlines, and late building permits. Glad to escape it all, she looked forward to beginning her new workout regimen at the gym.

After the stitches were removed from her leg, she desperately wanted to get back out to the park and continue her regular jogs, but Miles did not approve. He felt it was unsafe for her to go jogging by herself, so he suggested she join a health club.

Elise knew Miles was only trying to help, but she thought gyms were so commercial. Health clubs advertised fitness, but it was a multi-million dollar scam. Over ninety percent of members who frequented the gym regularly never obtained the results they desired. It amused her to watch a 250 pound woman cycle on the bike for thirty minutes while eating an entire box of Krispy Kreme donuts.

She would choose the park over a crowded gym any day.

Elise also didn't want to lose the time she spent in the park talking with God, but that wasn't the only reason she wanted to return to the park. She secretly looked forward to running into the man who rescued her like a damsel in distress. Images of his muscular body flashed in her mind. It was hard for her to concentrate on anything besides him.

Elise arrived at the gym and went straight to the treadmills. She started her workout by doing a light one-mile jog to increase her heart rate. Afterwards she followed a strict cardio routine.

After her strenuous workout, she retreated to the locker room to take a shower. She put her hand underneath the spray of water to test it. It was just right. Before she stepped in she noticed that the complimentary towel rack was barren. Elise knew she could use her own towels, but the club kept their towels heated and she savored the feeling of stepping out of the shower and wrapping her body in a warm towel. She left the water running and ran out to the receptionist's desk.

"Excuse me, could you ask someone to bring some fresh towels into the ladies locker room? We've run out," Elise explained.

"Sure, I'll have someone bring some in right away," the young receptionist replied.

As Elise turned to retreat to her shower, she heard a man call out, "Elise."

She recognized the voice, but hoped that it wasn't who she thought it was. She turned around and it was him—her hero—standing before her eyes.

Embarrassed, her face quickly turned red. Not only had he caught her wearing only a towel, but she also had a stupid shower cap on her head. He walked over to her smiling that handsome, devilish smile.

"Hi," he said, sounding as if he were approaching his high school sweetheart.

"Hello." She flinched at the sight of seeing him. She wanted to run and hide. "What are you doing here?" she asked.

"The fellows and I usually come here to play basketball." He pointed to a group of guys entering the men's locker room. "How's that leg? Are you all better?"

"Yes," Elise flexed her leg in and out. "It's all better. I've been waiting on you to send me the hospital bill."

"I put it in the mail a few days ago. You should have gotten it by now. Don't worry, you'll wish I never sent it once you get a look at it."

"You're probably right about that." She laughed. Elise noticed him staring at her and it made her more uncomfortable. "Well I must be going. I was about to take a shower."

"I'm sorry," he said. "I didn't mean to keep you." She turned to run back into the locker room.

"Elise, wait a minute," he called out to her. He walked back over to her. "Would you care to join me for a cup of coffee?"

Elise intended to turn down his offer, but her mouth betrayed her. "Sure, I'd like that," she replied.

"Great. I'll wait for you out here."

She walked back into the locker room. *What have I just done?* she thought. *I should have said no. I was supposed to say no.* But the excitement that danced in his eyes while he talked to her changed her mind.

An hour later, Sheridan and Elise sat in Starbucks sipping French vanilla lattes. Sheridan watched Elise as she drank from her coffee cup. He couldn't believe his luck. He thought he was never going to see her again. Since the day of their accidental meeting, his mind had been consumed with thoughts of her. He hadn't spent that much time with her, but what he did know intrigued him. He couldn't figure out what was so alluring about her, or why he asked her out for coffee, but he did know that he couldn't allow her to vanish from his life again. He knew she was married, but it was hard for him to fight the magnetism he felt toward her.

"You know I really shouldn't be drinking coffee. I won't be able to sleep tonight," Elise commented.

"Neither should I, but sometimes I find it's best to stay up and work."

"What do you do?" she asked.

"I'm a sports agent. I represent a lot of the Philadelphia sports figures—McNabb, Iverson, Randy Wolf."

"That must be interesting work."

"It can be. It can also be stressful. It's hard trying to keep my clients on top. I have to always present my clients in a positive light, whether it's to another sports team, or for an endorsement deal. And that's not always easy. When Kobe got into all that legal trouble out in Colorado, he lost a lot of money. Everything an athlete does is scrutinized by the media, so I try to make sure my players stay out of trouble."

"Doesn't your job require you to travel a lot?"

"Yeah, I do travel a lot of the time, but since a majority of my clientele resides in Philadelphia, I'm able to work from home through the use of e-mail and fax machines. What about you? What do you do?"

"I work for the city. I'm director of the Urban Enterprise zoned areas in Philadelphia."

"What does that mean?"

"I'm responsible for strengthening the more impoverished areas of the city economically by recruiting businesses into those areas."

"How do you do that?"

"Well, I contact large retail stores, companies, or businesses that are interested in setting up regional distribution centers in Philadelphia. Ultimately, if they agree to establish their business in the city, they are entitled to certain tax breaks. For instance, all materials needed to build the outside structure or furnish the inside of office buildings can be written off. It's one hundred percent tax-free. Plus businesses receive an additional fifteen hundred dollar tax break for every city resident they employ."

"That's a real bargain," Sheridan said.

"Yeah. A lot of smaller businesses that are trying to grow can benefit from these types of incentives." She took another sip of her coffee. "You know you never told me your name."

Those lips curved into that devilish smile that caused her heart to flutter.

"I was wondering when you were going to ask me my name. It's Sheridan."

"Sheridan. That's different."

"Yeah, it's a really old name. My full name is Sheridan Reed the Fifth. It's a name that has been passed down from my great-great grandfather. It's a tradition, and when I have a son of my own he will be named Sheridan Reed the VI."

"So you don't have any children?"

"No not yet; maybe someday. What about yourself?"

She solemnly replied, "No." It was torture every time someone asked her that question, a painful reminder of the problems she and Miles were having. She quickly changed the subject. "I'm glad you invited me out."

"I'm surprised. I didn't think you were going to accept my offer."

"At first I wasn't."

"What changed your mind?"

"I thought there was no harm in having a cup of coffee. Plus, I wanted to thank you for coming to my rescue in the park."

"It was my fault that accident happened in the first place. I should have been more careful."

Her cell phone rang. She knew it was Miles calling to make sure she was all right. She glanced at the clock. She was usually home by this time. She answered.

"Hey, honey. Is everything all right?" Miles inquired.

"Yes, I'm fine. I ran into an old friend at the gym and we stopped for coffee. I should have called to let you know I'd be late."

"No, that's okay. I'm sorry if I intruded. I just

wanted to make sure you were all right. When I didn't hear from you I began to worry. I'll let you get back to your girlfriend. Enjoy yourself. I'll wait up until you get home."

"All right, I shouldn't be much longer." She hung up the phone. Sheridan smiled back at her.

"You are very beautiful," he told her.

"Thank you." His obvious attraction to her sent up warning signs, but she ignored them. She enjoyed his company so much that she didn't want to leave.

"You realize I am attracted to you, right?" he asked her.

"You realize I'm married, right?" she playfully replied.

"Yes, I do realize that and I don't want to interfere with your happy home. I just want to get to know you better. You have been on my mind a lot since you left my house."

Scared of what he might confess to her next, she abruptly announced, "I must be going."

"Let me walk you to your car." He walked over to the trash can to discard their cups. Elise stood at the door and stared at him from behind. *He looks so good in those jeans.* Elise closed her eyes and said a silent prayer. *Lord, please get me out of this.*

"Will I get to see you again?" Sheridan asked as they walked to her car together.

"No, I don't think that would be a good idea."

Disappointed by her response, he said, "I understand you're married. I respect that."

Elise could clearly see the hurt in his eyes. Her heart ached for telling him no.

They stopped in front of her car. "You be careful going home," he told her. He softly kissed her on the cheek and walked away with his head down.

Elise got in her car and sat there for a moment. Contemplating her next move, she lowered her window and yelled out, "How about I meet you here next Wednesday? After my workout we can go for another cup of coffee." *It was just coffee*, she told herself. She could handle being in his presence for an hour or two.

That brought an immediate smile to his lips. "I'll see you then."

"I don't understand how two people can accumulate so much laundry in one week." Val sat in the family room folding two laundry baskets full of clothes while Julian stretched out across the couch with the television remote in his hand.

"Babe, you know I change clothes two to three times a day. I get dressed, go to practice, come home, take a shower, and get changed again."

"I've noticed," she replied sarcastically. "You've been changing clothes and going out so much that I barely see you."

"I told you I'm sorry. I'm going to make it up to you. I promise." Julian pulled on her pants leg and blew her a kiss. She jokingly blew his kiss back at him. "Okay," he said. "Don't come over here later trying to cuddle up next to me because I'm going to remind you of what you just did."

Val folded the last of the laundry and headed upstairs to place his clothes in their bedroom. She opened Julian's dresser drawer and moved aside some white T-shirts. She noticed an envelope marked "Colorado." She opened it, and inside were two airline tickets along with brochures of Aspen. Julian didn't say anything to her about going to Aspen. She quickly retreated back downstairs.

He was laughing at the television when she walked back into the family room. "Julian, what is this?" she demanded.

Caught off guard, Julian looked up and his mouth fell open. "What are you doing with those?" he asked.

"That's the question I ought to be asking you. When were you planning on telling me about Colorado?"

For a moment, Julian was speechless. "I . . . I was going to tell you," he stammered. "I just forgot. The team is going to a health clinic in Colorado to make sure we stay healthy for the season. We're going down during the NBA All Star break."

"What about the brochures to Aspen?"

"The fellas thought it would be nice if we did a little skiing while we were there."

"Oh, OK." She stared at the tickets in her hand. "Well, I'm glad I finally found out because I need to go buy some ski gear." Val turned to leave the room.

"Wait a minute." He stopped her. "For what?"

"Our trip to Aspen. You have two tickets here."

"No, the other ticket is for David Childs. He asked me to pick up his ticket for him. I'm sorry, honey, but this trip is for team players only. No women allowed."

The light that filled her eyes quickly faded away. She couldn't believe he was leaving her again. She had made plans for them to fly home together for a quick visit during NBA All Star week. Now she would have to make the trip alone.

"All right," she replied. She walked back to the bedroom and replaced the tickets. Thoughts of what Pilar had said to her weeks ago filled her mind. She stared at the tickets for two. She hoped Julian wasn't lying to her.

Later that day Pilar and Val were out shopping in downtown Seattle. When Pilar called Val earlier and invited her to go shopping, Val initially declined the invitation. Monday was the only day of the week that Julian didn't have practice or team business to attend to. She liked to reserve Mondays as their special time alone, but when she told Pilar that she'd have to take a rain check, Julian interrupted her and insisted that she go.

"Val, why don't you go? You'll only be gone for a few hours. You're always complaining about how you don't get out the house enough and Pilar was nice enough to invite you to go with her," Julian pointed out.

Val knew he was right. She did complain about how she spent most of her time in the house. "Are you sure? I don't want to leave you alone."

"Go. I'll be fine. I'll be here when you get back."

Persuaded, Val went, unaware that Pilar would buy so many things. Pilar managed to buy herself and her children over fifteen thousand dollars worth of clothes, and that was only in one store.

She had so many bags that store security had to help carry her bags out to her Escalade.

"Thanks for going with me. I really hate going shopping by myself, and I would never bring the children with me," Pilar said to Val as she adjusted her seatbelt. "Every time I bring Alec he has to go to the bathroom every ten minutes. I never get anything done."

"I enjoyed this. Maybe we can go out again sometime next week. I really need to go furniture shopping," Val commented.

"Oh! I know the perfect place. It's called the Fine Furniture Gallery, and everything in there is one of a kind. I bought just about every piece in our home from there. Are you redecorating?"

"No, just decorating. Since we moved into the house we barely have any furniture. The house is so hollow and cold. I've tried to wait on Julian so we could go together, but he's been so busy he told me to go buy whatever I wanted. I need to buy something to give the house a warm feeling."

"I understand. Whenever you want to go, just give me a call," Pilar offered.

All afternoon, Val tried to think of the best way to ask Pilar about Colorado. She needed to know if Carlos had mentioned anything to her about him going. She knew that once she asked her, Pilar would know that Val didn't trust Julian as much as she said she had, but the truth was that she did believe Julian's reasoning behind the two tickets. She just wanted to reassure herself.

"Pilar, did Carlos mention anything to you about going to a rehabilitation clinic in Colorado?" Val asked.

"Oh, yes! The team goes every year," Pilar responded. "Why? Were you worried Julian was up to something?"

"No, I just thought that since both Julian and Carlos would be out of town, that maybe we could do something," Val responded, covering up her real suspicions.

"Oh, that sounds like fun. How about we spend the whole weekend together? We can go to the spa and to the theater."

"Okay," Val replied. Her heart had slowly returned to its normal pace. She had been afraid of what Pilar's answer would be, but as usual she knew she had no reason to doubt her man.

CHAPTER 7

"Yo, Bryant!" Danyelle yelled as she attempted to shake Bryant from his daydream. Immersed in his own thoughts, Bryant took the blunt that she was passing to him.

"So how does it feel to be a father?" Danyelle asked.

"It doesn't feel any different than before he got here, except we have a whole lot of shitty diapers lying around and midnight feedings," he remarked.

Danyelle noticed Bryant's distant behavior toward his son. Bryant barely fed, played with, or held Bryce. He was completely withdrawn from the parenting experience. The only time she had seen him take any interest in his son was when Olivia took the baby to the doctor. He insisted on going with them. Olivia said that he grilled the doctor about the baby's progress and health. He wanted reassurance that Bryce would grow up to be a normal little boy.

Danyelle hoped the new father did not resent his son. A lot of Olivia's time was being taken up by the baby. Morning, noon, and night, she fed, washed, and cared for her son. It was hard being a first-time mother. She barely had any time for herself.

Olivia stuck her head out into the living room. "Is it safe to come out?" Olivia asked, holding the baby close in her arms.

"Yeah, Livie, it's okay," Danyelle replied.

Danyelle got up and tried to fan away the smoke from the blunt they had just finished smoking. Olivia had hoped that once the baby was born Bryant and Danyelle would stop smoking in the apartment out of respect for the baby, but they didn't care. Bryant didn't see anything wrong with smoking around the baby, and Danyelle claimed that since she paid half the rent she was entitled to smoke anywhere she pleased.

Bryant said Olivia was uptight and she needed to relax more, but she disagreed. She didn't think she was the problem. The problem was that she didn't have enough space. It was hard being confined to her small bedroom with a baby because they refused to smoke outside. Olivia constantly nagged Bryant about getting their own place, but he argued that he didn't make enough money. Olivia knew he was right. They couldn't afford an apartment with the expense of a new baby, but she still wanted to try and find them their own affordable apartment.

Olivia sat on the couch next to Danyelle while

the baby slept soundly in her arms. Danyelle could see the dark circles beneath her sister's eyes. The T-shirt she had on had the baby's vomit spattered in different places. Her hair, which was usually neatly pressed straight, was wild and uncombed.

"Pass me the baby, Livie," Danyelle said.

"All right, but don't blow smoke in my baby's face, like you did last time." Olivia handed Bryce over and grabbed the television remote.

"He liked his first hit of weed from Auntie Danyelle. Didn't you?" Danyelle asked the baby.

Olivia ignored her and pointed the remote at the television. She noticed a large brick of marijuana sitting on the floor to the left of the television.

"How many times do I have to ask you two to be more careful where you leave that stuff?" Olivia pointed to the weed. "I do have a baby now," Olivia said huffily. "In a few more months the baby will be crawling and getting into stuff. I don't want my baby eating or playing with marijuana at the age of six months," she complained.

"Sorry, baby, that's my fault," Bryant responded. "A guy I know wanted to buy it from me, but when I took it over to his house, he wasn't there. So I brought it here."

"Oh, so now you're a drug dealer," Olivia said mockingly.

"No, it's not like that."

Olivia could not believe that Bryant was selling drugs. Not wanting to argue in front of Danyelle, she asked Bryant if they could speak in their bedroom.

"Bryant, if you're selling drugs out of this house

then I have to ask you to go. I will not have you endangering our son's life."

"I'm not selling drugs." He defended himself. "I just thought that if I sold a few bundles of weed I could make a few extra hundred dollars. Things are kind of tight around here with the baby and you wanting to move into our own place."

Olivia sympathized with what he was trying to do, and realized that he was only trying to provide for his family and keep her happy, but selling drugs was not the answer.

"Bryant, I want us to be a family." She reached out for his hand. "You don't have to sell drugs to take care of us. We'll make it as long as we have each other."

Realizing he was wrong, he replied, "All right, let me go see if this guy is home so I can drop this stuff off to him." He moved over to kiss her on the lips and left. A few seconds later Olivia heard the front door slam shut.

Thirty minutes had passed. Olivia, Danyelle, and the baby sat in the living room watching a movie.

"I wish Mommy and Daddy were here to see how beautiful Bryce is," Olivia said.

"Daddy always wanted a boy. He would have spoiled Bryce rotten," Danyelle replied.

Suddenly, a loud crashing sound came through the front door. Olivia looked up to witness a squad of police run into her living room with guns drawn and pointed directly at them. One officer came over, pulled the baby from Olivia's arms, and handed him to another officer. The same officer then grabbed her aggressively and forced her up against the wall.

Olivia was paralyzed with fear. She didn't know what to do.

"Officer, what is going on?" Olivia asked. She could hear her baby's cries in the distance. "That's my baby. Can I please get my son? He's scared."

"Sorry ma'am, I can't allow you to do that. We'll have someone take care of him until we're done here," the officer replied.

Olivia could see several officers scouring her house. They appeared to be looking for something. They searched the closets, kitchen cabinets, and drawers.

"What is going on?" Danyelle screamed.

Detective Collins walked up behind the girls as they were being body searched by female officers. "Can I ask who lives here?" the detective asked.

"I do," Olivia replied. "Me, my sister, my baby, and my boyfriend."

"Is that your sister?" the detective asked.

"Yes."

"Where is your boyfriend?"

"He was just here. He ran out for a second."

"I can question him later. Ladies, please have a seat on the couch," the detective instructed. He knelt in front of them. "Do you know Darnell 'Drake' Duncan?"

Olivia shook her head no.

"We got an anonymous tip that Drake Duncan was selling drugs out of this apartment. Drake is a very dangerous man and is a fugitive who's been on the run for months."

"Officer . . ." Olivia started.

"Detective. My name is Detective Collins."

"I'm sorry. Detective Collins, we don't know any Drake Duncan."

"What is your boyfriend's name?"

"Bryant Winters."

The detective scribbled Bryant's name on a note pad. "Ladies, so far we have confiscated four bundles of marijuana and a few ounces of cocaine. He pointed to the drugs sitting on the table. Olivia didn't realize that those drugs were in the apartment. She had made sure that Bryant took the marijuana sitting next to the television with him.

"Who does the marijuana belong to?" the detective asked.

"I plead the fifth," Danyelle said.

"Detective, I don't know who those drugs belong to. I didn't even know they were in the apartment. Where did you find that?" Olivia began to cry.

"I found it in a closet in the back bedroom underneath the baby's things."

Olivia knew he was referring to her room.

"Ladies, you two could be looking at jail time. We already have the evidence. A year or more of jail time would mean your son would be placed in a foster home until you were released."

The detective looked at Olivia. "If you tell me everything you know I'll let the judge know how cooperative you were with us and he may just give you probation."

Olivia was confused and didn't know what to do. If she confessed that the drugs belonged to Bryant, he could go to jail and her son would lose his father. If she didn't say anything, then she would go to jail and her son would lose his mother. She knew it was better for Bryce to lose his father rather than his mother. Prepared to tell the officer everything she knew, Danyelle interrupted before she could say a word. "Detective, can my sister and I speak privately for a moment?"

"Sure." He got up to leave them alone.

"Livie," she whispered. "Drug possession is not a big thing. This is our first offense. They can't send us to jail over drugs that don't belong to us."

"But what about everything he said?"

"That cop was just playing with your head. Trust me, I know people who were caught with ten times as much as us and all they got was probation. Look, let's go down to the station. Let them arrest us. They'll set our bail. We can call Bryant, have him bail us out, and then we can get a lawyer."

"Danyelle, are you sure?"

"Trust me."

"What about the baby?"

"He'll be put in temporary custody of the state, but when we get in touch with Bryant, we'll tell him to go get the baby first. He's the father. He has rights."

Olivia agreed to go along with Danyelle's decision to remain silent.

Danyelle called the detective back over. "Detective, we're going to ask to speak to a lawyer before we say anything," she said confidently.

The detective shook his head as if they were making a big mistake. "Stiles, read them their rights," he barked.

The officer came over, put the handcuffs on the two sisters, and led them out of the apartment. Once they got to the station, they each made one phone call. Olivia called Bryant on his cell phone, but his voice mail picked up. She left him an urgent message telling him what happened and where she was. She also told him where to get the baby from.

Afterwards, they put Danyelle and Olivia in a holding cell where they sat and stared at the clock, waiting on Bryant to come and bail them out.

The next morning Olivia and Danyelle were taken down to the courthouse and escorted into a small, cold room. Inside was a white guy who looked no older than twenty-five. The officer who escorted them in took the handcuffs off and ordered them to sit down on the hard wooden chairs.

"Good morning, ladies." He smiled at them while looking through their file. "My name is Wilson York and I'm your public defender."

"We don't need any public defender," Danyelle informed him. "We're going to get a lawyer."

"Yes. Well, until you're able to obtain suitable legal counsel the state has assigned your case to me. I'm here to advise you of your rights, make sure you're aware of the charges being brought against you and answer any questions you may have."

"Mr. York" Olivia interrupted. "Did my boyfriend ever come down to the station? He was supposed to come and bail us out last night."

"Oh yes," York said. He opened the file and read off a sheet of paper. "A Mr. Winters. He did come down to the station. He was questioned and released. He gave a statement to the police. He claimed that the drugs belonged to the two of you. He denied any ownership of them."

"There must be a mistake. He wouldn't have said that," Olivia said. She looked at Danyelle, who shrugged her shoulders unknowingly.

"He also stated that he didn't live with the two of you."

"All his stuff is at my house."

"That may be true, but his name is not on the lease, is it?" the young lawyer asked.

"No," Olivia responded softly.

"And because his name is not on the lease, he is not responsible for the drugs found inside the unit."

"Shit!" Danyelle screamed.

"So now what?" Olivia asked.

"Well, we're going to ask the judge to grant you O.R."

"What is that?" Olivia asked.

"O.R. is when the judge releases people who have been accused of crimes on their own recognizance. Basically, he's giving them a free pass to go home, trusting that they will appear back in court on their assigned court date. If you don't show up, a warrant will be issued for your arrest. If he doesn't grant you O.R. today, he will. It may take a few days."

"A few days? I can't sit in jail for a few days. I have a son to care for," Olivia said, tears welling in her eyes.

"Well, you may not have any other choice. I will make a plea to the court on your behalf that you have a child to attend to, but I can't guarantee anything." The lawyer got up and grabbed his briefcase. "So let's go see what the judge has to say."

Several days later Danyelle and Olivia were released on their own recognizance. They immediately went down to the Department of Family Services. Olivia was in a hurry to get Bryce back. She approached the receptionist and explained the reason she was there. After Olivia finished her story, the receptionist picked up the phone and made a call. She turned to Olivia. "You can have a seat in the waiting area and someone will be out to speak with you shortly."

The two women waited approximately ten minutes before a woman came out to greet them. She was a black woman who appeared to be in her mid-fifties.

"Hello, I'm Mrs. Johnson. I was told that you were looking for your baby," the woman said.

"Yes, I was arrested a few days ago and the public defender told me that I would have to put in a petition to get my son back."

"Yes, that is usually how it works, but your son is no longer under our care. The baby's father came down here the same night he was brought to us. He had the baby's birth certificate stating that he was the father, so we had no choice but to release him."

A sharp pain pierced Olivia's heart. She knew that something was not right. She ran out of the office to hurry home. Danyelle thanked the lady for her time and followed Olivia out the door.

They arrived home to find their home in disarray; chairs were knocked over, clothes were thrown everywhere. Olivia walked into her bedroom to look for Bryant and the baby. All his clothes were gone and so were the baby's. Danyelle walked in behind her.

"They're gone. He took my baby and left," Olivia cried.

"Don't worry. We'll find them."

"How?" Olivia screamed. "I don't know where to begin to look. I don't know any of his friends. I've never met any of his family."

"You never asked?"

"Of course I questioned him about his past and his family. He told me he didn't have any family. He said that the baby and I were all the family he had. Now he's taken off with my baby and I don't even know why or where."

Olivia cried while Danyelle hugged her sister. Olivia felt closer to her sister than she ever had. Growing up they had never been close, but when a crisis arose, they were there for one another.

"I think Bryant is the one who set this whole thing up," Danyelle told her. "Who would call the cops and tell them that we had drugs in the apartment? I knew there was something strange about him. Every time we got high together he never spoke a word. He got unusually quiet like he was plotting something."

"You really think Bryant is responsible for sending us to jail? But why? Why would he do this?" She wiped a few tears from her eyes. "I need to call the police to report the baby missing." Olivia went into the kitchen and grabbed the cordless phone off the wall.

"I'm going to look around and see if Bryant left anything behind," Danyelle said as she walked back into Olivia's bedroom.

It wasn't long before a uniformed officer, along with the same detective who had arrested them a few days prior, showed up at their apartment.

"Hello Ms. Benson," the detective uttered when Olivia answered the door.

She was surprised to see him.

"I heard the call come in over the radio and I was in the neighborhood. I wanted to come by and see if there was anything I could do to help. I hope you don't mind?" He smiled back at Olivia.

"No, it's fine. Please come in."

While the uniformed officer sat on the couch and asked Olivia a series of questions, the detective looked around the apartment at photos of Bryant and the baby.

"Can we have this photo?" The detective pointed to a photo of Bryant holding the baby in the park.

"Sure." Olivia replied.

The detective handed the photo to the officer and the officer got up from off the couch.

"Ma'am, I'm done with my report. I'm going to knock on a few of your neighbors' doors and see if anyone heard or saw anything," the officer told Olivia.

"MacKenzie, I'm going to look around here," the detective informed the officer.

"So, Bryant is the baby's father?"

"Yes."

"The same guy I interviewed down at the station and said that the drugs belong to you?"

"Yes."

"Do you think he set this up?"

"My sister does."

"What do you think?" he asked.

"I don't want to believe Bryant would do this, but I don't have any choice."

"Why would he want to falsely accuse you of selling drugs?" the detective asked.

"I don't know," Olivia responded.

"If this was a setup, I promise that I will get to the bottom of it, but I have to be honest with you." Olivia braced herself for the worst, "Bryant has got a huge lead ahead of us. He's probably been gone since the night you were arrested. He could be anywhere in the country. The longer he's gone with the child, the harder it's going to be for us to find him."

Olivia's eyes turned sad.

"As soon as I get back to the station I'm going to contact the National Center for Missing and Exploited children. I'm going to transmit all of Bryce's information and hopefully they can help. They have a whole lot of resources that we don't have. So if Bryant left the state, at least we can alert other police agencies throughout the country."

"Detective Collins, do you think you're going to find my baby?"

"I'm not sure, but I sure hope so." He handed her a card. "Here is the name of a guy who has had a lot of success in finding missing children. A lot of parents invest in hiring private detectives because it's good to have someone looking for your child who can devote their full undivided attention.

Don't think I'm going to stop looking for Bryce, but the Philadelphia Police Department can't put its full manpower on one case."

"Thanks, Detective."

Olivia stared at the card. It read "Desmond Murray, Private Investigator."

Payce sat inside his car and stared at First Nazareth Church. He knew he couldn't sit in the car all morning long, Tressie was expecting him. He promised her that he'd attend Sunday services with her this week, but he wasn't ready to face Reverend Kane.

After seeing Reverend Kane at The Dollhouse, he would never be able to look at her again without being reminded of that night. The woman whose curves nicely filled out that black, leather, cat-woman outfit was not the same woman he met wearing a pastor's robe a few weeks ago. If she approached him, he wouldn't know what to say. He wished he had never gone out with Darshon that night.

Payce got out the car and walked up the church steps. He placed his hand on the doorknob and quickly let go before opening the door. The courage he had built up inside of him a few minutes before quickly deflated out of him like air from a flat tire.

He stood outside the church wishing he could turn around and go back home, but he couldn't. For three weeks straight he had made up excuses why he couldn't attend services with Tressie. Once he ran out of excuses, he had no choice but to go. He looked at his watch. It was getting late.

He opened the church doors and stepped inside the vestibule. The ushers immediately opened the doors and allowed him to enter. Inside the sanctuary Reverend Simms prayed over a woman. He held his hand over her head. "Lord, fill the emptiness left in Sister Monroe's heart from the loss of her husband," he shouted.

Payce looked around and found Tressie sitting in the last pew. He slid into the seat next to her and gently caressed her hand. As Pastor Simms prayed, Payce looked around the church for Reverend Kane. She wasn't in the pulpit. *Perhaps she missed service today,* he thought. A moment later, Reverend Kane rose from out of one of the pews. Payce watched her walk over to Pastor Simms and also laid hands on Sister Monroe's head. Suddenly Reverend Kane's eyes darted in Payce's direction and he quickly bowed his head. *I hope she didn't see me.* After prayer concluded, Payce hoped that the remainder of the service would go quickly.

"Hey, sweetheart," Tressie greeted Payce after church services ended. "I'm glad you made it." She kissed him lightly on the lips.

"So am I." He grabbed his coat in a hurry to leave. "I'm going outside to heat up the car. I'll wait for you out there."

"Payce, I know you're ready to go, but I need to speak with Danyelle about the Sunday school class she's going to teach for me. Can you wait for me? I won't be long." She quickly walked away.

Payce sat quietly, trying to make himself invisible to everyone around him.

Minutes later, he heard her voice behind him. "Hello, Payce."

He turned around in the pew. "Hey, Reverend Kane." He turned back around.

"How are you doing?" she asked.

"Good," he replied, hoping that his one-word answers would be a subtle hint that he didn't want to be bothered.

She sat down next to Payce in the pew. "Payce, I need to talk with you about what you saw a few weeks ago."

"Reverend Kane, I would like to pretend that didn't even happen," he whispered. "What you do is your business. You won't have to worry about me saying anything to anybody because my lips are sealed."

"Well, I'm glad to hear that, but I figured you wouldn't say anything to anyone about where you saw me because then you would have to explain what you were doing there. But that is not the only thing I want to speak to you about. How about we meet for lunch tomorrow?"

"Reverend Kane, I'm awfully busy. I have a new job and I'm trying to stay focused. I don't know if I'll be able to make it," Payce explained.

"Payce, I just want to talk. I have an offer that might be of interest to you. I just want to run it by you."

"I doubt I'll be interested."

"Payce." She grabbed his hand lovingly. "Please, can you just come to hear me out? It's not going to hurt to hear what I have to offer."

Her sincere and loving tone changed his mind, "Where do you want to meet?"

"There's a place called Caribou Café on Walnut Street. I'll be waiting for you at noon."

Someone called her name from across the room. "See you then," she said and strolled away.

"Payce, I'm ready," Tressie announced from behind him.

A minute too late, Payce thought to himself.

The following day Payce walked into the lunch eatery prepared to cut his meeting with the reverend short.

"Hi," Payce said to the hostess, "I'm looking for a woman in her early thirties. She might have a reservation under . . ."

"Reverend Kane?" she asked.

"Yeah, that's her," he replied.

"She's waiting for you. Follow me, please."

Payce trailed the hostess to a booth in the corner of the restaurant. She placed two menus on the table. "A waitress will be over shortly to take your order," she informed them and walked away.

"Glad to see you could make it," Reverend Kane remarked.

Payce removed his coat and took a seat. "Reverend, what's up? You wanted me here. Now I'm here. What do you want to talk about?"

"First, I want to thank you for not telling your father about my extra-curricular activities. I think that if my secret ever got out it could do nothing but hurt the church."

"Then why do you do it?" he asked.

"It's not my choice to be gay. I'm naturally attracted to women just like you are."

"I don't care that you're gay. I want to know why you work at The Dollhouse."

"I started going there because it was a discreet place to meet other people like myself. It allows me to hide my real identity. When I work at The Dollhouse, Sandy Kane emerges and Reverend Kane suppresses herself." She pointed to herself. "After I started working there, a few customers began asking for me by name. I brought in a lot of revenue, so the owner asked if I would be interested in working full time. Being a minister, I saw a conflict of interest and I confessed to her about who I actually was. That's how we came up with the idea of me wearing a mask to keep my identity concealed just in case someone came in who knew me. Plus, she thought I could act out some of the women's fantasies of making love to Catwoman."

"But you took the mask off."

"I know. That was the first time I've ever done that. It instinctively felt right to expose my identity at that moment."

"Maybe you should think about revealing yourself to more than your customers."

"Maybe you're right," she replied.

A waitress came over and placed a glass of water in front of each of them. "Are you ready to order?" she asked.

"Yes," the reverend replied. "I'll have the chicken salad. What about you, Payce?"

"Nothing for me," he replied.

The waitress retrieved both menus and walked away.

"Payce, the reason I asked you here is because I'm aware of your past. And I've experienced first-hand how hard it is for someone who is just getting out of jail to get a job."

"You've been locked up?" he asked.

"No, but I had a nephew who did time in New Jersey. He was locked up in Trenton State for ten years. When he got out he had a hard time finding a decent job. That is why I wanted to make you a job offer."

"Thanks, but I have a job."

"I heard you got a job parking cars down at the Westin Hotel, but is that enough to support yourself, not to mention your girlfriend? Wouldn't you like to take her out and buy her nice things? Trust me; working at The Dollhouse would eliminate a lot of financial problems."

"The Dollhouse!" he shouted. "That lesbian joint!"

"Would you keep your voice down?"

He looked around to see if anyone was looking. "What am I supposed to do at a lesbian spa? Watch y'all eat each other out?"

"Would you listen to me?" she whispered. "That place is making thousands of dollars every night. There has not been a night that I haven't left there with at least two thousand dollars."

"What does that have to do with me?" he asked.

"The place is making so much money that now they're thinking about expanding."

"I'm not giving no man a massage," Payce thundered.

"And I wouldn't ask you to. Have you ever heard of the term 'swing couples'?"

Payce shook his head no.

"It's when married couples or anyone in a committed relationship has sex with someone outside their relationship. You have sex with their partner while the spouse or mate watches."

"I've never heard of it."

"Well, the owner of The Dollhouse has had lots of requests from customers who are interested in it. She is recruiting men to come and participate in the swinging."

Payce started laughing. "You want me to be a male prostitute?"

"No, it's not prostitution."

"Yes, it is. I'm getting paid for having sex with strangers."

"No, you're getting paid for helping a couple live out their fantasies."

"Reverend Kane, you're sicker than I thought." He got up to leave.

"Payce, they're willing to start you off at fifteen hundred tax-free dollars a night."

Payce froze in his tracks.

"That is just to start. If you do a good job and couples return to see you, they will pay you more."

He sat back down in his seat.

"If you don't like it, you can quit, but I'm telling you it's easy money."

Fifteen hundred dollars, he thought.

"What about Tressie?" he asked.

"Tressie doesn't have to know. I'm not going to say anything to her."

Payce thought about having fifteen hundred dollars cash in his pocket. He hadn't seen that much money since he was hustling on the corner. Reverend Kane waited for Payce to accept her offer.

"Let me think about it and I'll give you a call," he told her.

"Don't make me wait long," she replied.

CHAPTER 8

Miles's facial expression said "I'm sorry." This was another failed attempt by Elise to resuscitate her husband's limp rod back to life. She held his manhood in her hand and wished for a miracle. She prayed that he would have a positive reaction to her touch, but her efforts were unsuccessful. She got up and moved to her side of the bed.

The doctor had prescribed Miles medication to assist with his treatment, but so far they saw no improvements.

They lay in silence and stared at the ceiling. Thoughts of Sheridan drifted through Elise's mind. She wondered how an innocent cup of coffee could turn into nights of hot and heavy sex.

A part of her was ashamed. She was a Christian woman who was responsible for pointing out the sins of others. Now she was the one committing sin. This was an unfamiliar place for her in life, a place she had never thought she would be. An extra-marital affair had been inconceivable, but Sheridan's touch electrified her body. The worst part was that she didn't want it to end. She had fallen in love with him.

It started with Sheridan coming into the gym on Wednesday evenings. He would act as her personal trainer by assisting her with the weight machines and demonstrating different techniques to get the most out of her workouts. Those techniques often required that he touch intimate parts of her body. The feel of his hands made her nervous. She knew that their relationship was getting more personal, but she didn't stop it. She enjoyed the attention he showered on her. Then came the night when their relationship took a dramatic turn.

It was a typical Wednesday night, and Elise was expecting Sheridan to walk into the gym at any second, but he never showed. She thought that he might have been running late, but by the end of her workout there was still no sign of him. Disappointed that he was a no-show, she hated the thought of having to wait another full week before she saw him again.

In no rush to go home, Elise chose to sit in the sauna for a while. The warmth from the sauna wrapped itself around her skin. She sat against the far wall, leaned her head back and closed her eyes and enjoyed the quiet, serene atmosphere. She was alone for a while before someone came in, interrupting her solitude. She kept her eyes closed and tried to block out the presence of someone else in the small-boxed room.

"Is this seat taken?" the stranger asked abruptly.

Elise was startled and wasn't aware that her un-invited guest was so close. She looked up. The steam slowly cleared away from her eyes.

"Sheridan?" she called out.

"Yeah, it's me. I hope I didn't scare you."

"Yes, you did scare me, but how did you know I was in here?"

"I asked the receptionist if she had seen you and she told me that you were in here. I'm sorry I was late. I had to go out of town to Miami unexpect-edly and my flight was delayed."

"Miami? That must have been a nice trip. Was it business or pleasure?"

"Business, unfortunately." He sat down next to her. "There's this kid who goes to school down there and he is withdrawing from school early to enter the NFL. My firm is eager to represent him. So they asked me to fly down there to give a quick presentation. He's a good kid, comes from a stable home, and has parents who care. The father is the one who actually contacted us. He wants the kid to be represented by a black sports agency, but I got the impression that the kid had his sights on some of the larger agencies."

"What does the father have to do with anything? Isn't it the kid's decision?"

"Ultimately, yes, it is the kid's decision, but his father played in the pros and has had a lot of re-grets for putting his trust in a lot of people who would never understand what it's like to be a black man playing in the NFL. He's just a father who wants to help lead his son in the right direc-tion."

"Well, I hope you get the account," Elise replied. "So do I."

They sat in silence for a moment. She felt uncomfortable sitting next to him with nothing on but a towel. At least when they were at the coffeehouse she did have clothes on. She looked down at the towel wrapped around Sheridan's waist. *What do I do if he touches me or worse, kisses me? Calm down, Elise, the man has made no indication that he would ever hit on you. Every time he's been alone with me he has been a perfect gentleman.*

Another five minutes of silence passed before a throbbing feeling began pulsating between her legs. She glanced over at him. He seemed unaware of what she was thinking. Elise couldn't hold back the desire that burned deep inside her. Lust had taken over her body and she was at its mercy. Throwing all caution to the wind, she quickly climbed on top of Sheridan and ferociously kissed his lips. Sheridan responded to Elise's advances by removing her towel.

The heat from the sauna created tears of sweat on their bodies. The sex was invigorating for both of them. He grabbed her tighter and tighter. He tried not to release his seed inside of her, but he couldn't withstand the feeling. He finally burst like a dam.

Elise leaned her head against his. The realization of what she had just done hit her like a ton of bricks. She had broken her wedding vows and deceived her husband. She got up and sat next to Sheridan. She held her head down and placed her hands on her head. Her remorse filled the room. He could sense her guilt.

"I know you regret what just happened," Sheridan said. "If you say you don't want to see me again, I'll understand."

Elise didn't say a word, nor did she look his way. Sheridan wrapped his towel back around himself and got up to leave.

"Sheridan!" Elise stopped him. She walked over and hugged him. "I'm scared of what's happening to me. I've never done this kind of thing before. I don't know what came over me," she whimpered from the embrace of his arms.

They continued to meet, not only on Wednesday evenings, but also on Monday and Friday evenings. She stopped going to the gym and began having her workouts in Sheridan's bedroom. Fortunately, Miles was not suspicious of her sudden appreciation for going to the gym. He encouraged her increased workouts and wished that he could go with her, but Elise intentionally scheduled her time at the gym during his therapy sessions with Dr. Johnson.

Elise glanced over at her husband. *He is such a good man.* She felt guilty for having thoughts of another man while her husband lay next to her, but there was no way she could stop it. All thoughts started and stopped with Sheridan. She and Sheridan had made plans to get together on Tuesday night before he went out of town on business. It would be their last night together for two whole weeks, and Elise couldn't wait to see him. When she spoke with him on the phone, he hinted that he had a surprise for her.

"Elise, what do you think about us purchasing a few sex toys?" Miles asked. "Honey?" Miles shook his wife lightly, trying to wake her from her day-dream.

"I'm sorry, honey. I must have been a million *Miles* away. What were you saying?"

"Are you all right?" he asked. "You seemed so deep in thought."

"I was just thinking about Olivia," she lied. "I hope she's able to find Bryant and the baby."

"Yeah, that must be hard—to be wrongly accused of a crime, go to jail, and then have your baby disappear."

"We'll have to keep her and the baby in our prayers. Now, what were you saying?" she asked.

"What do you think about us getting some sex toys? Do you think they could help out with the problems I've been having?"

"Sweetheart, I'm not sure, but it's worth a try. Before, I forget, on Tuesday after Bible Study I'm going to go over to the gym and work out a little, so I may be a little late getting home."

"Why are you going to the gym on a Tuesday night? That's usually your night off."

"Yeah, I know and I'm going to cut back on my workouts a little, but I want to get in there early this week and then I'll have the rest of the week to spend extra time with you."

Miles was glad that his wife was going to be spending more time at home. Lately, she had been spending so much time at the gym that they barely spent anytime together. Also, he noticed a change in Elise's behavior that worried him. She frequently daydreamed and was unfocused. At first he thought she was having an affair, but he later dismissed that as paranoia.

He mentioned Elise's distant behavior to his therapist, who provided him with several logical reasons why his wife could be behaving oddly. She explained that impotency was not only psychologically damaging to him, but also to his spouse. The best thing he could do was to give her space and allow her to deal with the problem in her own way. If things continued or got worse, he could always suggest Elise talk to a counselor or therapist.

Miles turned to his woman. "Elise, would you like to say a prayer with me?"

Elise wanted to pray with him. Prayer was the one thing in their life that had always brought them closer together, but she just wasn't up for it today. "I'm really tired," she replied. "Maybe we can pray together in the morning."

"No problem," Miles said. He leaned over and gave her a quick kiss on the lips, turned over, and went to sleep.

MARCH 2004

Pilar and Val luxuriated at the spa while they received their weekly beauty regimen of facials and body scrubs. They sat with avocado masks smeared over their faces.

"This feels soooooo good," Pilar said aloud. "I love to get the avocado scrub on my face. When I was pregnant, I looked forward to one of these every week. I love the way it opens my pores."

"Is Carlos glad to be back home?" Val asked.

"Oh yes!" she replied. "Since his return from Colorado he has been so attentive to the children

and me. I think he missed us while he was away. He
has been spending so much time with the children, and last night he even got up in the middle
of the night with the baby."

Val was envious of Pilar and Carlos. They were
married and had a family. She wanted that from
Julian.

"I can't wait for Julian and me to have a house
full of kids."

"Did you start with your wedding plans yet?"

"I started while he was away. I contacted several
places in Philadelphia to have our reception, but I
haven't had a chance to mention it to him. Since
he got back from Colorado he's been away from
home more than before he left."

Troubled with doubts of what Julian could be
doing while away from home, Val asked, "Pilar, do
you think Julian is cheating on me?" she finally
asked.

Ever since Pilar warned her about the numer-
ous affairs that go on in the NBA, Val had been
very suspicious of Julian's whereabouts.

Every time he went out she questioned where
he was going and with whom. She checked his coat
pockets for hotel receipts or phone numbers. One
night she stayed up until four o'clock in the morning waiting for him to get home. When he finally
walked in the door, she pretended to be asleep on
the couch. He came in, checked on her, and went
to bed. After she thought he had fallen asleep, she
snuck out into the garage to search his car. When
she didn't find anything, she knew she had
reached a point where she didn't trust him, and it

had to stop. She had to find out one way or another what he was up to.

"I wouldn't jump to that conclusion," Pilar said. "His time away from home could really have to do with business."

"I've been trying to convince myself that he is actually working, but intuition tells me there's something more," Val replied.

Pilar and Val had finally made it out of the spa and were on their way back home. Before leaving the spa, Pilar insisted on treating herself to a detoxifying body mud wrap. The spa services coordinator told her that it would make her feel twenty years old again.

It was Val's first time sitting in a tub full of mud. The mud didn't make her feel twenty years old, but it sure was relaxing. It relieved so much stress; her back, neck and shoulders were less tense. The strain of worrying about Julian had been temporarily lifted.

Driving home, Pilar pulled into the grocery store parking lot. "Do you mind if we make a quick stop? I have to have something good and hot waiting for my man when he gets home, besides myself," Pilar joked.

Inside the store, Pilar quickly scanned the aisles and found the ingredients she needed for her family's dinner. The two women chatted while waiting in the express checkout line.

"You cannot go to Julian with suspicions about his behavior. You have got to have some evidence to prove he's been unfaithful. Trust me, if there is evidence out there, it will come to you."

"How can you be so sure?"

"Trust me. Right after Carlos and I were married, I got pregnant with our first child. I was so busy decorating the nursery and preparing for our daughter's birth that I missed a few of Carlos's games. At the time he was playing for Chicago, so one night I thought it would be a nice surprise if I unexpectedly attended that night's home game. Only I was the one surprised. I arrived at United Arena and sitting in Carlos's reserved seats was an eighteen-year-old redhead. I thought I was going to lose my mind. I politely asked her who she was and do you know what her reply was? She said, 'You know who I am.' I knew in my heart the young girl had been sleeping around with my husband. I grabbed her by her arm and she shoved me. Carlos saw us arguing from the bench and climbed the stands to defend me. He publicly cursed her for putting her hands on his pregnant wife."

"What happened?" Val asked.

"Well, you know that the media taped everything that happened. It was on the news and in the paper. Carlos was fined for leaving the game and I was ready to leave him. Furious, I went home and packed my bags. He begged me not to go and swore that he would never cheat on me again."

"It must have been painful to come face to face with Carlos's mistress," Val replied.

"It did hurt. I hope no one ever has to go through having their personal lives aired throughout the media like we did," Pilar remarked.

Val noticed the corner of a magazine in the

newsstand. She couldn't see the entire cover clearly, but the letters "ian" and "ington" caught her attention. Val held up one finger to Pilar and walked over to the magazine stand. She pulled out a celebrity gossip magazine. On the cover was a full color photo of Julian in a loving embrace with a woman. The headline read "Seattle Sonics star rookie and his snow bunny." A short blurb beneath the photo said, "An unidentified witness told the magazine that Pennington and his new girlfriend were vacationing in Aspen and they looked very much in love."

Pilar glanced at the photo from over Val's shoulder. "Val, don't let this upset you. These types of magazines tell nothing but lies. Do you know how many times Carlos has been in this magazine?"

Val heard Pilar talking, but the words were suppressed in her mind. She couldn't believe Julian would do this to her. Her heart dropped, and so did the glass bottle of olive oil she held in her hand. It shattered on the floor.

She ran out of the store and into the rain. Pilar called out after her. Val got into Pilar's truck and watched the rain fall against the windshield. She was hypnotized. Those photos were the proof she needed to confront Julian, and she needed to confront him. Now.

Pilar climbed into the driver's side.

"Can you take me to the team's practice?" Val asked.

Pilar wanted to comfort her friend, but she thought that maybe the best thing she could do for her right now was to say nothing at all. She knew how devastating it was to find out the man you loved had been unfaithful.

The drive over to the team's practice gave Val time to think about what she was going to say. Her mind spun around in full circles. It was hard for her to accept the fact that Julian had lied to her. The foundation of trust that they had built over the years had crumbled.

They pulled into the parking lot, but before Pilar put her truck in park, Val jumped out and stormed into the auditorium. The team was running drills up and down the court. Val walked straight onto the middle of the court. Julian didn't notice her until she walked over and hit him in his chest.

Tears ran down her face as she screamed, "Who is she, Julian?"

"Valencia, what is wrong with you? You can't come down here causing a scene! I'm in the middle of practice!" He tried to shield himself from her punches.

Coach McGee saw the commotion that was going on at the opposite end of the gym. "Pennington, what the hell is going on down there?" Coach thundered.

"I don't give a damn, you've been cheating on me, and I want to know who she is," Val screamed.

"Pennington, this is practice, not *Dr. Phil!*" Coach screamed across the gymnasium. The rest of the team laughed at Julian's domestic dispute.

"Sorry, Coach, just give us a few minutes." Julian grabbed Val by the arm and pulled her into a small corridor off the gymnasium.

"What is wrong with you?" Julian demanded.

"Did you sleep with her?" Val asked.

"Sleep with who?"

"The girl you took to Aspen."

"Valencia, I don't know what you're talking about."

"Julian, you were caught on camera. The paparazzi took pictures of the two of you together. You and your mistress are on the cover of every tabloid magazine from here to Philadelphia."

Julian's face sank with guilt.

"Valencia, go home," he said. "We can discuss this later." He pointed in the direction of the door.

Val refused to budge. "Did you sleep with her?" she asked again.

Julian turned his back to her. She knew the answer was yes, but she wanted to hear him say it. She wanted him to acknowledge the wrong he had done.

"I slept with her once."

Rage flashed in her eyes.

"You're lying," she said, her teeth clenched. "Why would you take a one night stand to Aspen? You've been seeing her for a while, haven't you? That's why you're hardly home and when I call you don't answer your phone. How long has this been going on behind my back?"

He laid his head against the wall but didn't answer her question.

Val was so angry. She wanted to dig her nails into his skin and hurt him the same way she was hurting. The dark cloud that had been following her around finally poured rain down on her head, clearing her mind so she could see what was going on.

There was nothing more to be said between the two of them. What she thought they had was nothing but a lie. She marched back out into the gymnasium and all eyes settled on her. She could feel their stares. Everyone waited to see if she would lose control again.

Val slowly walked back out to the truck, and Pilar followed. Once they were back on the road, Val broke down in tears. She couldn't hold back her overwhelming sorrow any longer.

"Julian slept with her. He shared his body with a woman he barely even knew. We vowed to wait for each other. I saved myself for him. I feel so stupid." She poured out her heart.

Pilar pulled off to the side of the road. "Val, everything is going to be okay."

"How can everything be okay? I'm three thousand miles away from my friends and family. Julian and I are through. I have nowhere to go."

Tears continued to fall from her eyes. Her breathing became uncontrollable. She couldn't catch her breath. Val opened the door and ran over to a nearby bush just in time for it to catch her vomit. The rain beat down on her back. She grabbed her stomach to stop the pain.

Pilar ran to her side. "Let it all go. Once you let go of all the hurt, you will feel so much better." Pilar wrapped her arms around Val as the rain soaked their clothes. She was not going to leave Val until she was feeling better.

Five minutes had passed before Val could calm herself down. She walked over and leaned against the side of Pilar's truck.

"Val, I'm going to bring you back to my house. You can stay with us tonight," Pilar yelled. The rain had gotten heavier and it was hard for Pilar to see what was in front of her.

Val was too tired to put up any argument. She graciously accepted Pilar's invitation.

It wasn't long before Pilar pulled up into her three-car garage. She parked between a 745 Beamer and a Maybach.

They entered the house through a door from the garage that led straight into Pilar's family room. Val admired the view from the family room. Looking through three large bay windows, Val could see acres of land that had an in-ground swimming pool, a tennis court, and basketball court.

Out of nowhere a cute little toddler ran up to hug Pilar. "Mommy's home," he squealed.

Pilar put her hands out and stopped him. "No Alejandro. Mommy can't hug you right now. I'm wet."

The inquisitive three-year-old stared at his mother. She spoke to her children in Spanish and waved her two oldest daughters over.

"Children, this is Ms. Benson. She will be staying with us for a while, so I expect everyone to be on their best behavior," Pilar said to them. "Valencia, these are my two oldest daughters, Nina and Tia."

Each girl politely shook Val's hand.

"And this is the little man of the house." She pointed to her son. "This is Alejandro, but we call him Alec. Say hello, Alec."

He walked up to her. "*¿Hola, usted querría jugar conmigo?*"

Valencia looked up at Pilar for help. She couldn't speak Spanish.

"Alec, Ms. Benson doesn't speak Spanish. Speak English," she instructed him.

"Hi, would you like to play with me?" he asked Val.

Those innocent words melted her heart, and for the first time since her altercation with Julian, she smiled.

"Alec, Ms. Benson is tired. We can ask her to play a little later, after she's had a chance to rest." Pilar turned to the girls. "Where's the baby?" she asked.

"Mrs. Gonzalez has her," Tia responded. "Mommy, why are you so wet?"

"We got caught out in the rain. I'm on my way upstairs to change now." Pilar turned to Val. "You can meet the baby later. Come on, I'll show you to your room."

"Alec is so cute," Val commented as they climbed the stairs.

"Yes, I love all my children, but he's my favorite. He's a momma's boy."

Pilar led Val to a guest room that was larger than her and Julian's master bedroom. She looked around at the bronze interior room. Circular ceiling lights brightened the room. On the nightstand a crystal vase showcased lilies in bloom. *What an elegantly decorated room*, she thought. Against the far wall hung a full length mirror and a forty-two-inch plasma television was mounted above the fireplace.

"There's a bathroom through that door if you want to take a shower."

"Yes, I would love that."

"While you're in the shower, I'll make you a cup

of hot tea and I'll get you one of Carlos's T-shirts to sleep in."

"Thanks for everything, Pilar. I don't know what I would have done without you today."

Pilar smiled.

Val got in the shower and turned the faucet until the water was steaming hot. She loved taking a hot shower. The steam usually cleared her mind, but not today. Today her mind was full of memories of her and Julian. She turned her back to the steady stream of water, allowing it to loosen her back muscles. Taking the washcloth to splash water on her face, she remembered how she and Julian met.

Val and Olivia, both freshmen at Philly High, were excited about the school's first basketball game of the season. It was going to be an exciting game against Dobbins High School, and the entire student body was attending.

Before the start of the game, Julian paraded out onto the court to demonstrate his ability to ignite screams from the female spectators.

"That must be Julian Pennington," Val whispered to Olivia.

"Yeah, that's him. He's cute, isn't he?"

"He's all right."

"Stop lying. That boy isn't just cute—he's K-ute."

K-ute was their private definition of a guy that was a 10 or better.

"Okay, I'll admit he is K-ute, but let's see if he's a real *baller*." She laughed at her emphasis on baller.

From the time the official tossed up the ball until the very last second ticked away on the game clock, Julian put on a performance for his fans. He broke three school records that one night: the highest number of points in one quarter, the highest number of points in a single game, and the highest number of assists.

"That boy can really play," Val commented.

"They said he's good. A lot of people say he's a shoo-in for the pros."

Val watched Julian celebrate with his teammates. *He is K-ute,* she thought, *but he probably has girls lined up around the block.*

Val and Olivia waited inside the school for Val's father to pick them up. They stood not too far from the boys' locker room where, indeed, a pack of girls had assembled, waiting for Julian. Val watched as Julian walked out of the locker room. The flirtatious and obviously excited females pushed and shoved to get closer to the handsome ball player.

Julian looked up and saw Val standing close by. He broke away from the crowd and stepped to her. "Hi, what's your name?"

"Valencia," she replied. "Valencia Benson."

"That is such a beautiful name." He batted his long eyelashes at her flirtatiously. "I saw you in the stands. Did you enjoy the game?"

"Yes, I did. You played very well."

"Thanks." He smiled boldly. "Would you like to get something to eat?"

Val shied away from the handsome young man and pulled Olivia closer to her. "I'm sorry. We're waiting for my father to come pick us up."

"I understand," Julian replied. "Can I get your phone number? Maybe we can go out another time."

"I'm sorry, but my father doesn't allow guys he hasn't met to call the house."

Julian was disappointed. Soon the girls heard a car horn.

"I have to go," Val announced. "It was nice speaking with you, Julian." Val and Olivia rushed out to the car.

Julian watched them get in the car, but before she closed the passenger side door Julian yelled out, "Valencia!"

Val looked in his direction as he ran out to the car and over to her father.

"Hello, Mr. Benson, my name is Julian Pennington. I attend school with your daughter." Julian held out his hand for a handshake. "I was just talking with your daughter and she told me that you don't allow guys to call your home whom you haven't met yet. So I wanted to take this opportunity to introduce myself. I hope that sometime in the near future you will give me permission to speak with your daughter on the telephone."

Mr. Benson was impressed by Julian's respectful manner, and was amused by how smitten he was with his daughter.

"Val is right. I don't allow boys to call the house I haven't met, but now that I've met you and I see that you are a nice young man, I don't have a problem with Val giving you the house number." He turned to Valencia. "Baby girl, give him the house number."

Valencia was shocked. She could not believe her father had been charmed by Julian so quickly. Her father never gave out their phone numbers to boys without him first giving them a long lecture on responsibly dating his daughter. Val was impressed.

She knew anyone who could get past her father on the first meeting was someone special.

After being in the shower for nearly an hour, Val decided that it was time for her to get out.

She walked back into the bedroom and moved Carlos's shirt that Pilar had placed on the bed. She lay across the bed in her towel.

Val heard a soft knock at her door. "Come in," she said softly.

Pilar walked in carrying a hot cup of tea. She placed it on the nightstand and sat on the edge of the bed.

"Are you feeling better?" she asked.

"A little," Val replied.

"Don't blame yourself for what has happened. I already told you that I went through a similar incident and the entire time I blamed myself. I wondered what I had done wrong to make him want someone else. After a while I realized that I had to stop blaming myself. I couldn't take responsibility for his actions. I made him dinner, took care of the kids, and gave him sex." She snapped her fingers. "On demand." They laughed together. "I knew I was the best wife I could be, but if our marriage was going to survive, he would have to realize that I was second to none, and that our family took precedence over everything. And eventually he did."

"I do feel like this is my fault." Val told Pilar. "If I didn't insist we wait until after we were married to have sex, then this would have never happened."

"Don't think that way, because no matter what

you had done, this could have still happened. You can't live your life on the assumption that everything you do or don't do will prevent Julian from stepping outside of your relationship. You have to live your life for yourself."

Val absorbed Pilar's words of wisdom.

"Now it's up to you to decide whether or not you think your relationship is worth fighting for. Remember you said that you and Julian shared something special. If you really believe that, then the two of you can work through this together. You have to remember that just because you two are in love doesn't mean that either of you won't make mistakes. I stayed with Carlos because I knew that I could never love anyone the same way that I love him, but some women can't get past infidelity."

Pilar got up and grabbed Val's clothes from the bathroom. "I'm going to take these downstairs and put them in the washer. If you need anything, just yell. My room is right down the hall."

She was finally left alone. She closed her eyes and thought about Pilar's advice. *Should I forgive Julian? Or will I allow one mistake destroy what we have?*

CHAPTER 9

"Ladies, I'm going to be completely honest with you," Desmond Murray, the private detective, told Olivia and Danyelle. "You haven't really given me a whole lot of information on Mr. Winters. I'm pretty sure that I can find him, but it may take me a while."

"How long do you think it will take?" Olivia asked.

"I could find him next week, or it may not be until next year. It depends on how careful he's been about leaving a paper trail. It looks like he's done this before, because he left this apartment with no signs of him ever living here. But you did say he worked for Amtrak, correct?"

Olivia nodded her head. "They won't give you any information. I tried," she said. "I called them and all they kept saying was, 'We cannot release any past or present employee information.'" Olivia mimicked the woman she spoke to on the phone.

"Let me try. I may be able to persuade them to help us out," Murray replied. "Give me a call if you happen to find or remember anything that could help me find out his whereabouts, like an old phone bill or pay stub. I'll start by going down to Amtrak. I'll show his picture around to a few people. Hopefully someone will recognize him."

"Mr. Murray, I just remembered something," Danyelle said. "I'm not sure if this will be of any help to you, but Bryant took a trip over the summer to Chicago for a family emergency."

"Oh, yeah, I had forgotten about that," Olivia added.

"There's not too much more we can tell you. He went to Chicago and returned a few days later," Danyelle said.

"I don't suppose he left a phone number where he could be reached?" Mr. Murray asked.

"He did leave me with a number to the Best Western. I think that's where he was staying."

"Great, let's just pray that he used the phone there or maybe even rented a car. This is a great lead. Olivia, I'll call you in a few weeks and let you know my progress."

Val opened her eyes and was surprised to see Alec on the floor next to her bed playing with a handful of toy soldiers. She smiled at his cuteness. "Good morning, cutie."

"Can you come play with me? My mommy said not to bother you while she was gone, and I was really quiet while you was sleeping."

"Yes, you were very quiet." She looked at the

clock. It was past one o'clock in the afternoon. "Wow, I didn't know it was so late." She sat up and stretched her arms. Alec stood up next to her. "Alec, why don't you go to your room and set up a game for us to play while I get dressed? I'll be there in a bit."

The boy gathered his toy soldiers and raced out of the room. Val grabbed her cell phone. It had been a week since she had confronted Julian about his infidelities, and she was surprised that he hadn't once tried to call her to work things out. She knew that Carlos had told Julian she was staying with them, but she still wondered why he hadn't called her.

Sitting on the lounge chair next to her bed was another set of clothes from Pilar. Val had been borrowing clothes from Pilar all week long. She knew she was eventually going to have to go home and get her own clothes, but she was trying to put off facing Julian for as long as possible.

Forty-five minutes later Val walked down the hall and found Alec watching an episode of *Sponge Bob Square Pants*. Stacked high on his bed were Candy Land, Chutes and Ladders, Blue's Clues Room Talking Game, and at least three more games. He noticed Val enter and he ran to greet her.

"You can sit right here," he said, pointing to a small miniature chair.

"Alec, I don't think I'm going to fit in this chair. Why don't I sit on the floor?"

"All right," he replied. He quickly turned his attention back to the television.

Val looked around Alec's brightly colored room. The walls were painted lime green and or-

ange. Stenciled on the walls were different characters from Nickelodeon. Against the far wall was a
bookcase full of different books. Closer to the television was a miniature chair and desk set with lots
of paper, crayons, markers, and paints. Val admired several drawings hanging from the wall, all
done by Alec. She glanced at a few unfinished pictures on his desk when she came across a red
paper heart. She opened up the heart and inside
were the words "i like u" in a child's handwriting.
It brought back memories of her and Julian's first
Valentine's Day together.

Julian and Val had attended their school's annual Valentine's Day dance. At the end of the
night the DJ announced the last song and Julian
asked her to dance. He held her close while Val listened to the beat of his heart. Balloons and miniature confetti hearts fell from the ceiling, covering
them and making it a moment she would never forget. Julian made it even more memorable by kneeling down in front of her unexpectedly. She thought
he was going to ask her to marry him, but they were
only fourteen-years-old. He pulled a box out from
his coat pocket and opened it. Inside was a heart
locket. "Will you be my Valentine?" he asked her.

She knew that moment marked the beginning
of a true love story.

"Alec, where'd you get this?" she asked the
child.

He walked over to see what she was referring to.
"Some stupid girl at school gave it to me."

"Why you call her stupid?" she giggled.

"Because she bugs me. She is always messing
with me and she tries to sit next to me on the bus."

"Maybe she likes you."

"I don't like girls."

"You like me, don't you? And you like your mommy, and we're both girls."

"Yes, I like both of you, but I don't like my sisters. They're always telling me what to do and making fun of me. I don't think they like me." His face turned sad.

"They're your sisters. I'm sure they love you."

"Then why are they so mean?"

"Just because a person does something to hurt you doesn't mean that person doesn't love you." Val was surprised by her choice of words. She paused for a moment. "Let me tell you what you should do. The next time either of them is mean to you, you should be nice to them. They will feel bad for mistreating you, and try to make it up to you by being nice. It's hard being the youngest." Val gave him a hug. "Why don't we play a game?"

Alec walked over to his bed and pulled out Candy Land. They played two rounds and Alec beat her both times. After the second game, he set up the board again.

"Here you are," Pilar said to Val as she walked into Alec's room. "I should have known that Alec would have taken you hostage. How are you feeling today?"

"I'm doing much better. Alec has been keeping me company."

"I hope he hasn't been bothering you."

"No, he's been a good boy. I really enjoyed my time with him. He helped me realize a few important things that I need to apply to my own life."

Pilar sensed that she was referring to her and Julian. "Would you like to use my car?" she offered.

"If you don't mind, that would be great."

"No, go ahead. My keys are downstairs on the kitchen counter," Pilar told her.

Val walked toward the door when Alec called out her name. "Ms. Benson, you're leaving?" he asked.

Val forgot all about Alec and the board game. Fortunately, Pilar intervened on her behalf. "Alec, Mommy will play with you. Ms. Benson has to run out. We will see her when she gets back."

Val shot Pilar a thank you smile and dashed out the door.

Val pulled up in front of what used to be her home. It seemed like months had passed since the last time she was there. She felt like an intruder as she inserted her key into the door and entered. Val looked around at the familiar home furnishings. Nothing had changed. She walked into the family room, expecting to find Julian laid out on the couch. Instead, she found a spotless family room. The last time she was here the room was a total mess. Julian used this room as his dining room, bedroom and kitchen. He always left a trail of dirty dishes, newspapers, and clothes lying around. *He must have cleaned up himself after he realized that I wasn't coming home,* Val thought to herself.

She walked toward the stairs, but stopped when she heard a noise coming from the kitchen. She could smell the aroma of tomatoes and cheese drifting from the kitchen.

"Julian?" she called out.

She strolled into the kitchen and was surprised to find a blonde-haired girl pulling out a pan of lasagna from the oven. The young woman was so preoccupied with the phone conversation she was having that she didn't notice Val enter the room.

She turned around and jumped when she saw Val's piercing stare. "Melissa, I'll have to call you back." She hung up the receiver. "Can I help you?"

Val recognized her immediately. She was the girl in the photo with Julian. She was the one he took to Aspen—his mistress. "I'm Valencia," she replied. "Is Julian here?"

"No, he's not here right now." The woman's crystal blue eyes stared right through Val. "He mentioned that you might stop by to pick up your things. He asked me to tell you that they're up-stairs."

Val was unprepared for the way the woman ad-dressed her. She treated Val like she was a guest in the house Val had shared with Julian less than a week ago. Unsure of how to react, Val decided it would be best if she gathered her things and waited to speak with Julian later.

Val walked up the stairs. "If you need any help, just yell," Julian's new friend called out. "My name is Caitlyn." Val ignored her and continued up the stairs.

She walked into the bedroom that she used to share with Julian, and into the walk-in closet. She pulled her suitcase down from the top shelf and went toward her side of the closet. Lying in the trash she noticed a shirt she had bought a few years back with both her and Julian's names air-brushed on it. Val kneeled down and lifted up the shirt. *Maybe Julian never did love me.*

Upset, she began pulling things off the hangers and throwing them into her bag. Once she was almost finished packing her things, she looked a little closer at the things she was throwing in her bag. None of these clothes looked familiar to her. "Where are all my clothes?" Val asked out loud.

"They were moved down the hall," Val heard a voice say from behind her.

Leaning against the door was Caitlyn. She sashayed into the master bedroom and sat on the edge of the bed.

"When I moved my things in here, Julian said it would be all right if I moved your things down the hall."

Val's mouth dropped open. "You live here?" Val questioned her.

Caitlyn shook her head yes. "I moved in a few days ago."

Val looked toward the bed and images of Caitlyn and Julian making love flashed in her mind. She quickly turned her head to erase the images from her head. In an attempt to escape Caitlyn's company, Val grabbed her bag and stormed down the hall to the guest bedroom. She quickly found her things and began to pack, slamming skirts and blouses into her suitcase. Val felt a pair of eyes watching her and she didn't have to turn around to know Caitlyn was eyeballing her again.

"Can I help you?" Val asked with her back turned toward Caitlyn.

Dynah Zale

"I just wanted to make sure you found everything. I wouldn't want you to forget anything."

"I think I can handle packing my things by myself," Val said emphatically.

"You don't remember me, do you?" Caitlyn asked.

Val quickened her pace to hurry up and get her things packed so she could leave. "No, I don't. Should I remember?"

"I attended school in Kentucky with Julian. I ran into you a few times when you were visiting."

"You knew Julian at the University?" Val stopped packing her things. She turned toward Caitlyn. *If he was dating her while he was in school, I'm going to kill him.*

"No, I tried to get to know him better, but he wasn't interested."

"So you decided to give it another try after he got drafted into the NBA. How convenient," Val commented sarcastically.

"No, you don't understand," Caitlyn said, laughing. "My uncle is Theodore Haas, the owner of the Seattle SuperSonics.

Val suddenly remembered the party thrown by the owners of the team earlier in the year. Caitlyn was there. She was the one who was flirting with Julian.

Caitlyn continued. "When I found out Julian was leaving school to enter the draft I—"

"You don't have to finish." Val cut her off midsentence. "You wasted no time coming after my man."

"It's not like it was hard. From what I've been told you were too good to satisfy *your* man. So I satisfied him for you."

Val stepped up in Caitlyn's face. "Julian never complained to me."

"What do you expect, Val? He would go out and play ball every night. He'd come home tired and needing to relax and relieve stress. You two shared a bed, but you never shared yourself. You never even touched him—no foreplay, no teasing, nothing. I just gave him what he needed. Trust me, it wasn't hard."

Val looked at her with disgust. How dare an outsider tell her what she did wrong in her relationship? This interloper had no idea what kind of relationship Julian and she shared. It was a special kind of love that allowed them to wait for one another.

Val was about to slap her, but she stopped herself. She knew Caitlyn wasn't worth the effort. Val went back to packing her things.

"Valencia, don't be upset. If I didn't go after him, eventually someone would have and it probably would have been a white girl. The owners provide lots of women for the players to play with when they're on the road. They prefer to see their players with pretty white wives with long, straight hair." She stepped in Val's face and said, "instead of dark-skinned wives with kinky hair."

Val lost all self control. Caitlyn had definitely crossed the line. Val wrapped her hands around Caitlyn's throat and squeezed hard. Val knocked her to the floor, grabbed her hair, and banged her head over and over again. Her anger was so strong; she had the strength of a man and fire in her eyes.

Out of nowhere someone lifted Val up off Caitlyn. "Valencia, what are you doing?" Julian yelled.

Caitlyn held her head as blood seeped into her hand.

Julian walked over to her. "Caitlyn, are you okay?" he asked.

"Is she okay?" Val screamed. She walked up to him and pushed him. "What about me? She verbally attacked me."

"And you physically assaulted her. You didn't have to put your hands on her," he responded.

"You don't know what she said to me," Val cried.

Caitlyn wrapped her arms around Julian. "She attacked me for no reason."

"Julian, is this . . ." she pointed at Caitlyn, " . . . what you want? Did you forget about what we had? What we meant to one another? You're going to end our relationship like this?"

He didn't say anything.

"Did you ever love me?" she yelled.

"Of course. But right now I need a break. I can't explain what's going on with me, but I need some time to sort things out."

"Julian, take your time, because when you do figure things out, I won't be here for you." Val looked over at Caitlyn. "And neither will she." Val grabbed her suitcase and left.

On the way back to Pilar's, she knew it was time for her to go back home, back to Philly. Everything she had done was for Julian. Now it was time she did something for herself.

CHAPTER 10

Olivia looked at the message indicator on her answering machine. There was one new message. She hit the playback button.

"Olivia, I have some news for you." Mr. Murray's deep voice echoed through her apartment.

"Good news, I hope," she said out loud.

"I found the hotel you said Bryant stayed at in Chicago. I managed to get a copy of his phone records and he called a Ms. Daneesha Oaks several times. I also have a North Carolina number, but I haven't tracked down to whom that number belongs yet. I'm going to try to get an address for Ms. Oaks and pay her a visit. I'll try to find out what her relationship with Bryant is. I'll keep you posted with any updates. Talk to you later."

Olivia lay on the couch hoping to soothe her aching head. For the past two weeks she had been nursing a headache that wouldn't go away. The stress from worrying about Bryce had put Olivia in a state of depression. She hadn't slept in days. She had lost her appetite and had isolated herself inside her bedroom.

Aside from her worry about the baby she had also been suspended from her job, pending the criminal charges pressed against her.

"Oh God! What have I done to deserve this pain?" she cried. Elise's words of wisdom filled her mind. *. . . by not maintaining an intimate relationship with God through daily prayer and reading of the Word, distance will grow between you and the Lord, resulting in trials and tribulations.*

"Lord, I'm sorry," Olivia prayed. "I was always too busy with the baby to pray. God, have mercy on me and my baby. You promised that whatever we ask for in prayer, we shall receive. So I ask for the safe return of my son. Bring him safely home to his mother. Amen."

A knock at her front door told her she had a visitor, but Olivia wasn't in the mood to see anyone, so she ignored it. The knocking continued and she soon realized that her unwanted guest was not going away, so she lifted herself up from the couch and answered the door.

A beautiful, tall woman with long, black, silky hair pulled back into a ponytail stared back at her. The pecan color of her skin blended well with the earth tones of her make-up.

She shivered from the cold chill of the air. "Hello," the woman said. "I'm looking for Bryant Winters."

Olivia was surprised by the woman's inquiry. This was the first time anyone had ever come to the house looking for Bryant.

"Bryant?"

"Yes, Bryant Winters."

"You're a friend of his?" Olivia asked.

"No, I'm his wife."

Olivia's heart dropped. She couldn't believe Bryant had a wife and she was standing at her door. She didn't know he had ever been married. She was speechless. It took her a few seconds to regain her composure.

"Would you like to come in?" Olivia said, offering the stranger a seat. "My name is Olivia."

"Hello, I'm Taima."

Olivia sat across from her. "Bryant never told me that he had a wife."

"We've been married for four years," Taima said. She hesitated before she continued. "I've been away for a couple years and I'm trying to get back in touch with him." She looked over her shoulder to make sure no one else was in the room. "If you don't mind me asking, what is your relationship with Bryant?"

Olivia wondered whether she should answer Taima's question truthfully.

"If you're intimately involved with him, it's okay," Taima told her. "We haven't actually been husband and wife for a long time."

"I recently had a son by Bryant," Olivia chose her words carefully. She wasn't sure if she could trust Taima or not. How did she know she was really Bryant's wife? She may be working with Bryant to keep her son away from her.

By the look on Olivia's face, Taima knew there was something wrong. "Did Bryant steal your son away from you?" Taima asked.

"Yes, How did you know?"

"Two years ago he did the same thing to me. Bryant had me committed into a drug rehabilitation clinic in Wisconsin. He drugged me for months by putting Ecstasy in my food. He made sure I was so high that I couldn't tell the difference between reality and fantasy. He filed a petition with the court for full custody of our daughter and had me declared an unfit mother. That's when he had me institutionalized. It took me two years to get clean and get out of there. By the time I returned home, he had taken our daughter, Niya, and left town. I've been searching for them ever since."

Olivia couldn't believe the story she had just heard. Finally, here was someone who actually shared her pain. Olivia could see how visibly upset she was. She handed Taima a tissue to wipe her tears. "How did you get my address?"

"It's a funny thing. I've been searching for him for over a year. I filed a missing persons report, put up flyers, and I even did a little investigation of my own, but nothing I did turned up any leads. A few weeks ago I was searching through the closet for something I had lost and I came across a bunch of old sports magazines Bryant used to subscribe to. I remembered him telling me once that he had been a regular subscriber to that magazine since he was thirteen-years-old. Well, I got an idea and asked a male cousin of mine to call the magazine's customer service number and act like he was Bryant. He told them that he had a new credit card number and needed to change the one they had on file. They immediately took the new number and before he hung up, he asked them to verify his current address." She then held up a copy of the sports magazine that lay on the coffee table. "It's a blessing that Bryant changed his subscription address to here."

"Taima, unfortunately, I don't know where Bryant is. I hired a private investigator and he called today with some leads, but he hasn't found them yet. Did Bryant ever introduce you to any of his friends? Maybe a distant relative? Anyone who could help us find out where he has disappeared to?" Olivia asked.

"No." She slowly shook her head. "When Bryant and I were married, we didn't know each other too well. We had only been dating for five months before he proposed. Everyone who attended our wedding was either a friend or relative of mine. I did ask him about his mother and siblings. He said his mother passed away when he was young and that he didn't have any brothers and sisters. He was a loner in life."

Olivia shook her head, "He pretty much told me the same story. Why don't you leave your name and number with me and the next time the investigator calls to give me an update I can ask him to give you a call. You may be able to give him some information about Bryant that I couldn't."

"No problem."

Payce was tired of working seventy-five hours a week and bringing home less than three hundred dollars. He knew he had to start making some real money. That's why he called Reverend Kane and accepted her offer to work at The Dollhouse. Glad that he had accepted her offer, she immediately arranged for him to interview with the owner, Natasha Brown, the following day.

Payce walked into The Dollhouse. Sitting at the front desk was the same girl who was there when he and Darshon were there.

"Hello, I'm here to see Natasha," Payce said to the young woman.

"I remember you," she said, smiling. "Are you going to be working here?"

"If things go well, I will."

She picked up the phone and dialed a three-digit extension. "What's your name?" she asked.

"Payce Boyd."

"Natasha, Payce Boyd is here to see you." A minute later she hung up the phone. "Follow me."

Payce and the young woman walked through a maze of halls until they stopped in front of a door with "Natasha Brown" written on it. The reception-ist knocked before opening the door slightly. She whispered to Payce, "Natasha is really cool and laid back." She took a few steps back toward the re-ceptionist area. "Good luck," she called out.

Payce pushed the door open and walked into the cluttered office. Papers and files were piled high in all four corners of the office. Natasha was entering information into her computer from var-ious papers scattered over her desk.

Payce glanced at Natasha and thought she re-sembled a black Cher. Her hair was long, silky, and straight. It reached past her butt. Her head was buried so far down into her computer that he couldn't see her face.

"Hello," he said.

"Have a seat," Natasha commanded. She never looked up, and continued to type on her computer. "So you're a friend of Kane's?"

"Yes ma'am."

"Have you ever done this kind of work before?"

"No."

"Another amateur." She sighed. "But that's all right. You'll learn." She immediately went into the details of the job. "The job pays fifteen hundred per session. You can work as long as you want, when you want. You can work once a week if you want, or three sessions a night. It's up to you. Three sessions equal a total of forty-five hundred dollars. Each session ends at the couple's discretion. One couple may just ask you to have sex with the wife once, and then you're done. Another couple may ask you to stay for eight to twelve hours. It's their prerogative. Sometimes couples enjoy role playing. You may have to dress up like a cop, handcuff the husband, and do the wife. Condoms are provided in all the rooms and I leave it up to the employees on whether or not they want to divulge their names. Since this is a business, I would recommend keeping your identity a secret. You can pick up your money at the end of every session or at the end of the night. The receptionist is responsible for distributing compensation. Any questions?"

Payce shook his head no.

"Good." Natasha got up and walked over to a closet. She pulled out a huge trash bag. "What's your waist size?" she asked.

"Thirty-eight," Payce responded.

When she stood up Payce got a good look at her enormous silicone breasts that toppled out of her baby doll T-shirt.

She grabbed a pair of small, leather shorts. "Here you go." She threw them at him. "The men's locker room is down the hall. Change your clothes, and there is a couple waiting for you in Room 18."

"I start now?" he asked. Payce was surprised that she wanted him to start so soon. He thought he'd have a day or two before he began work.

"In this business you quickly learn that time is money," she replied.

Payce changed into his new work uniform, which was a bit too tight around the ass. He wasn't used to this. He felt really uncomfortable walking around with nothing on but a pair of small leather shorts and his Timberland boots.

He found Room 18 and knocked on the door softly. A woman's voice yelled from inside, "Come in."

He opened the door to find a beautiful woman wearing a sheer, black negligee lying on the bed. *This job might not be so bad,* he thought. She was absolutely stunning. Her hazel eyes and lean body aroused him. Her long legs resembled an athlete's and her abs were perfectly defined. He walked into the room and up to the bed.

"What's up?" he said to her.

"What's going on?" A man's voice startled him from behind. He turned around to see a man sitting in a chair. Her husband—or who Payce thought was her husband—resembled a football player. He had broad shoulders, a huge body, and hands twice the size of Payce's.

"Hey!" Payce replied. He felt awkward knowing that he was supposed to have sex with the man's beautiful wife while he watched. Payce wasn't exactly sure how he was supposed to address the man, so he walked over to him and reached out to shake his hand. The man stared back.

"Man, we both know why you're here. So go ahead and get started."

Payce walked back over to the edge of the bed. Without hesitation, the wife pulled him down on the bed and began taking his shorts off. She touched Payce in places that made him feel so good he wanted to shout, but he was scared that if he did it would make her husband angry. Payce didn't want to have a confrontation with the enormous man, so he closed his eyes to hold back all emotion. The only sounds in the room could be heard from the wife moaning. Payce wondered what the husband was doing. He was awfully quiet. He opened his eyes and snuck a quick look over at the husband who was watching his wife. His expression was cold and hard.

The woman lay back on the bed and Payce went to her. He gave her his all. He looked into her face and pretended that she was his wife. He thought about how much he would enjoy making love to her every night.

"She likes it doggy style," the man said from his chair. Payce looked over at the husband and stopped what he was doing. "Did you say something?" Payce asked.

"I said she likes it doggy style," he bellowed.

Not wanting to upset her husband, he did as told. He turned the woman over on her knees.

Payce thought that this was some weird shit. It was already difficult trying to please another man's wife with the husband in the room watching, but for him to request a specific position was crazy.

"You like that, don't you?" she asked. Payce thought she was talking to him, but when he looked down at her she was talking to her husband.

Payce wasted no time in getting the job done. Afterwards, the three of them stared at one another in silence. The husband got up, laid on the bed, and the wife wrapped herself up in his arms. Payce felt strange watching them enjoy their time together when he was the one who did all the work. He slid into his leather shorts and exited the room. He was exhausted and had enough for the day. He put his clothes back on and stopped by the receptionist's desk to collect his pay. As he was reaching for the door, he turned around to see Reverend Kane dressed in a robe, escorting a red-headed woman into one of the rooms.

Tressie was surprised to see Olivia and Danyelle kneeling at the altar when she walked into the church. With everything that was going on with the baby, she thought Olivia wouldn't want to see anybody. Tressie took a seat in one of the pews and waited for them to finish praying.

Olivia got up with tears in her eyes but a smile spread across her face when she saw Tressie. She walked over and gave her a big hug.

"Hey girl, how are you feeling?" Tressie asked.

"I'm doing okay. I'm taking one day at a time."

"Have you heard anything about the baby?"

"The private detective we hired left a message on my answering machine last week, but I haven't spoken to him. I did leave a message on his voice-mail about Bryant's wife."

"Danyelle told me about that," Tressie replied. Danyelle had been giving Tressie daily updates on what was going on with Olivia, Bryant, and the baby. "Keep your head up. That detective will bring Bryce home to you."

"That's why I'm here. I was home feeling sorry for myself when I finally picked up my Bible. All throughout the New Testament are stories of how Jesus healed people and performed miracles, all because they had faith. There was the woman who believed that all she had to do was touch the hem of his garment and she would be healed. And then there was the blind man whose eyes Jesus touched, and he could see again. These are all things that happened because people believed. So I'm here because I believe. I believe God will send my baby back to me. I prayed that the Lord would send me a clue about Bryant, and seconds later Taima knocked on my door. Don't think I'm not worried about my son, because I am but I trust that the Lord will provide. I just need to continue to pray."

"You have really been blessed," Tressie replied.

"I sure have," Olivia said.

"I wonder where Elise is," Danyelle said.

"She must be running late. She is usually the first one here," Olivia remarked.

Tressie sat and wondered whether or not she

should tell them what she had seen. She might have been mistaken. Maybe it wasn't Elise after all.

"Last week Payce took me to see a drive-in movie in Atlantic City," Tressie told them.

"I didn't even know they still had drive-in movies," Danyelle replied.

"Neither did I, but that's not what I wanted to tell you. We were watching the movie and I happened to look over into the next car, and I could have sworn I saw Elise making out with some guy in the backseat."

"Uh!" Danyelle cried. "I need a blunt."

"That's ridiculous!" Olivia replied.

"I'm telling you, it was her."

"Did you talk to her?"

"No."

"Then how do you know it was her?"

"What did you want me to do, get out the car, walk over, and knock on the window? It was her. I would know Elise anywhere."

"Tressie, you know Elise would never cheat on Miles. She loves her husband. I'm not saying you didn't see what you saw, but I'm saying maybe you were mistaken."

"I know what I saw."

"Are you sure you weren't high? Maybe Payce slipped a little something into your soft drink when you weren't looking," Danyelle laughed.

Olivia's cell phone rang.

"Hello?" she answered. "Yes, Elise, we're all here at the church waiting on you." She looked at Tressie. "Oh okay. Is everything all right? Okay, we'll see you next week."

Olivia hung up the phone. "That was Elise. She

said that something else came up and she won't be able to make it here tonight. She told us just to say a prayer, and we'll pick up next week."

"Something must be really important for her to miss Bible Study. We all know how she feels about being here every Tuesday night," Tressie added.

CHAPTER 11

Miles walked into the kitchen with a pile of bills from the mailbox. "Elise!" he bellowed. Miles's voice echoed against the still silence in the house before he quickly remembered it was Tuesday night. *Elise said she was going to the gym tonight.* He thumbed through a few bills: electric bill, credit card bill, credit card bill, another credit card bill. "I have got to remind myself to sit down with Elise and get rid of some of these credit cards," he said out loud. A Victoria's Secret catalog had also arrived for Elise. Aware that his wife liked to browse the catalog and shop online simultaneously, he thought he would do her a favor and place it in the den next to the computer. As he walked into the den he browsed through the pages. The lovely Tyra Banks modeled a few items that he wouldn't mind seeing his wife in. Before he laid the catalog down he looked around for a pen. He wanted to mark a few of the things he liked, just in case Elise decided to surprise him one night. He pulled open a drawer to search for a pen and was surprised to see a bill lying inside the drawer.

After Elise and Miles were married, Miles took on the responsibility of paying all the bills, including Elise's. Anything that needed to be paid, she usually gave straight to him, so it was unusual for him to find a bill Elise had not mentioned.

He examined it closely. It was a hospital bill that detailed the injuries Elise had incurred from the accident she had at the park a few months ago. He reviewed the bill and noticed the admittance date was November second and the discharge date was also November second. *She told me she stayed overnight at the hospital for observation. If she didn't stay at the hospital, where did she stay?* He turned the bill over. It was addressed to a Mr. Sheridan Reed.

He took the bill and ran out of the house. *Who is Sheridan Reed?* He jumped in his car and drove to the address on the envelope. He was unsure of what he was going to do once he arrived, but he couldn't wait until Elise got home to question her. He needed answers now. Perhaps Sheridan Reed could explain why his wife lied and hid the truth about where she spent the night of November second.

He thought about how Elise's behavior toward him had changed over the past few weeks. When he touched her, she would pull away. When he made suggestions of things they could do to arouse him, she acted as if she didn't want to be bothered. He gave her intense foreplay to stimulate her sexually, but after several minutes she would get up and leave him to lie alone in the bed.

Elise's disinterest left him physically and mentally wounded. He thought that the stress of his impotency was wearing her down.

He pulled up in front of the address and parked his car on the next block. As he walked back toward Sheridan's house he noticed Elise's car parked out front. His heart pounded against his chest. Elise had lied to him, again. She was supposed to be at the health club.

He stared at Elise's car for a moment. He was being irrational. Elise would never intentionally lie to him. There had to be a logical reason why she wasn't at the club. She could have stopped here to drop off a friend, or maybe she worked with Mr. Reed.

He turned around to get back in his car, but something stopped him. He wanted to put his trust back in his wife, but something was telling him to stay. He walked up to the door and listened for a moment. He tried to hear voices, but he couldn't hear anything. He raised his hand to knock on the door, but again he stopped himself. He wasn't ready to face what was on the other side of that door. He stood outside the residence for ten more minutes before he lost his nerve. He couldn't do it. He was too scared about what he might have to face. He decided to wait in his car until she came out, and then he would find out who Sheridan Reed was.

Inside the apartment Elise sat on Sheridan's couch. Since her arrival he had been busy preparing something special for her in the bathroom.

She heard the water running in the tub and him moving things around.

"Just wait one more minute!" he yelled from the bathroom.

It was not unusual for Sheridan to plan something special for their rendezvous together. She always looked forward to a candlelit dinner, a dozen roses, or something pretty and pink from Frederick's of Hollywood. The week before he suggested they go see a drive-in movie together. She was hesitant at first because she feared someone might see them together. Sheridan tried to reassure her that no one would see them, but to ease her mind he took her to a drive-in movie theater in Atlantic City, sixty miles away. It was such a romantic night. He bought popcorn and soft drinks and they even made out in the backseat like high school kids. Elise loved his spontaneous side.

She loved spending time with Sheridan, but the guilt of lying to her husband was beginning to weigh heavily on her conscience. She wasn't sure how much longer she would be able to keep it up.

She wasn't just lying to her husband. This affair had also affected different areas of her life and had led her to do things she wouldn't normally do, like cancel Bible Study. The one constant thing in her life was her Bible Study group, but when Sheridan asked her to skip Bible Study and come straight to his house, she agreed.

"Elise, come here," Sheridan shouted, breaking her from her thoughts.

She walked into the bathroom and was surprised by the number of lit candles that were positioned around the bathtub.

"I would appreciate the pleasure of your company," Sheridan said to her. He was sitting in his oversized bathtub that was big enough for two.

Elise quickly undressed and slipped in with him. She squeezed between his legs and lay back on his chest. The warm bath water was filled with bubbles and rose petals. Various colored candles illuminated the room, while Luther Vandross sang in the background.

Sheridan slowly washed her body. They kissed and the magical moment brought them closer together.

Elise moved her leg to get a little bit more comfortable, and she hit it against something hard. She moved her hands underneath the water to search for the foreign object that was in the water with them.

"Be careful, searching around underneath there. You never know what you'll find," Sheridan commented.

She finally found what she was looking for and revealed a bottle covered in suds.

"What's this?" she asked.

Sheridan shrugged his shoulders in response.

She looked closely at the bottle. Written on the outside of the bottle were the words 'A Message in a Bottle'. She opened the cork and pulled out a scroll. Elise unrolled the paper. It read, "I love you." Her heart sank to the bottom of her stomach.

"I love you, too," she whispered in his ear.

After their romantic bath together, they moved to the bedroom. Still dripping wet with water,

Sheridan kissed her neck. He continued to please her, but after a while she stopped him.

"I need you," she told him.

He obeyed and they made love for over an hour.

Afterwards, they lay tangled in his bed sheets. He slowly rubbed her arm.

"That was amazing," Elise said.

"Yeah, I enjoyed it myself," he replied.

Sheridan could sense that there was something on her mind, but he wasn't sure what it was. He hoped she wasn't thinking about her husband. He wanted their time together to only be about them. "What's wrong?" he asked.

"I have something I need to tell you," she confessed. "I hope you don't think I do this kind of thing on the regular."

Sheridan knew from the first time he saw her that she was far too sophisticated to have random affairs with anyone. He also knew that she loved her husband.

"My husband and I have been having problems in our marriage. He's been experiencing temporary episodes of impotency."

"I'm sorry to hear that. Has he gone to see a doctor?" Sheridan asked.

"Yes, the doctor told us that a man his age usually experiences impotency for psychological reasons as opposed to physical. There could be a number of reasons why this is happening to him. We didn't start having these problems until we planned to start a family. He's been seeing a therapist, but so far there has been no change."

Sheridan knew there was a reason why every time they were together she would devour him sexually. Her husband hadn't been able to satisfy her for months. Sheridan felt sorry for her husband, but happy for himself. He knew it must have been upsetting for her husband to have such a beautiful woman at home and not be able to make love to her.

"How are you handling this situation?" he asked.

"I'm not the one with the problem," she replied.

"I realize that, but having your husband shut down on you like that has to have some psychological effect on you."

"When he first began having problems, I felt like it was my fault. I thought maybe he had lost interest in me. If I touched him he would get hard, but just before we were ready to make love, he would go limp. Of course he apologized and insisted that it wasn't my fault, but I didn't believe him. I thought I wasn't being sexy enough, or adventurous enough. For months I wasn't sure if he still loved me. I even thought he might have turned gay. I just didn't know. It was hard for me to get through that time until he went to go see a doctor, and that's when I realized it wasn't me."

"I'm glad you told me," Sheridan said, and hugged her a little tighter.

As Miles walked down the stairs that led from Sheridan's front door he heard a door open. He quickly hid beneath the stairs and immediately recognized Elise's voice.

"I love you," Elise said.

"I love you, too," Sheridan responded.

Miles could hear them kiss. They walked down the stairs together. Sheridan held Elise as if he didn't want to see her go. Miles watched as a stranger lovingly embraced his wife.

"I wish you didn't have to go," Sheridan said to her.

"I'll see you in two weeks," she replied as she gazed into his eyes.

Miles watched the love scene unfold before his eyes. He could see the look of love in his wife's eyes. It tore his heart apart to witness the truth. He didn't want to believe that Elise could betray him. He knew that the love they had for one another was real. How could she throw away what they had?

He took a deep breath and stepped out from behind the stairs. "Elise," he called out.

Elise turned around, shocked to see Miles standing before her. She was terrified, speechless, and her heart beat rapidly. She was scared of what Miles would do. She knew he wasn't a violent man, but she didn't know what he was capable of when finding his wife in the arms of another man. Apologetic tears formed in her eyes.

Miles stared at her. He hadn't planned on confronting her, but a minute ago it seemed like the right thing to do. Now that he stood in front of them he didn't know what to say. "I knew there was something going on, but I thought it was my imagination." Miles spoke in a solemn tone. "I'm not mad. I couldn't expect you to wait for me forever."

"Miles, this is not what you think," Elise told him. Natural instinct told her to deny everything.

"Elise, don't lie to me any longer." The pitch of

his voice rose and got deeper. It made him mad to hear her lie to him again. "Elise, I heard you say you loved this man. Is it true? Do you love him?"

She didn't want to hurt him by confessing her feelings for Sheridan.

"Elise, do you love this man?" Miles yelled.

"Yes," she whispered.

Those words hit his heart like a ton of bricks. He grabbed his hand and squeezed tightly. He knew he had to calm himself down before he lashed out at her. Hurting her would make him feel even worse.

"Elise, I don't blame you," he said. "This isn't your fault. I understand why you went looking for satisfaction elsewhere. I can't blame you when I'm the one who failed. It was my responsibility to take care of you."

Elise held her head down in shame. Tears rolled down her face. Sheridan watched in disbelief.

"You didn't fail me," Elise responded. She stepped toward him. "Miles, can we go home and talk about this in private?"

"No, I can't do that. I can't leave here with you thinking that once we get home everything will be okay when I know you're in love with another man. Us going home together is not going to change what has happened here tonight."

A teardrop escaped Miles' eyes and rolled down his cheek.

"Elise, you have to believe that I tried. I wanted so badly to give you the baby you wanted, but for some reason God said I was not the one. Perhaps I'm not the one destined to give you a baby. Maybe it was meant for Sheridan to . . ." He looked in

Sheridan's direction. ". . . make your dream a reality."

"Miles," Elise whimpered.

"I'm not going to stand in the way of your happiness. That's why I'm walking away."

"Miles, don't say that. Think about what you're saying before you make irrational decisions."

"I know what I'm saying. I'm saying good-bye."

Elise could not believe what she was hearing. Miles was stepping aside so she could fulfill her dream of having a baby with another man.

"Miles, don't do this. We can fix this," she begged and reached out for him, but he pulled away.

"I love you, Elise. I would give you anything. Even your freedom."

Miles's eyes held a look of determination. Elise knew there was nothing more she could say to change his mind.

Miles held out his hand to Sheridan. Sheridan looked at Miles's shaking hand. He couldn't believe that Miles was giving his wife away to another man. He was skeptical of Miles's true intentions. Scared that at any moment Miles would pull a gun out and kill them all, Sheridan reluctantly shook his hand.

"Make sure she's happy," Miles said to Sheridan, and he turned to leave.

APRIL 2004

Tressie was surprised to see a limousine pull up in front of her house. The chauffeur got out and walked to the front door.

"Hello, I'm here to pick up a Ms. Montrese Cox," the chauffer informed Tressie's father.

"Tressie!" Mr. Cox yelled out.

She hurried from her bedroom and into the living room.

"Mr. Boyd has arranged for me to drive you to your date tonight," the driver announced.

She knew tonight was going to be special when Payce asked her to wear something sophisticated and classy. She spent her entire savings on a black strapless dress by Nicole Miller. She wore a pair of diamond stud earrings her parents had given her for her sixteenth birthday, and she borrowed a single diamond pendant necklace from her mother.

Her parents waved good-bye as the limo pulled away from the curb. On the ride there she wondered what Payce had planned for the night. Payce's choice of mystery impressed her. She knew he went to a lot of trouble to arrange tonight, and that meant a lot to her.

The limo pulled into Penn's Landing. The chauffeur ran around to her side and opened her door.

Payce was waiting curbside for her. "You look beautiful," he declared.

"You look rather nice yourself," she replied.

Payce wore a pair of black dress slacks with a white dress shirt. His gold cufflinks were engraved with his initials.

Payce held out his arm and escorted her to the Spirit of Philadelphia, a dinner boat known for its delicious cuisine and breathtaking view of the Philly skyline from the Delaware River.

They walked onto the boat and Payce gave his

name to the hostess. She escorted them to their seats. "The ship will be sailing in a moment. Once we're on the water a waiter will be over to take your order," she informed them.

"Payce," Tressie whispered once the hostess walked away. "Are you selling drugs again?"

"Why would you ask me that?" he asked with a confused look on his face.

"You have been spending a lot of money lately. You don't make that much money parking cars at the Westin. Every time I see you, you have on a new pair of sneakers. You traded in that old Chevy for a new Lexus, and now we're having dinner at one of the most expensive and exclusive restaurants in Philadelphia. What's up?"

Payce realized that his lifestyle had improved dramatically since he had started working at The Dollhouse. He knew Tressie was eventually going to wonder where he was getting the money, and he had an answer already prepared for her. "I'm not selling drugs. Before I got locked up I put some money away. I didn't want to come home from jail broke. Since I started working I thought it wouldn't hurt to spend and enjoy a little of my savings."

"I was just concerned, that's all. I don't want you to get locked up again," Tressie demurred.

"Baby, you don't have to worry. I'm never going back there again."

After they finished their meal, Payce asked, "Did I tell you how beautiful you look?"

"Yes, you did. But you can tell me again." She laughed.

Their waiter approached her with a card in his hand. "Excuse me, ma'am. This is for you."

Tressie took the card and wondered what was inside. She opened the card and written inside it said:

Tressie,
   Since you've walked into my life my heart has been filled with so much love. I never thought I could love someone as much as I love you. With all the wrong things I've done in my life, it's hard to believe that God has blessed me with something so right.

                                        I love you,
                                        Payce.

Payce had never told her he loved her before. She looked over at him with tears in her eyes. He held a jewelry box, and inside was a diamond tennis bracelet.

"It's gorgeous!" she exclaimed.

"This bracelet represents only a tenth of how much I love you."

"Payce, I . . ."

"Don't say it. I don't want you to tell me you love me just because I told you. I want you to tell me when you're ready and when you mean it."

He took the bracelet from her and put it on her wrist. He got up and held out his hand. They walked out together onto the deck and watched the moonlight shine against the water.

"I want to make love to you tonight," he told her. "Can we spend the night together?"

She nodded her head yes.

After the ship docked, Payce escorted her back

to his car and they rented a room at the Hilton Hotel.

"I love you," he told her again.

"I . . ."

"Don't say it." He put his finger to her mouth. "I told you, don't say those words until you really mean it."

Payce slowly undressed her and laid her on the bed. He lovingly admired her body. He took his time with her and kissed every inch of her body before making love to her.

Her body throbbed with pleasure as he kissed her lovingly.

After they made love, she lay in his arms and thought about how many times she had dreamed of making love to Payce. It was better than she had imagined.

"I love you," she finally confessed.

"I love you, too."

CHAPTER 12

It had taken Murray a while, but he had finally gotten Daneesha's home address. He wasn't sure if the young girl at the supermarket where Daneesha used to work was going to believe his story about him being her long lost uncle. Well, he must be a good storyteller, because it didn't take much convincing for the cashier to give up Daneesha's address.

Murray sat outside Daneesha's home, keeping the house under close surveillance. No one had approached the house all afternoon except for the mailman.

At the start of each new assignment, Murray liked to verify that he was monitoring the right residence because of a mistake he had made three years prior. He had been hired by a wife who suspected her husband was having an affair. After three weeks of watching the husband have one-night stands with different women, he later discovered that he had been trailing the wrong person. He had been following the wife's neighbor, and not his client's husband. That one mistake hurt his business. So he made it routine practice to verify the residence he was watching.

Once the mailman left the block, Murray snuck up to the house. He stepped onto the porch and was startled by the presence of a sleeping dog. Murray was terrified of dogs and he hadn't realized they even had a dog because the mutt hadn't made a sound all afternoon.

The dog woke from his sleep and looked at Murray. Frightened, Murray was about to turn and run when the dog slowly closed his eyes and went back to sleep. Thankful that the beast did not attack, Murray quickly stuck his hand in the mailbox and looked at the envelopes. All bills were addressed to Daneesha Oaks. He quickly replaced the mail and hurried back to his car.

From his car, Murray stared at the small house. The harsh Chicago winters had badly deteriorated the exterior of the home. The blue paint had lost its luster, each window was covered with plastic, and the front screen door was hanging off the hinges. He had also noticed a few floor panels on the porch were missing. It wouldn't be long before the house collapsed.

The sunlight was soon replaced by evening's darkness. It was quitting time for a lot of hard-working people, and he expected Daneesha would be arriving home shortly. He wished to speak with her about Bryant, but doubted she would willingly tell a stranger any information about her relationship with him. He knew he was going to have to watch her for a few days and devise a plan on the best way to approach her.

At exactly six o'clock, a CTA bus stopped a few feet behind Murray's car. A woman and two small children got off and walked toward the Oaks' residence. He watched as they passed by. The young mother struggled with an armful of groceries while trying to keep an eye on her children. The little girl, around three-years-old, held her younger brother's hand tightly as they ran to keep up with their mother. Murray could hear their mother repeatedly yell for them to keep up. The family walked onto the porch and their black Labrador Retriever came alive. The dog stood up and welcomed them home by wagging his tail and licking their faces.

"Hey, Kobe," the little girl sang out.

The mother struggled to get her key in the door. Once she successfully opened the door, she ordered the children to go inside.

As the mother held the door open for her children, Murray could see a front view of her full, round belly. "She's pregnant," he said to himself.

Murray watched the house, hoping Bryant would show up, but no one else entered the home for the remainder of the night.

The following morning, Murray watched as Daneesha and the children left the house. He sat in his car, calculating his next move. He speculated that Daneesha lived alone with the children. He thought about how he could get a pregnant woman to tell him what he needed to know without raising suspicions. He knew he had to think of a subtle way to approach her. *How was he going to do it?* Out of nowhere, an idea popped into his mind that just might work.

Later on that evening Murray knocked on Daneesha's front door. The family dog barked loudly. Murray whispered to the dog, "Calm down, fellow. You don't recognize me? I was here yesterday. I'm not here to harm you."

The dog growled. Murray was surprised at the dog's sudden emergence as a watch dog. He was disguised as a deliveryman and was thankful he had remembered to pack his bag of disguises. He had on a body suit that made him look twenty pounds heavier, and he wore a plain blue uniform. He held a hand truck loaded with a huge box.

The commotion the dog made caused the little girl to run to the door and open it wide.

"Hello, can I speak to your mommy?" Murray asked the child.

"Mommy! Mommy!" she screamed through the house.

Moments later Daneesha appeared at the door. "Yes, can I help you?"

"Good evening, ma'am. I have a delivery here for a Daneesha Oaks."

"That would be me. What is it?"

"Well ma'am, I believe they said it was a crib."

"A crib? I didn't order any crib."

Murray looked at the fictitious paperwork on his clipboard.

"Well my delivery sheet says to deliver this crib to Daneesha Oaks at 19 Holman Way," the man said.

She eyed the unexpected delivery suspiciously. Murray moved the box to the other hand. "Ma'am, if you don't mind, this box is very heavy," he said to her in hopes that she would accept the delivery.

Hesitant to allow him to enter her home, she finally relented. "I'm sorry. Children, move your things from the middle of the living room floor!" Daneesha commanded. She opened the door wide for Murray to bring in the box.

He walked into her home and the interior of her house was worse than the exterior. The kitchen ceiling had several holes, and the wallpaper that lined the walls had turned yellow and was beginning to peel. The children watched a small black and white television that sat on top of a large floor model television. A small wire hanger substituted as the television's antenna to keep its reception.

"Where would you like it?" he asked.

She pointed down the hall. "You can put it in the second room on the right. That's my daughter's room." She rubbed her belly. "This one is going to be a girl, so they might as well share."

Desmond pulled the large box into the room. Daneesha walked in behind him. "Do you have a name of the person who ordered the crib?" she asked.

He looked down at his clipboard. "I'm sorry, ma'am, the office didn't include the buyer's name on my work order."

"That's all right. It was probably my fiancé, Bryant. He likes to surprise the children and me."

"That's a beautiful thing ma'am, a man who loves his family." He pointed to the crib. "This crib is really beautiful. A lot of couples choose this one." Murray began to open the box and pull out the contents.

"You're going to put it together?"

"Yes ma'am. Set up is free of charge when you order one of these cribs."

"Oh! I wasn't aware. Do you need any tools? I'm sure Bryant has some tools lying around here somewhere."

"No, that's all right. I have everything I need right here." He pulled out his tool kit and the directions to assemble the crib. Once he started, he regretted his decision to put it together. He hadn't put a crib together in over twenty years. He had purchased a deluxe crib with the most sophisticated gadgets. It took him a whole hour just to sort out the different pieces.

Daneesha came to check on him. "Are you okay back here?"

"Yeah! I'm all right. It should be done shortly," he responded.

She glanced at the lopsided crib and hoped that it wasn't supposed to sit that way. She stood and watched him for a moment.

He knew that this would be the best time to strike up a conversation with her. "So, when are you due?"

"I'm only six months pregnant. I have three more months."

"I'm sure your fiancé is excited, but he's probably a pro by now since you two have been through this twice before already."

"Actually my two oldest children aren't his. This is his first child, so he is really excited."

"Children really are a joy. My kids are grown,

but it seems like just yesterday they were falling asleep in my arms. Kids grow up so fast. Make sure you spend as much time with them as you can."

"My fiancé and I both try to spend as much time with the children as possible, but his job requires him to travel a lot."

"I hope he's going to be around for the baby's birth?" Murray questioned the young mother.

"Oh, yes sir, he should be back home in a few weeks. Once he gets home, he promised me that he wouldn't leave again until after the baby was born."

The phone rang. "Mommy," her daughter screamed. "Grandma wants you."

"Excuse me." Daneesha waddled to the phone.

Murray overheard her telling her mother about the mysterious crib that arrived and how it was a blessing because she could not afford to buy a new crib for the baby to sleep in. By the time she returned back to the bedroom, he had finished the crib.

"I'm all finished."

"It looks good," she responded.

The crib was perfectly assembled after hours of trial and error.

She walked him to the door. "You have a good night, sir."

"You too, ma'am, and make sure you take care of that little one."

"Thank you. I will."

"Player, I'm surprised you could get away tonight. You've been a hard man to catch up with. Every time

I call you, I get your voice mail," Darshon said to Payce.

They stood in line at Pinnacle, the liveliest nightclub in the city. They were there to help their friend, T.J. celebrate his birthday.

"I know. I started school and I've been working a lot. Any extra time I have after that is spent with Tressie," Payce responded.

"You still working at the Westin?"

Payce nodded.

"They must be paying really well at the Westin— brand new car, brand new watch," Darshon pointed at Payce's Rolex. "Are you sure you're not hustling on the side?"

"Man, I told you I'm legit this time. Everything I bought, I worked for."

"You wouldn't lie to me, would you, man?"

"Man, I'm not hustling." Payce knew he wasn't being completely honest with Darshon, but he couldn't tell him about working at The Dollhouse. Darshon was his best friend, they had been through everything together, but this was one secret he had to keep to himself. If anyone ever found out what he was doing, he knew he would be jeopardizing his relationship with Tressie and the respect he had earned from his father.

"Well, I'm glad to see you, and I'm sure the fellows will be happy to see you, too."

"You know I couldn't miss T.J.'s birthday."

After a twenty-minute wait, they finally reached the front of the line and paid the admittance fee. Inside the club, lights flashed, music bumped, and the place was crowded with people.

"How are we going to find T.J.?" Payce screamed above the loud music.

"Just follow me," Darshon instructed.

He pulled Payce through the crowd of people. A few girls winked and tried to get Payce's attention as he walked by. *Nothing's changed*, he thought to himself. Darshon led him straight to a table where T.J. sat by himself.

"What's up, player?" Darshon screamed out. He slapped hands with T.J.

"Payce, my man," T.J. yelled. "Welcome home, my nigga. I haven't seen you since you were released."

"I've been trying to stay out of trouble," Payce replied.

"I understand."

"Why are you sitting over here by yourself? I thought you would have sweet talked one of these honeys in here into coming over and helping you celebrate your birthday."

"Me and John just got here. He's already out there on the dance floor with some chicken head. I was just about to order a bottle of Cristal." T.J. pulled out a wad of bills from his pocket. Payce stared as T.J. peeled off a few hundred-dollar bills. He could see that T.J. was still reaping the benefits of a drug dealer's lifestyle.

T.J., Darshon, John, and Payce began selling drugs while in high school. It wasn't long before they realized that they could make more money on the streets than in school. As a result, they all dropped out, except for John. When John told his mom that he was quitting school, she lost it. She grabbed her frying pan and chased him around

their house. Scared that he might wake up one day
to find his mom standing over him with that black
skillet, he decided to finish out his education. He
was the only member of the crew who graduated
from high school.

Even with John's absence, their pockets got fatter and fatter. Each one of them bought themselves a car, jewelry, and plenty of new clothes.

They called themselves the GT Hustlers. Unfortunately for Payce, that all came to an end two
years ago. T.J., Payce, John, and Darshon were at
their centralized hub distributing drug packages.
The fellas were no longer standing on the street
corners. They hired workers to make the money
for them. They operated like a legal business.
When a worker needed to replenish his drug sup-
ply, they dispatched a runner to come and pick up
the package. The runner, usually a neighborhood
kid between the ages of nine and eleven, was good
at transporting drugs from one place to another
because of his quick speed and ability to elude the
police.

One night a guy called in and said that his runner was sick and he didn't have anyone to pick up
his replenishment package for him. He was quickly
running out, and he needed someone to bring the
drugs to him.

"Fuck that. If he can't get someone to come and
get it, then he's going to have to come himself. We
ain't no delivery boys," T.J. yelled.

"I'll take it to him," Payce said.

"Man, you know the rules. We don't transport
drugs for nobody," T.J. shot back.

"I know, but it's this one time. I'll have a talk

with him when I get there." Payce grabbed the
package of drugs and jumped into his car. He got
no farther than five hundred feet away from the
hub when the cops surrounded him and aimed
their guns. He was charged with possession, intent
to distribute, and carrying a controlled substance
in a drug-free school zone.

Since it was his first offense, he got only eighteen months in lockup, but that was enough for
him.

"I got it, man." Payce also pulled out his wad of
bills.

T.J. looked at the money and put his arm around
Payce's shoulder. "My man must have stashed some
loot before he went away," he said.

"Yeah, I managed to save a little something."
Payce called a waitress over to their table and threw
her five one hundred dollar bills. "Cristal, please."

Payce walked over to the balcony and looked
out over the mob of dancers on the dance floor.
He saw John grinding on some girl. She was shov-
ing her exposed breasts in his face. Payce took a
sip from his glass. He watched all the hot girls with
their short skirts and low-cut blouses. It had been
such a long time since he had been in the club.
When he was locked up, he dreamed about hanging out at the club until three o'clock in the morning. He knew he could never take his freedom for
granted again.

He was about to walk away when he spotted a
girl leaning against the far wall staring at him. At
least he thought she was staring at him. He wasn't
sure until she waved. He called her over and she
slowly made her way through the crowd.

"Hey, shorty, what's your name?"

"Kai," she said. The young woman was dressed in a sequined, backless, pink shirt and a pair of black low-rise pants. Her hair was pulled up into a pony-tail.

"Are you here by yourself?" he asked.

"No, my friends are around here somewhere."

"Why were you staring at me?" he asked.

"The way you stood on the ledge watching everyone made you look powerful. That turned me on."

Payce liked her. She was aggressive and she ob-viously wanted him.

"What are you doing after you leave here?" he asked.

"Probably going home? Why, what's up?"

"I don't know. I thought maybe we could hang out for a while. It's my friend's birthday and he rented a hotel room. I was hoping you and your friends could follow us back there and help us cel-ebrate."

"That sounds like fun."

"Good, meet me out front after the club closes."

She tempted him with her eyes, and left to find her friends.

"Yo, T.J., did you get that hotel room?" he yelled.

"Yeah, what's up?"

"I just invited a few friends over." He smiled.

When Payce walked out of the club he found Kai and her girlfriends waiting for him just like he told her. Payce pulled Kai to the side. "Listen, go get your car and pull up in front of the club. I'm going to go get my car and you can follow me back to the hotel."

T.J. had reserved the penthouse suite at the Marriott, and it was huge. It had three bedrooms and three bathrooms. There was a living room and dining room area and a huge flat-screen television with a wall full of DVDs.

Payce was not surprised by T.J.'s expensive taste. T.J. was known for always reserving only the very best.

"Everyone make yourself at home," T.J. yelled from the kitchen.

Payce pulled Kai closer to him. He didn't want anyone pushing up on her. She was his for the night. T.J. came out with glasses full of Hennessy. "What's your name?" he asked one girl.

"Delilah," she replied.

"As in Delilah and Sampson?" T.J. asked.

She smiled and shook her head yes. He looked at her naturally curly, shoulder-length hair. She was pretty. A little shy, but pretty. "Delilah, can you do me a favor and pass out the rest of these drinks? I need to go get some ice."

When T.J. returned, he called Delilah over to him. He whispered in her ear and made her laugh while Darshon and John talked with the remaining two girls.

"So what made you call me over?" Kai asked Payce.

"When I saw you staring at me I thought to my-self, that girl is hot."

"Do you still think I'm hot?" she asked. She pressed against his pelvis with her body.

His cell phone vibrated against his hip. He

pulled it out and looked at the caller ID. It was Tressie. He hit the ignore button and turned his attention back to Kai. "From what I can see, you are more than hot." He sat his drink down. "Why don't we go into one of the bedrooms for some privacy?"

He grabbed her hand and yelled out to the girls, "Don't worry about her. I'll make sure she gets home in the morning."

CHAPTER 13

MAY 2004

Elise got up from bed and walked into the kitchen. She quietly poured herself a glass of water and wiped the perspiration from her head. Weeks had passed since Miles had discovered her affair, but her mind kept replaying the scene of Miles stepping from behind the stairs and catching her in Sheridan's arms. She repeatedly heard those words fall from his lips: "Do you love him?"

That night she saw Miles's spirit crumble and his six-foot frame shrink right before her eyes. Ordinarily, her husband's presence dominated any arena, but that night her infidelities left him a weak and defeated man. The man she vowed to love for life walked away from her, his marriage, and their happiness, so she could fulfill her dream of having a family.

Her self-indulgent behavior over the past few

months disappointed her. "How did I get here?" she wept.

Awakened by her cries, Sheridan rushed to her side. Hugging her tightly, he said, "Everything is going to be all right. Why don't you go lie down in the bedroom and try to get some sleep?" he offered.

"No, I'm all right," she lied. She broke away from his loving embrace.

He knew her mind held lingering memories of the night Miles had confronted them. Elise had withdrawn from their relationship. Her body was with him, but her mind was with Miles. When they talked she became easily distracted and responded back to him with one word answers. A number of times he had caught her vacantly staring into space.

"Sheridan, I'm all right. I just need to be alone. You can go back to bed."

Unsure if he should abide by her wishes, he hesitated.

She grabbed him by the shoulders and pushed him in the direction of his bedroom. "Really, I'm fine."

Convinced, he slowly went back to bed.

Elise lay on the couch and stared at the ceiling. Lately she had been reminded of the day she married Miles. The church was elegantly decorated in all white. Pink and lavender roses adorned the end of each pew. Her Vera Wang gown, unlike the traditional Cinderella wedding dress, gracefully fell to the ground and cascaded around her feet. That day Miles had surprised her with vows he had written himself.

I promise to always make you happy and never make you sad.

I promise to cherish your love as a gift from God.

And I promise to never allow a day to pass without telling you 'I love you.'

Elise tried to think through the situation in her head. She couldn't understand why or how she had gotten into this predicament. Being an individual who always held high moral standards, was a member of the church, and a woman who never stumbled in her Christian walk, she thought that the sins of the world were beneath her.

But it was becoming clear to her that the same lessons she preached to her Bible Study group were the same lessons she failed to apply to her own life. She often lectured the young adults of First Nazareth on the importance of allowing God to have complete control over your life and not just the parts you want him to have.

Elise was guilty of believing she could withstand the temptations of Satan by herself. Now that her life was spinning out of control, she wanted to call on God. She knew he was the only one who could fix everything.

She wanted to fall to her knees and repent, but she was ashamed and embarrassed to bow before God and admit the wrong she had done.

Elise closed her eyes and dreamt that Miles had found her with Sheridan again. Only this time, he pointed a gun at the two of them. Elise begged him to put the gun down, but before he could the gun went off and the scene turned black. She couldn't see anything. Suddenly a ray of light shone down on Miles in the distance. He lay on the ground, unconscious.

"Miles!" Elise cried. "Wake up." She felt his hand for a pulse but couldn't find one. She searched his body for a gunshot wound, but found nothing.

"Dial 9-1-1!" She screamed from the couch. "Someone please dial 9-1-1."

Sheridan raced in from the bedroom and shook her lightly. "Elise, wake up. You're having a bad dream."

Frightened from her dream, she looked at him, panic-stricken.

Her nightgown was drenched in sweat.

"Here, drink this." Sheridan handed her the glass of water that sat on the coffee table. "You must have been having a nightmare. I heard you screaming," he yelled. "Are you all right?"

She thought about her dream, and instantly she realized the importance of trying to save her marriage. She knew it was not going to be easy, but she had to try. She just hoped that Miles would listen to her once she got there.

"I need to go." Elise grabbed her shoes, purse, and coat.

"Elise, where are you going?" Sheridan asked.

"Home." And she walked out the door.

Elise walked into her house and a cold breeze wrapped itself around her.

"Miles!" she screamed. "Miles?" He did not answer. "He has got to be here. His car is in the garage."

She walked into the dark kitchen and the only noise she heard came from the water left running in the kitchen sink. She moved her way over to the faucet to turn it off. When she turned to her left she discovered blood splattered across the kitchen counter.

"Oh God!" she screamed. "What is going on? Miles!" She yelled. A butcher knife lay in a puddle of blood. She quickly pulled her cell phone out of her purse and attempted to call the police, but before she did her home phone rang. Startled by the ringing sound, she was scared to answer it, but she reluctantly lifted the receiver. "Hello."

"Hi, can I speak with Mrs. Lewis?"

She heard the official tone in the caller's voice. *Please God,* she silently prayed. *Allow my husband to be all right. He is such a good man. He doesn't deserve to be harmed in any way.*

"This is she," she replied.

"Mrs. Lewis, this is Nurse Frazier from Albert Einstein Hospital. Your husband was brought in here a little over an hour ago."

"Is he all right?" she asked.

"Yes, he's going to be fine. He apparently called 9-1-1 and told the operator that he had amputated his penis."

Elise thought for a moment she misunderstood the nurse. "Excuse me, can you repeat that?" she asked.

"Your husband dismembered his own penis," she stated.

Elise looked over at the blood drying on her counter. "I'm on my way."

* * *

Elise rushed to the nurse's station. "Hi, I'm looking for a Miles Lewis."

"Are you his wife?" the nurse asked.

"Yes, I am."

"Dr. Bancroft has been waiting for you. He asked me to page him when you arrived. You can have a seat in the waiting room."

Minutes later, Dr. Bancroft approached her. "Mrs. Lewis, thanks for coming so quickly. Before you see your husband I wanted to speak with you about his condition." He took a seat in a chair next to hers. "I don't have to tell you how highly un-usual it is for a man to cut off his own penis. The EMT's who brought your husband in this evening managed to find his penis, and I was able to reat-tach it. In approximately three weeks he should have normal urinary function back and it will probably be a total of seven to eight months before it completely recovers. My biggest concern about your husband's case is his mental state. When he was brought in I had to heavily sedate him. Some-times under sedation, patients say some crazy things, but he insisted that he did not want his penis. He said it did nothing but cause him heartache."

Elise held her head down in shame.

"Can you explain his behavior? If I'm aware of what's going on, perhaps I can help."

"Doctor, my husband and I have been going through a few problems. He has been experienc-ing some impotency problems."

The doctor nodded his head to express his un-derstanding. "Has he seen a doctor?"

"Yes, he's been going to a doctor for months. Plus he's been seeing a therapist once a week, but nothing they've suggested has helped."

"If you don't mind, can you give me the name of his therapist? I would like to request that Miles start seeing his therapist five times a week. He needs intense treatment. I want to make sure that this doesn't happen again. The next time he might do something more damaging."

Elise closed her eyes to hold back the tears. Dr. Bancroft stood up. "If you need anything you can contact me here at the hospital," the doctor offered. "If you'd like to see your husband now, I'll walk you to his room."

Elise watched Miles sleep soundly in his bed. She held on to his hand, praying that once he woke up he would be happy to see her.

Hours later he slowly opened his eyes. "What are you doing here?" he asked groggily, surprised to see Elise sitting at his bedside.

"I was at the house when the hospital called to tell me what had happened."

He turned his head away.

"Did I do this to you?" she asked. "Am I responsible for driving you to do this?"

Tears welled up in his eyes. "Elise, after I left you, I went home to an empty house. Everywhere I looked I saw reminders of you. It drove me insane. I sat in the den and realized the reason this was happening was because I couldn't satisfy you. This impotency has destroyed my life and took the one thing from me worth living for—you. Before I knew it, I had laid it down on the cutting board in the kitchen and picked up the butcher knife. If the doctors couldn't help me, then I knew no one could."

She grabbed Miles's hand. "Listen, you amputating your penis is not going to make things any better. We . . ."

"We?" he interrupted her.

"Yes, *we* are going to battle this together. God brought us together and we can not allow any man or woman . . ." She pointed to herself, ". . . tear us apart." She leaned over and gently kissed him on the lips, " 'Til death do us part." She smiled. "Let's pray, and God will handle the rest."

A Month Later

"Man, she was a freak. I'm telling you. You name it, she did it," Payce told Darshon as he jumped behind the steering wheel of his car. They had just finished shopping at the mall.

"Well, I wish the rest of her girls were like her. Those other two girls wouldn't separate for the world. It was as if they made a pact that night not to leave one another's side. I was better off going home after the club."

Payce's cell phone vibrated. It was Kai, calling him again. She had been calling him nonstop since the night they were together. He sent her call to voicemail. It had been a month since they met, but he didn't want anything serious with her. He had already decided to hit it a couple more times, and then let her go. He couldn't manage to keep both Tressie and Kai.

"The easy girls are always attracted to you. Like this girl Najah you met in the mall," Darshon said, pulling a slip of paper off the dashboard.

"Man, can you put that number away? I have to pick up Tressie. If she sees that number I'll never hear the end of it."

"Sorry, man."

They pulled up to the corner of Broad and Cecil B. Moore. Darshon opened the door for Tressie, and he climbed into the backseat.

"Hey, baby," she said to Payce. She leaned over and gave him a kiss on the mouth. "Guess what I learned in school today?" Without giving him a chance to guess, she continued, "I learned that dogs have the same IQ as a four-year-old child. So do you know what that means?"

He looked interested in what she was saying, but he could feel his phone vibrating on his hip. He didn't want to answer it in front of Tressie because he knew it was Kai. Payce turned up the radio to drown out the vibration sound.

"Why are you turning up the radio when I'm talking?" she asked.

"Sorry, baby. Darshon likes this song."

Tressie turned around to look at Darshon. He was asleep. She turned the volume back down and continued.

"As I was saying, those mutts at your parents' house can fully understand what I'm saying when I tell them to get away from me. Every time I walk in the house they sit in my face and stare."

"Maybe they're mesmerized by your beauty," Payce replied. "You better start being nicer to them or the next time you come over they're going to have you for dinner," he laughed.

Weeks of watching Daneesha's house had finally paid off for Murray. At long last, Bryant had returned to the house. Like a long lost relative he strolled onto the porch and greeted Kobe as if they were old friends. He talked with the black Lab for a moment before entering the home.

Murray thought about calling Olivia and giving her an update, but quickly decided against it. He didn't want to get her hopes up. Just because he had found Bryant didn't mean he was going to find Bryce, especially since Bryant had arrived at Daneesha's alone.

Bryant's first week with Daneesha and the children consisted of many family outings. They dined out, went to the movies, and Bryant even took the kids to see Sesame Street on Ice. Murray tailed Bryant the entire time, never letting him out of his sight.

Murray also paid close attention to Daneesha and Bryant's relationship. It was obvious that she loved Bryant very much. The look in her eyes said forever, but the look in his eyes said never. Every time she grabbed for Bryant's hand, his response to her affection appeared forced and phony. Any displays of public affection initiated by him never seemed sincere.

The funny thing about Bryant was his attitude toward the children. The love and attention he showed toward Mar-quita and Marquise came straight from the heart. Murray was trained to read people's body language and he could clearly see that Bryant genuinely cared for those children as if they were his own.

One morning Murray pulled up on Daneesha's block and put his new rental car in park. He was still angry about the confusion at the rental car agency, and couldn't get it off his mind. Earlier in the week Murray had made arrangements to exchange his rental car for a different make, model, and color. In his line of business, it was mandatory to change vehicles as much as possible. Using the same car during an investigation was a sure way to tip someone off that they were being followed.

When he arrived to exchange his car they tried to replace it with a bright green Dodge Neon. He knew there was no way he would be able to go unnoticed in that car. He spoke with the salesperson at the ticket counter and she verified that they had made a mistake on his reservation. Unfortunately, they had rented out their entire fleet of cars, and the only vehicle left was the Dodge Neon. After an hour of arguing with the lady at the counter, and with the lot manger, a customer arrived to return their car. Once Murray heard they had another car available, he immediately took the keys and sped off.

Luckily he had arrived back just in time to see Bryant step out of the house wearing a suit. He wore a pair of brown wing-tipped shoes that shined brightly under the mid-morning sun, and he dangled a stogie from his mouth. Bryant's Sunday best caught Murray's attention, and he sat up to get a

better look. Normally, this was the time Bryant
would leave to take the children to daycare, but
today was different. Bryant called for Daneesha
and the children to hurry up. The three of them
walked out onto the porch looking charming.

Daneesha wore a simple white dress that allowed lots of room for her growing belly. On top
of her head she modeled a small, white hat with a
veil that partially covered her face. The children
were also dressed in outfits that closely resembled
Easter attire. Bryant helped Daneesha down the
steps while holding her son in his arms.

Murray followed them to City Hall, where he
watched a small, intimate wedding ceremony take
place from the balcony, presided over by the county
judge. The only witnesses were the children and an
unidentified woman who stood for Daneesha as her
maid of honor. Once the ceremony was over, she
hugged Daneesha and wished the newlyweds the
best.

Immediately after leaving City Hall, Bryant
stopped by a lawyer's office. He quickly ran in carrying a brown envelope, and seconds later he was
back in the car. They stopped at a nearby restaurant to have dinner. Murray sat at the bar while
they were seated not too far from him. The restaurant was crowded and very noisy, but he could still
hear Bryant make a toast.

"I'd like to make a toast to the newest members
of the Winters family. My new wife . . ." he leaned
over and kissed Daneesha on the lips, "and our
children."

"Yeahhhhhh," everyone screamed in unison.

A month after they were married, Bryant walked out onto the porch with a small travel bag in his hand. Daneesha followed closely behind him. Bryant said a few final words and kissed her one last time before he got into his car and drove away.

Murray watched the couple say good-bye. He remembered Daneesha telling him that Bryant wouldn't leave her again until after the baby was born. Something important must have come up to make him leave her so close to her due date. He started his car and followed Bryant to the airport. From a safe distance, Murray watched Bryant return his rental car, take the escalator to the airline terminal ticket counter, check his bag, and walk straight into the Delta terminal.

Wondering where Bryant was going, Murray walked over to the list of flights that were posted on the departure board. There were so many flights leaving that it was going to be hard to determine where Bryant was going. He stared at the list of destinations until one name caught his attention. Greensboro, North Carolina. That flight was scheduled to leave in a little over an hour. Murray rushed over to the ticket counter and purchased a one-way ticket to Greensboro. He quickly went through security and rushed toward his gate number. He looked around, but Bryant wasn't there. Murray thought maybe he had made a mistake and picked the wrong flight. His eyes scanned the area until he spotted Bryant sitting inside a small bar.

Murray strolled into the bar and grabbed a seat

right next to Bryant. He ordered himself a beer and watched the Bulls play basketball on TV.

"The Bulls will never be the same without ole' Mike," Murray said to Bryant.

Bryant looked around and realized the old fellow was talking to him.

"When Jordan was playing, everybody was happy," Murray continued. "The city of Chicago was rich, Mike was rich, even I was rich. I own a restaurant located right outside the United Arena. Every night the Bulls played a home game customers would line up around the corner to get something to eat before they went home, but since Jordan retired, business has slacked off considerably." He took a sip of his beer. "That loss of income has affected me and my family."

Bryant nodded his head but kept his attention focused on the game.

Determined to initiate a conversation, Murray continued talking. "So now I'm headed to Greensboro, North Carolina. A friend of mine referred me to a real estate agent who said he has some great properties at a really cheap price. If everything works out, I'm going to relocate down there. Financially that would be the sound thing to do because the cost of living is cheaper."

Bryant turned to face him. "Greensboro. That's where I'm from."

"A country boy?" Murray asked, glad that he had finally said something to get Bryant's attention.

"Yes sir, born and raised. Where's the property located you're going to look at?"

"You know, I'm not sure. But the agent did say that the building was located in a very busy part of town. He mentioned a mall. I can't remember the name right now."

"It must be Four Seasons Mall, and if your property is located outside the mall that is definitely a busy area."

"I'm glad I ran into you. Now I can call my wife and tell her not to worry. You know how women can be."

Bryant nodded his head in agreement.

"Are you married?" Murray asked.

Bryant smiled. "Yes, sir, I've been married for about a month, now."

"So you're a newlywed. Congratulations." Murray signaled for the bartender to refill Bryant's glass. "Where's your wife? Is she accompanying you?" Murray looked around the small establishment.

"No, it's just me. I had some business to take care of. Like you said, I now have a family to provide for."

The bartender placed a drink in front of Bryant just as their gate number was announced over the loud speaker.

"That's me," Bryant said. He downed his drink and gathered his things.

"Me too," Murray replied. The two men got up, left the bar, and walked toward the gate.

"It was nice talking with you, sir. I hope everything works out for you."

"You too, son."

CHAPTER 14

Once their plane landed in Greensboro, Bryant rushed off. Murray noticed that he repeatedly checked his watch while waiting for the luggage to come through baggage claim. Murray retrieved his bags and went to rent a car. Luckily he had made reservations ahead of time. He just prayed that he wouldn't have the same problems he had in Chicago.

Bryant merged onto Interstate 85 and traveled south. He drove to a small residential community and pulled into the driveway of a blue bi-level house. Murray watched Bryant grab his things from the trunk and knock on the door. He watched carefully as someone opened the door and welcomed him in. Over an hour had passed before Bryant emerged from the house, and he wasn't alone. He carried a baby in his arms. Bryant strapped the infant into the car seat and pulled out of the driveway. Murray's intuition told him that the baby

Bryant carried in his arms was Bryce, but he had to be sure.

Before Bryant pulled away, Murray quickly wrote down the license plate number of the car he was driving. Murray waited fifteen minutes before he got out of the car and knocked on the door. An older woman with graying hair answered.

"Hello ma'am," Murray said with a deferential nod. "I'm a friend of Bryant's and he asked me to come back here to see if he left the baby's blanket behind."

"Oh! Come in." She held the door open for him.

She looked around the living room. "I didn't think he left anything. We checked to make sure he had everything before he left. You can have a seat while I go look upstairs."

Murray was unsure of what to expect when he knocked on the door, but he was relieved when a senior citizen answered. The elderly were easier to get information from without them getting suspicious. He looked around her home. Her fireplace mantle held dozens of photos, mostly of Bryant. One photo was taken of Bryant wearing a little league baseball uniform, and another showed Bryant at his prom. He noticed a more recent picture of Bryant holding a little girl. Murray wondered who the child was.

"I'm sorry, but I don't see anything," the old woman reported. She slowly crept back down the stairs.

"Don't worry about it, ma'am. He might have it with him and not know it." Murray stood up to leave. "Did you enjoy your time with Bryce?"

She revealed a mouth full of dentures. "Oh yes. He is such a good baby. I can't wait until he comes back for another visit."

"Is Bryant coming back here tonight?" Murray asked.

"No, he said he had something to take care of and that he needed to get the baby back to his mother. Him and the baby are going to stay the night out by the airport so he can catch his plane in the morning."

"Oh yeah, that's right. We do have an early morning flight to catch. I guess it would just make more sense to stay out by the airport. I'm sorry if I bothered you, ma'am."

"That's no problem. Be sure to give my best to both my nephews."

"No problem, ma'am. And you take care of yourself."

Murray left the home in a hurry. Now that he knew Bryant had Bryce, he had to find out at which hotel they were staying. Once he found that out, he would call the police.

He drove out to the airport and searched all the area hotels for Bryant's rental car. He finally found it parked at the Ramada. Murray walked into the lobby and took a seat. He had followed enough people to know that front desk clerks never gave out guest information. He was certain that if he waited long enough the clues he needed to find Bryant and Bryce would come to him. He patiently sat for over three hours before he saw Bryant get off the elevators and walk over to the front desk. He watched Bryant say a few words to the clerk and turn back toward the elevators.

"Hey, man," Murray called out.

Bryant abruptly turned around and was surprised to see his old friend from the airport. "Hey man. What's up?" Murray noticed Bryant's jittery behavior.

"I'm surprised to see you here," Murray replied.

"Yeah, the business dealings that I had going on down here are being held at this hotel," Bryant said.

"I was sitting at the bar when I noticed you enter the lobby." The elevator doors opened and they both entered. "What floor you going to?" Murray asked.

"Five," Bryant responded.

Murray pushed the fifth floor button and the eighth floor for himself. "When are you heading back out to Chicago?"

"Sometime tomorrow," Bryant hesitantly replied.

"I have a few more days of business here," Murray replied. "Maybe we can hook up again in Chicago."

Bryant looked at Murray suspiciously. The doors opened for the fifth floor and Bryant stepped off the elevator.

"Yeah man, just leave your name and number down at the front desk and I'll be sure to pick it up before I check out," he shouted just before the elevator doors shut.

Bryant entered his room and watched his great uncle, Mayfield Winters, play with Bryce.

"Look at how handsome this little boy is. He's going to make us a lot of money," the old man said. He held the baby up to get a good look at him. "He is really a cute little boy. He almost looks too good to sell." Bryant grinned at his uncle's compliments about his work.

"He's a strong little fella." Bryce held on to his great-uncle's finger. "Do you have his paperwork?" Mayfield asked.

"Right here." Bryant pulled a brown envelope out of Bryce's diaper bag.

"What about the mother? Did you take care of her?"

"She's not an issue. She won't ever find me or the baby. Right now she should just be getting out of jail, and once she does, she won't know where to begin to look for me or Bryce."

"Good, and I have the adoption papers all drawn up. All we have to do is get the Richardsons to sign off on the contract and give us the check."

There was a knock at the door. "Bryant, take the baby into the bedroom and come back out here. I want you to meet our newest clients," Mayfield said.

When Bryant returned he was shocked by the sight of two men sitting on the couch holding hands.

"This is my nephew, Bryant. Bryant, this is the Perry family—Kendrick and Kyle." Bryant reached out to shake both of their hands.

It surprised Bryant to see a same-sex couple. He and his uncle had provided dozens of babies to a lot of couples, but this was the first time they had ever done business with a gay couple.

Mayfield pulled up a chair from the living room table and handed the couple a pile of papers.

Kendrick spoke up first. "Mr. Winters, I was surprised when you got back to us so soon. I didn't think that you were going to respond at all."

"Well, when I spoke with you on the phone, I appreciated the fact that you were completely honest with us about your situation," Mayfield said. "We did a preliminary background check on both of you and we saw nothing that would indicate a problem with you adopting a child or, in your case, children. That's why I arranged this meeting." He pointed to an envelope. "These are the contracts I need you to look over. I'll give you a week or two to get back to me, and if you want to proceed, give me a call and I will make the final arrangements.

"Is this adoption legal?" Kendrick asked.

"Yes. Is there anything that concerns you?" Mayfield asked.

"Well, the extreme price that you charge for this adoption process. It costs one hundred thousand dollars for one baby. That's a lot of money. Even an overseas adoption costs no more than ten thousand dollars. Why the extremely high price?"

"The reason we charge so much is because we guarantee healthy babies to couples who are usually denied by the standard adoption agencies, couples like yourselves. Everything is kept in the strictest of confidence, and we cater to an exclusive set of people. The process of screening all candidates is costly. I have to make sure that every child we place is going to be cared for properly. I would be deeply hurt if I later found out a child I provided you with was being abused or mistreated."

"I understand," Kendrick said. "Like I told you on the phone, a lot of adoption agencies, both public and private, have denied us the chance to adopt. A few agencies have even tried to discourage us from trying. They thought it was inappropriate for us to force a child into accepting our lifestyle."

"We don't discriminate here," Mayfield replied.

Bryant noticed Kendrick's professional manner, his speech, and his style of dress. It was obvious that Kendrick was not only intelligent, but also powerful.

"Well, I need to have my lawyer look these contracts over and we'll get back to you as soon as possible." He turned to Kyle. "Are you okay?"

"Yes, I'm just delighted. I can't believe we are finally going to have a family of our own," Kyle squealed.

"I invited my nephew here because he knows a little more about the children you are going to adopt," Mayfield explained.

"Well," Bryant spoke up, "right now it's only two children, but the mother is eight months pregnant with a third child. There's a little girl named Marquita, she's three years old, and a boy named Marquise. He's one."

Bryant handed them a picture of the children.

"They are adorable!" Kyle exulted.

Bryant continued, "The third child is also a girl."

Kyle was delighted at the news of three children.

Kendrick grabbed Kyle's knee. "We have always wanted a big family. I know that we do not represent the traditional family structure, but we think the most important thing to give a child is love. I shouldn't be denied the right to be a father just because I choose to share my life with a man instead of a woman." He grabbed Kyle's hand.

"As I said before, our number one priority is to find these children a safe, happy, and stable home environment," Mayfield affirmed. "The mother is young and is having a rough time, so the money that we charge will also be used to help her get herself together, possibly go back to school to make a life for herself."

"Can you provide us with any information about the mother?" Kyle asked.

"I'm sorry, but that information is confidential."

Kyle looked at Kendrick, concerned. "We had discussed the possibility of the children wanting to one day know where they came from, or who their biological parents were. We don't want to deny them that right."

"Well, it is highly unusual for us to allow the birth parents to contact the children after the adoption is final. But if at any time you want to find out who the children's parents are, just give us a call. If the mother allows us to release her identity, then we will gladly provide you with that information."

"Is the birth mother aware of our sexual orientation?"

"No, we just provided her with paperwork from the background investigation. From that she can determine what kind of home her children will be living in, but the names have been concealed."

"Could you please just give her our personal thanks?" Kyle asked. "She is giving us her most prized possessions, and she doesn't have to worry. We will take good care of them."

"Well, it looks like we can wrap things up. I almost forgot," Mayfield said, snapping his fingers. "I need to confirm the final price with you. I believe that I did tell you that the price for all three children, plus the adoption fees, would be three hundred fifty thousand dollars."

Bryant looked at his uncle with a surprised look on his face.

"Yes, Mr. Winters, and that will not be a problem," Kendrick responded.

"All right, well it looks like we've concluded our business here. Please make sure you give me a call when you're ready to proceed."

Mayfield walked them to the door and said a few final words.

"Unc, three hundred fifty thousand dollars!" Bryant exclaimed. "What do they do that they can afford that kind of money?"

"Kendrick is a very successful real estate developer in New York City. Kyle comes from a very influential family. He was born with money."

"Damn, that's a lot of money. The first thing I'm going to do is take a vacation to Maui."

"You did a good job and you deserve it." He quickly reminded Bryant, "Don't forget I need a copy of those adoption papers stating that those kids are legally yours. You did get the mother to sign off on those papers, didn't you?"

"Yes, sir. As soon as I get back to Chicago I'll get in touch with the lawyer to find out if the papers have been filed."

* * *

Murray walked around the fifth floor, listening at various doors. He was frustrated because he had no clue which room Bryant was in with the baby. Unsure of what his next move should be, he decided to go back down to the lobby and wait. If he found Bryant, once he'd find him again. As he stood waiting on the elevators, he heard a door open. He hid around a corner and listened closely.

"Mr. Winters, we appreciate you contacting us concerning the adoption and I . . ." Kyle playfully punched Kendrick in the arm, "I mean *we* will be in touch."

Murray watched the two men shake an older man's hand and walk toward the elevators.

"Bryant, I gotcha," Murray whispered. He pulled out his cell phone. "Yes, I would like to report a kidnapping."

"I'm expecting another couple, any minute now. Their names are Albert and Rosa Richardson, an older couple in their late fifties. They will be the ones taking Bryce home."

"What's their background look like?" Bryant asked.

"She's a housewife and he owns a chain of motels across the country. You've heard of Room and Board Motels, haven't you?"

"Yeah, I've stayed at a few of them."

"That's him."

It wasn't long before Bryant got to see what the Richardsons looked like. He thought they looked like a real life replica of George and Weezie Jefferson. He was a short, balding man, and his wife was a husky woman who towered at least a foot over her husband.

"Mr. and Mrs. Richardson, I'm so glad to see you," Mayfield welcomed them. "Please have a seat." The couple sat down around the dining room table, and Mayfield asked Bryant to get the baby from the adjoining bedroom.

When Bryant returned, he held Bryce up for them to see. Bryant wanted his son to make a good first impression on his new parents, so he had bought him a one-piece, blue striped outfit with a matching baseball cap. Bryce resembled a miniature baseball player.

"He is beautiful!" The wife held out her hands. "Can I hold him?"

"Sure," Mayfield said, nudging Bryant to hand her the baby.

Holding her son for the first time brought tears to her eyes. "I can't believe this is finally happening."

"You can take him home with you tonight," Mayfield replied. "We just need for you to sign a few papers." Mayfield pulled out the contracts and Bryce's medical records. Bryant watched the couple play with his son. Bryce was a friendly baby and took to them immediately. He grabbed at Mrs. Richardson's jewelry and talked to them in his own native baby talk.

"Do you have any other children at home?" Bryant asked.

"No! He will be our first. Does he have a name?"

"Yes ma'am. His name is Bryce."

She screwed up her face. "I don't like that name. Can we change it?" she asked Mayfield.

"Yes ma'am," he replied. "There is a line in the adoption papers for a name change."

"If you don't mind me asking, why did you wait so long to adopt?" Bryant asked.

"I realize that we are considered an older couple," Rosa replied. "My husband worked hard all our lives to make sure that we were financially secure. It wasn't until my fifty-seventh birthday that we realized that we had no children to inherit the business. It was too late for us to try and have children of our own, and that is when we began to look into adoption."

Mr. Richardson looked through the adoption papers and signed off on all the pages. He pointed to the last page. "Is this where we can change his name?"

"Yes," Mayfield replied.

"We've decided to name him Kevin," Rosa announced.

Bryant sat and watched the adoption transaction take place. He had been through this a hundred times before, but today was different. In the past, he had always felt a twinge of guilt for selling his children, but he had really grown to love Bryce. He guessed the reason he felt so close to Bryce is because of how much he cared for his mother. Olivia would always be special to him.

Bryant never had the opportunity to bond with any of his other children like he had with Bryce, except for Niya. Niya was his oldest daughter and the very first child he sold. He could still hear her cries in his sleep. The day he handed her over to her adoptive parents she cried out 'Daddy'.

Before Bryant became a baby broker he had a

good life. He was married to a beautiful woman, they had just bought a house, and his wife, Taima, had just given birth to a baby girl named Niya. Life couldn't be better, until Bryant lost his job and the monthly bills starting piling up. He missed several mortgage payments and the bank was threatening to foreclose on their home. Bryant went to his Uncle Mayfield to ask for a loan, but unfortunately his uncle was broke. That's when his uncle mentioned a couple he knew who was willing to pay top dollar for a baby girl. He suggested that Bryant give them Niya.

Hearing his suggestion infuriated Bryant. He couldn't believe his uncle would even think of such a thing. Until he heard that the couple was willing to pay one million dollars. *One million dollars for a baby?* He knew it was wrong, but it seemed to be the only solution.

Bryant agreed and his uncle handled everything. The only other concern Bryant had was Taima. What were they going to do about her? She would never allow Bryant to sell their child. Mayfield convinced Bryant that the only option they had was to drug Taima and sign her into rehab. He didn't want to do it, but he did. He still felt bad about what he did but the money helped make up for it.

"Kevin. That's a nice name," Mayfield replied. "Isn't it, Bryant?"

Bryant slowly nodded his head in agreement.

Mayfield looked through the contracts to make sure everything was signed. "Well, it looks like you have a new addition to your family. Here are his medical records." He handed the documents to Mr. Richardson.

"Here is the adoption fee," Albert Richardson said. He handed Mayfield a cashier's check.

"Thank you, Mr. and Mrs. Richardson. I feel good knowing that Kevin is in your hands." He stood up and they shook hands.

"Wait, let me get you his diaper bag," Bryant piped up. He ran back into the bedroom.

While they waited on Bryant, someone knocked on their door. "Bryant, are you expecting someone?" Mayfield called out.

"No," Bryant shouted back.

"Excuse me for a second." When Mayfield opened the door he came face to face with a Greensboro police detective and two other officers. "Hi, can I help you?" Mayfield asked.

"Yes, I'm Detective Denali. We received a tip that there was a baby who was kidnapped in this room."

"Detective, there is no baby here," Mayfield replied in a whisper.

"Well, if you don't mind, we'd like to take a look around." He tried to push the door open.

Mayfield pushed back against the door. "Officer, I don't mean to be disrespectful, but if you don't have a search warrant, then I can't let you in."

"Sir, you don't own this hotel room. We have the hotel manager's permission to search every room in this hotel if necessary."

The police barged their way into the room and found the Richardson's gathering their things to leave with Bryce.

"Excuse me, sir, is this your baby?" the detective asked Mr. Richardson.

"Yes, this is our son. We just adopted him," Mrs. Richardson interjected.

The detective turned around and asked Murray, "Is this the baby you were hired to find?"

"Yes, it is," Murray said.

Bryant came back out with the baby bag. "What is going on?" He looked at Murray. "What are you doing here?"

"That's him," Murray told the detective.

"Arrest them both," the detective commanded the other officers, pointing to Bryant and his uncle.

The handcuffs were put on Bryant. "What is going on?" he whined.

"You're under arrest for kidnapping a child," the detective informed him.

"I didn't kidnap him. He's my son. I have his birth certificate in the room."

The officer looked at Murray for confirmation.

"Yes, he is the father, but he did not have the mother's permission to leave the state of Pennsylvania with the child."

The detective picked up the adoption papers that lay on the table.

"I assume this was a private adoption?" the detective asked.

"Yes, detective, it was," Mr. Richardson responded.

"How much did you pay?"

Mr. Richardson looked unsure about answering. "I paid one hundred fifteen thousand dollars," he said.

"That's all I needed to hear. Take them away," the detective said. He pulled the baby from Mrs. Richardson's hands and handed him to Murray. "You won't be able to adopt this baby, because the adoption is illegal," he informed the couple.

"What about my money?" Albert Richardson asked.

"You will get your money back. Just come down to the station and provide me with a statement."

The detective walked up to Murray. "I also need for you to come down to the station."

"Sure," Murray said. "I just need to call the mother and let her know I found her baby." He dialed Olivia's number. "Olivia," he said when she answered. "I have some good news for you."

CHAPTER 15

Monday afternoon Payce dragged himself into work at The Dollhouse. The receptionist stood at her usual post watching an episode of *As the World Turns* on a small television set hidden behind the counter. She raised her eyes slightly and acknowledged his arrival by nodding her head, then turned her attention back toward the television.

Payce walked halfway down the hall before he turned back around. "What is your name?" he asked the receptionist. "I've been working here for weeks and I still don't know your name."

"Simone," she replied.

"Hi, Simone. I'm Payce."

"Oh, I know who you are. Just because you didn't know my name doesn't mean I didn't know yours." She grinned.

Payce liked her. Under different circumstances, he would have tried to get her phone number, but dating coworkers was not his thing, especially ones who worked at The Dollhouse.

He attempted to walk down the hall toward the locker rooms when Simone called out his name. "Payce, I forgot to tell you, Natasha wants to see you in her office."

Making a quick U-turn, he commenced walking in the opposite direction. He lightly tapped on his boss's door. "You wanted to see me?" he asked.

Natasha took off her reading glasses and pulled her attention from the magazine article she was reading. "Yes, Payce, come in and shut the door."

He took a seat in front of her desk. "What's up?"

"I have a favor I need to ask of you. Since you've joined our family, my clientele has increased. You have quickly become one of my most requested employees."

"I aim to please," he laughed.

"Saturday night I'm throwing a party. It's an exclusive party extended to wives only. Wives of various celebrities, music artists, athletes, famous politicians—you get the picture. I have already asked a few of the other fellas who work here to help me out that night and I was hoping you would also be interested in working."

"Sure, I'd be glad to help out. Will I be doing the same thing I do here?"

"Yes, except there will be no husbands around to watch you. No husbands are allowed." She stressed her words. "I put this event together because I hear a lot of wives complain about how their husbands are negligent to their sexual needs. Most have never experienced an orgasm. These women are looking for a good time. Give these ladies pleasure, and whatever else they may be looking for."

"No problem," he arrogantly replied.

"I'm calling the party, 'What goes around comes around.' I've got hundreds of responses. Women are bringing their friends and family. This party is going to be huge."

"How much are you paying?"

"I like that! You always have money on the mind." She pulled out two stacks of bills and placed them on the desk in front of him. "I'm willing to pay you in advance. That's how much I trust you. This is fifteen thousand dollars. Is that enough?"

"That is more than enough," he replied while picking up the stacks of money.

Payce pulled up in front of Natasha's home and a valet opened his car door. He grabbed his duffel bag from the backseat. When he stepped out the car he couldn't help but notice the exquisite landscaping done to her front yard. In the center of the circular driveway a water fountain housed a multitude of gold fish and a row of magnolia trees lined the driveway from the street all the way up to the house. Off to the side, a man-made pond sat underneath a small crosswalk and bright fluorescent lights revealed a path for guests to enjoy the beautiful grounds.

Payce slowly walked up the marble steps that led to the front entrance. A doorman greeted him and invited him inside. Payce passed through the archway and was blinded by a shimmering chandelier

that hung from the ceiling. Its reflection gave off
so much light that it took a moment for his eyes to
adjust to the shine. He glared up at the chandelier
when a topless waiter, wearing nothing but a pair
of white leather shorts, darted past him carrying a
tray of hors d'oeuvres.

"Hello, Payce." Payce turned around just in
time to see Reverend Kane coming in his direction.

"Reverend Kane." Payce checked out the dress
she was wearing. The midnight blue gown was very
tasteful and sophisticated. Her hair was pulled
into a single French braid, and the only jewelry
she wore was a large sapphire pendant that hung
around her neck. "You look nice tonight. Natasha
didn't mention you would be here."

"I'm working tonight. Natasha thought it would
be good if I was available just in case any of her
guests wanted to have the lesbian experience."

Payce hoped that he wouldn't have to do a
threesome with her. To watch the Reverend go
down on another woman would be embarrassing.

"Payce." Natasha descended her winding staircase in a Valentino original. The white, silk, floor-
length dress hugged her curves. "I'm so glad you
made it." She hugged him. "I thought you might
get lost with all the construction they're doing on
the interstate."

"No, you gave good directions."

"I'm glad." She pointed up the stairs. "You can
go upstairs to the first bedroom on the left and
change your clothes. Once you're ready you can
join us in the den."

Before he walked away, Natasha stopped him.

"Payce, let me tell you what to expect tonight." She walked back over to him. "Once you enter the den I want you to walk around, introduce yourself, mingle with the ladies, and get to know everyone. I have provided each woman with a black velvet bag full of small platinum boomerangs. If a woman is interested in your services she will place a boomerang in your hand. If it's a regular boomerang then she is allocated one hour with you, but if the boomerang has a diamond chip inserted in it, then she gets two hours. You can then escort her upstairs to one of the available bedrooms. Do you have any questions?"

He shook his head no.

"Good, I'll see you inside."

Ten minutes later Payce entered the den. Inside were women of every race, nationality, and creed—black women, white women, old women, young women and even a few well-known celebrity women in attendance. The place was swarming with women. It was standing room only. A few guys had three or four women on their arms. He saw Tariq, one of his coworkers from The Dollhouse, escorting a married pop star upstairs. They acknowledged one another with a nod and Payce walked around the room introducing himself to different ladies.

It wasn't long before a sexy, but mysterious woman approached him with a diamond boomerang in her hand. The way she walked up to him and never said a word, but allowed her eyes to talk to him, was alluring. She placed the boomerang in his hand and led Payce upstairs. He followed and watched her hips sway from side to side in a pair of tight fitting white Capri pants. They entered the room and she sat on the end of the bed. She quickly pulled her sea green blouse over her head. Her eyes beckoned for Payce to come closer to her.

Payce thought the woman looked familiar, but he couldn't remember where he had seen her before. Suddenly, it hit him. She was married to a famous football player who played for the Philadelphia Eagles. She was always seen on television at her husbands' football games, cheering him on. Now he was about to do the man's wife. Payce was so excited he wanted to ask her for an autograph.

He was anxious to get started. She lay back on the bed when the police burst into the room.

"This is a raid! Put your hands against the wall! You are under arrest for prostitution."

Not again, Payce thought. The police pushed him against the wall, put the cuffs on him, and led him away.

AUGUST 2004

A guard escorted Tressie into the visitor's room. She sat for five minutes on one side of a plexiglass partition before Payce walked in, looking shabby. He sat down in front of her wearing an orange jumpsuit, hair uncombed, and the whites of his eyes turned yellow. He gestured for her to pick up the telephone receiver sitting next to her.

"Hey," he said into the receiver. "I'm glad you came. I needed to see you."

"I didn't want to come, but I guess I needed to

see for myself that what everyone was saying was true."

"Tressie, don't listen to what people are saying out on the streets. If you have any questions, ask me. I'm right here. I'm the only one who can provide you with the truth."

"The truth? You're the one who has been lying to me for months. You lied to me, your parents, and yourself."

"I'm sorry."

"Sorry!" she screamed. "Payce, you were selling your body for money."

He looked down at the floor in shame.

"I thought we were *one*. Didn't you tell me you loved me? I thought you could tell me anything. Last night all I could think about was how many times you left my bed to go to work. I believed you when you said you were going to the Westin, when the truth was you were going to The Dollhouse to fuck somebody's wife."

"Don't talk like that. You're too much of a lady to talk like that."

"What do you care? You don't want a lady. You want one of those whores who paid you hundreds of dollars to fuck them."

"Tressie, I love you."

"I don't believe you have the audacity to sit in my face and say that. If this glass were not separating us, I'd spit in your face. How do you know one of those women weren't HIV positive?"

"I wore a condom, every time. Tressie, you have got to believe me when I say I'm sorry for what I did and I love you."

"You have a strange way of showing it."

"I know I made some mistakes and there is no way I can take it back, but no matter what you say, we are a part of one another. Like you just reminded me, we are one. Nothing can separate us. Not even these bars."

"What part of *us*," she stressed her words, "thought it was all right to sleep with other women?" she asked softly with tears in her eyes. She loved him so much, and she couldn't understand how he could betray her in such a way.

"Please don't leave me when I need you most," he pleaded.

Tressie hated to abandon him. She did love him and he deserved a second chance. Everyone thought the worst of him. *Maybe he just needed someone to care,* she thought.

"Tressie." He looked into her eyes. "Will you be there for me when I get out?"

"I guess I don't have any choice," she replied.

Tressie knelt at the altar and stared up at the cross. Tears had dried on her face. "King of Kings and Lord of Lords, I'm crying out to you today to watch over Payce. I need you to keep him safe while in jail. Protect him, Lord. I know that he did wrong, but I ask that you look past his mistakes and see what's inside his heart. Jesus, you have given so many of us a second chance—a second chance to serve you, a second chance to praise your name—and I know that if given the opportunity, Payce would take the second chance you give to him and use it to glorify your name. God, I ask that you intervene in our relationship. We cannot and will not last without you. We need your strength and your understanding. We are being faced with obstacles that I can't endure, so I ask that you take the burden from me. Amen."

Tressie stepped away from the altar as Elise walked into the sanctuary.

"Tressie, I heard about what happened with Payce."

"I don't know what to do," Tressie cried. "I love him and I don't want to lose him, but how can I trust him after this? What we had is ruined."

"I understand how you must feel right now, but you did the right thing by coming here to pray. When the Lord answers your prayer, open your heart to accept his answer. It may not be what you want to hear. He may tell you that you and Payce were not meant to be together. Are you prepared to accept that?"

"Elise, how can he not be the one for me? He's the bishop's son."

"Tressie, you know just as well as I do that being the bishop's son doesn't get you into Heaven. You have to be saved, and if I were you, I'd question whether or not Payce was saved by the things that he has done. Don't think I'm here to judge Payce because I'm not. But don't allow Payce's mistakes to be a burden to you. You deserve better than that. Remember II Corinthians 6:14: 'Be ye not unequally yoked with non-believers.'" Elise hugged her. "Just think about what I said. The Spirit will lead you in the right direction."

SEPTEMEBER 2004

Tressie ran out of the university library trying to catch the last bus home. If she missed this bus, the next one wasn't scheduled to come until after four o'clock. She had lost track of time doing research for a paper that was due tomorrow. Her classes were over for the day, but she still had a lot of studying to do. Three different instructors had scheduled exams on the same day, and she was prepared to pull an all-nighter and study until dawn.

Running down the sidewalk, she quickly turned the corner and was suddenly knocked to the ground. Her books scattered over the pavement and her purse slid a few feet away from her. Tressie sat on the pavement, ready to call the scoundrel who ran into her and made her miss her bus every dirty four letter word she could think of, when she looked up and was greeted by a familiar face.

Quinton Briscoe smiled back at her and gallantly rose to his feet. "Tressie, are you all right?" He held out his hand to help her up.

She grabbed his hand and brushed the dirt off her clothes. Onlookers who witnessed the accident asked if they were okay. Quinton reassured them that they were both fine.

Quinton Briscoe was Tressie's first boyfriend, first love, and first heartbreak. Tressie and Quinton dated for several months before he got bored and started dating a girl from New Jersey. Tressie was hurt, but she hid the pain in her heart and over time she recovered. She later learned that he had been arrested on drug charges and sent away for a few years.

An unexpected hot flash passed through her body, her face turned red, and her palms began to sweat. She couldn't control her body's reaction to seeing Quinton after all these years.

"Quinton, what are you doing here?"

"I came to drop something off to my sister."

Tressie stared at his wavy hair. She wanted to touch it. It looked so soft. "I have seen your sister around campus a few times."

"She forgot one of her books this morning and I promised I would bring it to her." Quinton bent down to pick Tressie's books up from the ground. "Were you late for class? I'm sorry if I stopped you."

"No, I was trying to catch the bus home, but I think I missed it."

"If you need a ride home, I'd be happy to drop you off. My car is parked right around the corner."

"I'd appreciate that," she replied.

Once they were in the car he inquired about her life. "So how is everything for you? Fill me in. Have I missed out on anything exciting? Are you married? Any children?"

"No kids. No husband. Just me. I've been study-ing a lot, trying to finish school. What about your-self?"

"I got a job in Jersey at a warehouse. They put me on third shift, which I'm not too happy about, but besides that I'm doing all right," he told her. "Just trying to get back what I lost. Being away all those years hurt me, but I'm trying to do right this time." Quinton merged onto the expressway north-bound. "I didn't hear you mention anything about a boyfriend."

She thought about Payce and was quickly re-minded of the promise she made to wait for him.

"I do have a boyfriend." She cleared her throat. "I'm dating Payce Boyd."

"Payce Boyd," he said out loud. "Payce Boyd, the bishop's son?"

"Yeah, that's him."

"I heard he was arrested for male prostitution."

Tressie slowly nodded her head. Her face turned red from embarrassment. Payce was mak-ing it hard for her to stand by his side.

"Tressie, I'm sorry, I shouldn't have said that. He's a lucky man to have you in his corner. I wish I had you when I was locked down."

Quinton pulled up to her house. "How are your parents doing?"

"They're doing well."

"Tell them I said hello."

"I will. I'll see you around."

She quickly got out of his car and rushed into the house. She breathed a sigh of relief when she saw his car pull away. *He still looks as fine as ever.* He had grown from a boy to a man. She walked into the kitchen and poured herself a glass of iced tea. She turned on the fan to cool herself down. "Payce, please hurry up and come home," she said to herself. "If I keep running into Quinton, there's no telling what a girl might do."

CHAPTER 16

OCTOBER 2004

Tressie sat in the school cafeteria eating her lunch. She had exactly twenty minutes before the start of her next class. She took a huge bite of her sandwich when a familiar voice interrupted her thoughts.

"Excuse me, miss, is this seat taken?" Quinton stood at her table with a bouquet of fresh wildflowers in his hands. She wiped the mayonnaise away from the corners of her mouth.

"Are those for me?" she asked.

"I brought them for the prettiest girl in school."

"Well then, they must be for me." She reached out for them. "They're gorgeous. Thank you, but why did you buy me flowers?"

"I was hoping to get a smile from you," he admitted.

"You didn't have to buy me flowers to get me to smile."

"I thought that my new cologne might do the trick, but I wasn't sure. So I bought the flowers just in case."

They laughed and he pulled up a chair next to hers. "Tressie, I was wondering if you were free this afternoon."

She looked at him strangely. Reluctant to answer his question, she asked him why.

"Don't get any ideas. You already told me you were involved with Payce. I was just hoping we could hang out for a little while this afternoon, like old times. It doesn't have to be anything special. Maybe we could just go for a walk?" he suggested.

He looked so innocent and sincere that she couldn't turn him down. Besides, she didn't see any harm in taking a walk.

"I'll meet you at Broad and Cecil B. Moore at three o'clock," she told him.

"I won't be late." He got up and left.

At exactly three o'clock Quinton pulled up to the corner, and minutes later they were riding rented bicycles in Fairmont Park.

"Slow down, Tressie!" Quinton shouted.

Tressie was attempting to finish the entire eight-mile perimeter without stopping to rest. It was her idea to rent bicycles. She hadn't ridden a bike since she was a kid, and she thought it would be fun. She stopped to allow Quinton to catch up.

He pulled up beside her, out of breath. "Girl, I

can see how you managed to stay in shape. Can we walk the bikes for a while? I see a bench over there." He pointed to a corner picnic area.

"If we must," she pouted.

They walked over to the bench and parked their bikes.

"I thought guys were supposed to work out in jail," Tressie said.

"Most do. But I was always in the library studying," he responded.

"Trying to be the good guy?" she asked.

"I remember at one time you used to like good guys."

"I did, but all that changed when I met you."

He laughed. "What would you call Payce?"

"Payce is MINE," she said with confidence.

"Do you love him?"

"I don't just love him, I love everything about him. Even when he does wrong, I love him even more because I know that he is human and is capable of making mistakes."

"Does he love you?"

"I believe he does."

"I hope you're right, because sometimes people confuse love with lust. Being behind those prison walls will make a man say things he really doesn't mean."

"Payce was in love with me before he went to jail, and when he comes home, he'll still be in love with me."

"I don't want to see you get hurt," he replied.

Tressie walked over to look out over the Schuylkill River. Quinton walked up close behind her.

"Didn't you just tell me not to confuse love and

lust?" She put some distance between the two of them. "I think you're lusting for me right now."

"I've been lusting for you for five years." He grabbed her and held her close. She didn't make any effort to break away from his embrace. He slowly brushed his soft lips across hers. He looked into her eyes and she quickly turned away. She released herself from his embrace.

"Quinton, what do you want from me?"

"I want you. I don't want anything but you."

"You know that's not possible."

"Why? Because of Payce. He's locked up and I'm right here." He walked up to her and held her hand. "Tressie, all I want is a chance, a chance to show you that we would be good together."

Unsure of what to do or say, Tressie played it safe. "Can you give me some time? I heard everything you've said, but I'm still in love with Payce, and while our relationship has hit some shaky ground, I can't just walk out on him. I need some time to sort out my feelings."

"Okay, I'll give you some space," Quinton responded.

Payce walked to the officer's desk and signed for his personal things. "You never told me who it was that bailed me out," he said to the officer.

"The lady standing behind you," the officer replied.

Payce turned around and saw Reverend Kane standing in the corner. He grumbled a few words under his breath, grabbed his wallet, and walked out of the prison facility.

Reverend Kane followed him outside. "Payce, you could thank me for bailing you out," she yelled.

Payce kept walking and yelled out, "Thanks, Rev."

"No thanks needed," she replied. "Natasha is the one who paid the bail money."

He stopped walking. "I thought she was in jail," he said. Then he realized something else. "Why weren't you arrested?"

"Can we talk in my car? I can give you a ride home." She motioned for him to follow her. He was reluctant to follow, but he knew that she was the only one who could answer his questions.

"When the police raided Natasha's house, I happened to be down in the wine cellar. Someone from the party requested a rare vintage wine, and Natasha asked me if I could go get it for her. That's when I heard the commotion upstairs. I hid out down there until the following morning. The first person I bailed out was Natasha. After she was released, she posted bail for the rest of her employees. You were the last person we had to get out."

"Why was I the last one to get bailed out? She told me I was one of her best employees. I should have been first."

"You are one of her best employees. I asked her to allow me to post your bail. I wanted to be the one to get you out of this mess, since I am the one who got you into it. Payce, I owe you an apology. I never meant for any of this to happen. The last thing I wanted was for you to go back to jail."

Reverend Kane sounded so remorseful that he couldn't allow her to take all the blame. He knew she was only trying to help him out. "Don't worry about it, Rev," Payce said. "I've been in worse situations and I came out of them just fine. Besides, it wasn't entirely your fault. I knew what I was doing was wrong, but again, I allowed money to lead me down the wrong path."

"I still feel guilty," she said. "Plus, I thought you should know I talked with your father."

"What did he have to say?"

"He's disappointed and mad, so be prepared for a long lecture when you get home tonight."

"I guess it's safe to say you didn't tell my father about you working at The Dollhouse."

Reverend Kane shook her head no. "I wanted to. I intended to tell him everything, but I lost the nerve at the last minute."

"Reverend Kane, are you going to continue to hide who you really are?"

"I'm still praying on it, and I know that God will forgive me because he forgives all sinners, but I'm concerned about the church. Will the congregation accept me for who I am, or will they reject me? I love that church too much to up and leave. I love the singing and the glory that is given to God in praise. On Sunday mornings I love to watch the children learn about who Jesus is, and you should see their faces when they realize what God has done for them. If I tell the church who I really am, I have to be ready for the repercussions that may follow."

"Have you ever thought about starting your own church?"

"I have, but it takes a lot to start a church. I need

at least one person to support me in an endeavor that large."

"You already have one. You have Jesus."

"Yes, I do." She smiled. "Plus, I've met somebody."

"That's great!" Payce replied. "You didn't meet her at The Dollhouse, did you?"

"No, actually she's been a friend of mine for years. We recently discovered our love for one another."

"That's great. I hope that means you'll stay away from places like The Dollhouse."

"No, I'm not looking to work at anymore lesbian spas. I think I'm going to retire from that line of business." Reverend Kane parked her car a few blocks away from Payce's home.

"I guess this is where we say good-bye," Payce said. "I have to face my father. I'm not looking forward to it, but it's something I have to do."

"Payce, I admire you for facing your problems."

"That is one thing my father has always taught me and my brother—to be responsible for the wrong we've done. Thanks a lot for the ride, Reverend Kane."

Several weeks had passed since that afternoon Tressie shared with Quinton, and since then he had showed her a side of him she didn't know existed. Quinton did everything he could to prove to Tressie that they belonged together. Every week he took her out to the movies, a play, or dinner. His heartfelt generosity was refreshing. He did all the things Payce didn't. He asked about her day, what she did in class, and he was even interested in her involvement at church.

The ultimate surprise came the day he whisked her off to a secluded lake in the suburbs for a picnic and washed her feet in fresh spring water.

Tressie was definitely impressed by how attentive Quinton was to her needs, but as much as she liked Quinton, she was still in love with Payce. Payce was her soul mate, her gift from God. She refused to end their relationship over a few mistakes.

Payce had called her a few times since his release from jail, but she wasn't ready to see him yet. She was still upset and needed some more time alone. Each time she spoke with him, he sounded so happy. Unfortunately, she couldn't return the enthusiasm. He kept asking to see her, but each time she made up excuses. She knew she couldn't hide forever. She was going to have to see him sooner or later, but in the meantime if Quinton wanted to continue to take her out and spend time with her, she wasn't going to deny herself the opportunity to have him treat her nice.

THREE MONTHS LATER

Payce and Darshon sat in Darshon's living room playing video games. They battled one another on PlayStation 2 for the championship title in *Grand Theft Auto.*

"What did your dad say?" Darshon asked.

"Of course he was ready to put me out, like so many times before. If it wasn't for my mom making such a big fuss about me not having anywhere to go, he would have put my ass on the curb."

"What about Tressie?"

"She said she forgave me, but I still feel the tension between us. When I call to ask her if we can spend some time together, she replies with one-word answers. Then I won't hear from her again until I call her. I have to find a way to make it up to her."

"Make it up to her?" Darshon exclaimed. "Man, I'm still mad at you. You were knocking women off three and four times a day and you didn't tell me. I thought we were tight. Not to mention the fact that you didn't try to share any of the wealth with me. I knew something was up. There was no way you saved that much money before you went away. But I would have never guessed this." He pointed to the front page of *The Philadelphia Inquirer*. The headline read "Madame Natasha Indicted on Twelve Counts."

Like a hurricane, Darshon's sister Lisa stormed through the front door. Her face lit up when she saw Payce sitting in her living room. "Payce, baby! I'm so glad to see you're okay. I was so worried about you." She knelt down at Payce's feet as if he were a king.

Payce laughed at her. "Lisa, would you stop?"

"I was worried about you. Wasn't I, Darshon?" She stroked the back of Payce's head.

"Lisa, leave the man alone," Darshon yelled.

Lisa ignored her brother and focused her attention on Payce. "I should be mad with you. You were working at The Dollhouse, my favorite hang out spot, and you never told me. You should have said something. I would have brought you in lots of business."

"That's all right, Lisa. I had enough clients."

"It never hurts to have more. Plus, we could have finally hooked up. I would have paid top dollar for your fine ass."

"Lisa, he doesn't want your big ass," Darshon screamed at his sister. "Go sit down somewhere. Let the man breathe."

"Sorry, Lisa. I work strictly with heterosexuals, not homosexuals," Payce told her with a smile.

"I would have jumped the fence," she replied. "Only temporarily, of course. Just long enough for me to get a taste of you." She got up and walked away. "Payce, just remember I'm waiting on you." She licked her lips and stuck out her tongue at him.

"That's nasty," Darshon commented.

"Man, reset the game. She broke my concentration," Payce told him. Then his cell phone vibrated on his hip. "Damn!" Payce said out loud. "Can I get in at least one game without any interruptions? He pulled out his cell phone and looked at the caller ID screen. It was Kai. "This girl has been calling me non-stop. She left me a million messages while I was locked up."

He flipped open the phone. "Hello."

"Payce, what's up? I'm glad I finally caught you."

"Look, Kai, I can't talk right now. I have a lot of shit going on right now. I'll have to get back with you when I have some time."

"I read about your problems in the paper, but that's not why I'm calling. I have something important I need to talk to you about and it can't wait."

"What is it, Kai?"

"Can't we meet someplace and I can explain then?"

"No," he replied. "If you want to talk, then do it now while you have me on the line. I don't know when the next time is that I'll be able to speak with you again."

She sighed. "I guess I don't have no choice but to tell you over the phone. I had a baby."

"Congratulations." He wondered why she was telling him that.

"And I think you're the father."

"What?" He jumped from his seat and walked into the kitchen. "How do you think I'm the father? Kai, I haven't seen you in months," he wailed.

"I know. I thought someone else was his father, but the paternity test results said he wasn't the father. The only other person I was with was you."

"You waited all this time to tell me?"

"I've been calling you for weeks. You wouldn't return my calls."

Payce's head began to pound. He couldn't believe this was happening to him now. "What do you want?" he asked.

"I need you to go down to the child support office and take a DNA test."

"Fine, make the arrangements and call me with the details."

Payce slammed his phone shut and sighed deeply.

"What's up?" Darshon asked.

"Man, I might be a father."

CHAPTER 17

Tressie ran down the subway steps and squeezed through the subway doors just before they closed. She carried her heavy book bag through the crowded train in search of an empty seat. She found a window seat next to a four-year-old boy who was coloring pages in a book.

Tressie sat by the window and watched the scenery turn from row homes to single family homes. The train suddenly made a sharp turn and forced the boy's hand to run straight across the page.

"Damn, I messed up again," he said out loud.

Tressie was shocked by the youngster's choice of words.

"Qua, didn't I tell you to color inside the lines?" a teenage girl who sat on the right side of him shouted out. Annoyed, she turned her back toward him and continued her conversation on her cell phone.

"Do you want to see the picture I did today in school?" he asked Tressie.

"I sure do." He pointed to a page in his book and she smiled at the child's creative drawing. "That's beautiful!" she exclaimed. "Are you going home to show your mommy?"

"I am his mother," the young girl shouted at Tressie.

Embarrassed, Tressie criticized herself for assuming the young mother was his sister. Tressie heard her cell phone ringing in her book bag and was grateful for the distraction. She dug around in her bag before she found it. "Hello?"

"Hey, Tressie."

Tressie closed her eyes at the sound of his voice. The person she despised the most was calling her.

"It's Payne," the caller said.

"I know who it is," Tressie snapped. "What do you want, Payne?"

"Why are you being so rude?" he asked.

She realized that she was being short with him. "Forgive me. I'm sorry. What can I do for you?" she asked.

"As I was saying before your rudeness stepped in, I've scheduled a mandatory meeting for Saturday in Harrisburg."

"Since when have meetings with you been mandatory?" she screamed.

"Since I've been conference president," he responded.

"I can't come." She refused to argue with him. "I don't have to attend. You should have listed this on the schedule."

"Tressie, you have to come. I have some important items on my agenda that I need to discuss about the next annual conference meeting. I've been working on changing a few things and I need to assign projects to certain individuals, and that includes you. Tressie, please come."

He had used the word "please." That caught her off guard. She couldn't believe he was actually being polite. This meeting must really be important to him. She hadn't made any plans for the weekend, so she could attend.

"Payne, don't do this again," she berated him. "I'll be there, but don't schedule impromptu meetings and expect everyone to rearrange their schedules to accommodate you."

He sighed heavily into the phone, irritated by her complaints. "The meeting starts at three o'clock. Don't be late." He hung up on her.

She placed her phone back in her bag. She couldn't believe she had agreed to attend an unscheduled mandatory meeting for Payne. Tressie looked around the train for the adolescent mother and her son. They must have reached their stop. Only a small handful of passengers remained on the train. Tressie laid back her head and rested until her stop.

Saturday morning Tressie pulled her car into the First District Diamond Center parking lot. It was five minutes past three and there were no other cars in the lot. She couldn't believe Payne wasn't there. He was such a fanatic about everyone attending his meetings on time. Lateness annoyed him.

Tressie tried calling Mariah before she left Philly to see if they could ride up together, but she couldn't reach her.

"Hello," Tressie called out as she entered the center. Her voice echoed against the hollow walls. "I better not be the only person who showed up. If so, I'm going to personally kill Payne." She walked down the hall to the office where their meetings were usually held. She opened the door. Inside a dozen roses and a card with her name on it lay on the table. She picked up the roses and read the card.

Tressie, this place reminds me of the first time I saw you. I looked at you not with my eyes, but with my heart and with my soul. The red roses represent the world and the single white rose in the center represents how you stand out amongst the world.

Tressie heard someone walk in behind her. She twisted herself around and Payce stood in the doorway.

She ran to him. "This was so sweet. Did your brother tell you I was going to be here?"

"No, I arranged this meeting to get you out of town. I had to pay Payne to call you and arrange this bogus meeting. It wasn't easy asking Payne to do me a favor. He drove me up here early this morning and opened the center for me. He kept reminding me how much I owe him for doing this."

"You did all this for me?" Her eyes danced.

"I knew you were still mad with me for getting arrested. I needed to make things right between us. Do you like the roses?"

"I love them . . . and the card."

"I meant what I said. No one in this world can measure up to you. I don't think I could live my life without you in it." They hugged. "Let's get out of here. I made us reservations at a nearby restaurant."

They left the church conference center and went to a nearby park.

"I thought we were going to eat," she said.

"We are. The restaurant is down that trail. It overlooks the river." They held hands through Riverfront Park, and once they arrived at the restaurant, they were seated in an enclosed balcony that revealed a magnificent view of the sun setting behind the river. The red and yellow colors from the sun sparkled against the water.

Three scented candles provided light for their table. While they waited on their order, Tressie stared at the stars in the sky.

"Oh my! Did you see that shooting star?"

"No, I missed it. Did you make a wish?"

"I wished that you would have told me you were working at The Dollhouse."

"I know I messed up. But I promised myself that I would never hurt you again." He stroked the side of her face. "I should have trusted you enough to tell you the truth. From now on I'm going to be completely honest with you at all times," Payce promised.

They finished their dinner and it was time for

them to head back to Philadelphia. Payce sat in the driver's seat and adjusted his seatbelt.

"I love you," Tressie purred.

"I love you, too," Payce replied.

He leaned over to kiss her and just before his lips reached hers, Tressie asked, "What's that?"

"What?" he asked.

"That. Inside your jacket."

"Oh! Nothing. Just something I had to pick up for T.J."

"If it's nothing, then show it to me. Didn't we just get done talking about trust?" she asked.

He reluctantly reached inside his jacket and pulled out a Ziploc bag full of cocaine. Before she could say anything, he tried to explain. "Don't be mad. I told T.J. that I would pick this up for him today while I was out here."

"So this trip wasn't about us. It was about drugs."

"No! I had already made arrangements to meet you when I mentioned it to T.J. He was going to come himself, but since I was already making the trip, he asked me if I would mind doing him a favor."

"And you just couldn't tell him no?"

"Tressie, he's done so many things for me in the past. What was I supposed to do?"

"Tell him no! You are out on bail!" she yelled. "You already have charges pending. What happens if you get caught with that on you?"

"Tressie, ain't nothing going to happen. When I get back to Philly, I'm taking this stuff straight to T.J."

"Didn't you just get done telling me that you would never hurt me again?" she asked.

Payce got quiet and stared straight in front of him.

"When did you have time to pick this stuff up? I've been with you all day."

"I met with the guy earlier this morning."

Tressie held her head to control her anger.

"What do you want me to do?" he asked.

"We don't have any choice but to go home with the drugs. But promise me that as soon as we get back to Philly, you will take those drugs straight to T.J."

"I promise." Payce started the car. "Trust me. We'll be fine."

Payce was on his way to Temple's main campus to pick up Tressie from school like he did every Thursday, but first he had to get rid of Kai and the baby.

"Kai, don't do this no more," he reprimanded her.

"Do what?" she asked innocently.

"You know what. You can't call me last minute and ask me to come pick you and the baby up."

"I had to take Cayden to the doctor's office and I thought that since you had only come to see him once since the paternity results proved you were the father, you'd be anxious to see your son."

"I told you I've been busy."

"Too busy to come and see your son?" she asked with an attitude.

"I told you I'll be over later this week to spend some time with him." He pulled up to the bus stop. "I'll call you tomorrow."

"You're dropping us off at the bus stop?" she screamed.

"That is how you got out here, isn't it?"

"I thought you were taking us home," Kai yelled, not budging from her seat.

"I would have, but you called me last minute. There is someplace I have to be. The next time the baby has a doctor's appointment, make sure you let me know and I will come and get the two of you myself, but today I have something to do," he explained. The baby let out a loud burp. Payce turned around to get a good look at him. He still couldn't believe that the beautiful baby was a part of him.

Payce's cell phone rang.

"I guess that's your someplace calling you," Kai replied.

Payce knew it was Tressie calling to find out where he was. "I have to go," Payce said out loud.

Kai continued to sit in the front seat, pouting.

"What are you waiting on?" he urged.

"I need some money," she shouted. "You haven't even asked me did the baby need anything."

He turned his eyes down in shame. He had forgotten to offer to buy anything.

"I need to get diapers and formula," she screamed at him.

"What happened to WIC? Can't they help you out?" he asked as he dug into his pocket.

"The last time I looked, WIC isn't the one who fathered our son," she replied sarcastically.

"Here." He shoved forty dollars in her face.

"Forty dollars! This isn't going to last long," Kai complained.

"Kai, you know my situation. You know I'm not working. I'll bring you some more money when I come over there later this week."

Kai got out and pulled the baby from the back-seat while Payce grabbed the baby's carriage from the trunk.

Meanwhile, Tressie stood on the corner of Broad and Diamond searching for Payce's car. *He's usually never this late*, she thought. She looked at her watch and called him again, but got no answer.

"He must be stuck in traffic," she said out loud. She stood on the corner for another five minutes before a light rain began to fall on her head. She had forgotten to grab her umbrella before she left the house that morning. If Payce didn't show up soon, she would be soaking wet.

The raindrops got heavier and heavier, and Tressie couldn't wait any longer. She hailed down a cab.

"Can you take me to the Gallery Mall, please?" she asked the driver.

She didn't know where Payce was, but once she got to the mall she would call and leave him a message to pick her up there.

Tressie looked out the window at each passing car, hoping she would see Payce's car. The cabbie drove south down Broad Street and stopped at a red light. Waiting for the light to change, Tressie looked out the window and was shocked to see Payce with a girl and her baby. She watched as Payce kissed the baby and handed the baby carrier back to the girl. The light turned green and the cabbie pulled off.

"Wait!" she screamed. "Turn around! You have to turn around."

"You told me you wanted to go to the Gallery." His strong Middle Eastern accent slurred his words.

"I know, but I changed my mind. I need for you to follow that car." She pointed in the opposite direction.

The cabbie made a U-turn in the middle of Broad Street, changing his course from south to north.

"Go faster!" she commanded. "I know you can go faster than this. I've seen you cab drivers drive like you were in the Indy 500."

She looked ahead until she spotted Payce's car. He made a right turn onto Diamond Street. She pointed. "There he goes. Follow that Lexus."

The yellow taxi sped up and trailed Payce's car.

"Blow your horn, flash your lights," she demanded.

The cab driver followed her orders. Payce finally noticed the taxi and pulled over. Tressie jumped out of the back of the taxi and ran over to his side of the car.

"Who were you just with?" she hollered.

"Hey baby, I'm sorry I was late . . ."

"I saw why you were late. I saw you with that girl and her baby. Who is she?" Tressie yelled. The rain poured down on her head. She pulled her wet hair out of her face.

Payce watched black mascara roll down her face. The cab driver pulled up alongside Tressie.

"Ma'am, could you pay me, please?" he asked. Payce got out of his car and paid the fare.

He walked back toward her. "Tressie . . ." He took a deep breath. "We need to talk."

The rain was drenching both of them.

"No! You are going to tell me who she is!"

"Okay, but can you get in the car first?" He tried to reason with her.

She opened the passenger's side door and slammed the door shut. He got into the car and turned toward her.

"There's something I need to tell you," he uttered.

She sat on her side of the car waiting for him to explain. Tressie knew that what he had to tell her was not good.

"That girl . . ." he began, "the baby you saw me kiss . . . he's my son."

"Son?" she shouted.

"Last year, I met his mother and we hooked up for one night. Cayden was the result," he told her softly.

"You cheated on me again?!"

"Tressie, it was only that one time."

"Why should I believe you?" she screamed back at him. Her cell phone rang. She looked at the caller ID and it was Danyelle. Tressie hit the mute button. She didn't want anyone to disturb her conversation with Payce. "You had a baby and never told me."

"She didn't tell me until after I got out of jail. I wanted to tell you but I didn't know how."

Her cell phone started ringing again. It was

Danyelle again. "Why do people call at inopportune times? Hello," she answered.

"Did I catch you at a bad time?" Danyelle asked. She could hear that Tressie was upset about something, but what she had to tell her couldn't wait.

"Danyelle, I really can't talk right now."

"Tressie!" she cried. "Don't hang up. I've got something important to tell you about Payce."

Tressie looked in Payce's direction. He pretended to be interested in the falling rain.

"Go ahead," Tressie responded solemnly.

"I was in Southwest Philly today getting high with this girl. We were sitting on her deck in the backyard smoking a blunt when her pregnant next-door neighbor walked out into her backyard. So Loretta, that's the girl I was getting high with, she asked me were you still dating Payce Boyd. So you know me, I'm like, 'yeah.' Well, she goes on to tell me that her neighbor, Najah, claims that she is pregnant by Payce. Girl, when she told me that news I had to put my blunt down. I almost choked on my inhale. That was some startling shit."

Tressie was silent. Danyelle wondered if she was still there. "Hello?" Danyelle called out.

"I'm here," Tressie replied. "Continue."

"Anyway, I asked was she sure and she said 'yeah' and that if I didn't believe her I could ask her myself. So I stood up and asked the girl, and she said she was pregnant by Payce Boyd."

Tressie sat in her seat sniffling, trying to hold back the tears. Danyelle regretted telling her friend this information. "Maybe I should have waited to tell you this."

"No, you did the right thing by calling me. Is he aware of this?" she asked.

Payce turned and looked at her when she asked that question.

"She said Payce knew, and he told her he would take care of his child."

"Thanks. I'll call you later tonight." She hung up with Danyelle and turned toward Payce.

"Payce," Tressie said very calmly.

He turned and looked in her direction. She swung her hand back and slapped him across the face. "You bastard. Who the hell is Najah?"

He stared at her with a blank expression.

She got out the car and walked toward the bus stop.

"Tressie, where are you going? Get in the car. I'll take you home."

"Fuck you. I'd rather walk!" she screamed.

CHAPTER 18

Tressie took one last look at herself in the mirror. The strawberry flavored lip gloss she bought at the mall added luster to her lips. She rubbed her lips together and stuck the tube of lip gloss in her purse. She and Quinton were going out and he wouldn't tell her where they were going, but he did promise her it would be a night she would never forget.

The day after Tressie found out about Payce's two children, she ran to Quinton for comfort.

"I hate him," she told Quinton.

"You don't mean that," he responded. "You're just really upset right now."

"You're right. I don't hate him, but he makes me sick and I don't want to see him ever again. I've had enough of being mistreated."

"Does that mean you're a free woman?" Quinton asked.

"Um . . . yeah. I guess it does." It never occurred to her that she was once again a single woman.

"Good, because I was serious when I said I wanted us to be a couple again."

"Quinton, I . . ."

"Before you say no, hear me out," Quinton interrupted. "I know you want to clear your head and get Payce out of your mind, but there is no better way to do that than to let me into your life. I can help you forget about Payce. I want a chance to make you happy. You deserve to smile all the time. Plus, if you and I are together, Payce will know that it is really over between the two of you."

Tressie was scared to jump into another relationship so soon after her breakup with Payce, but Quinton did have a point. She needed to show Payce that they were finished, and she knew Quinton would keep his promise to treat her good.

"All right, we can give it a try and see how things work out."

"I promise I will not let you down," he exclaimed.

Tressie heard Quinton's voice downstairs and glanced at her reflection in the mirror one last time. She ran her fingers through her hair and straightened out her skirt over her hourglass figure. "Perfect," she said to herself.

She ran down the stairs. "You look lovely," Quinton said.

"Thanks," she replied. "Are you ready?"

"Yes." He shook her father's hand and said goodnight to her mother. He held the door open for her and escorted her out to his car.

"Why are you acting so formal?" she asked. "I'm not used to you acting this way."

He whispered in her ear, "It's strictly for the parents. They want to make sure their only daughter is going out with someone respectable." Quinton turned around and waved good-bye to her parents, who stood in the doorway watching.

"You don't have to put on a show for my parents. You're considered a good catch after some of the other guys I've brought home."

"Well, I don't want them to see me as a good catch. I want them to look at me as their future son-in-law."

She laughed. "You're moving kind of fast, aren't you?"

"Not at all. I already know who I want to spend my life with. I just hope she wants to do the same," he replied.

Tressie felt uncomfortable talking about a future with Quinton when her heart still belonged to Payce. She quickly changed the subject. "Where are you taking me?"

"I told you it was a surprise."

"You can't give me a hint?" she pleaded.

"Don't do that. You make me hot when you do that."

"Pleeeeeeeeease," she whined.

"I can't win," he said. "I'm taking you to see AI."

"Stop playing. Are you for real?"

"Here go the tickets right here." He pulled out a pair of tickets he had stashed under his seat.

"Oh my gosh!" she examined the Sixers tickets. "These are floor seats," she screamed. "I'm going to be so close to Allen that I can see those gorgeous eyes and those pretty lips and . . ."

"Excuse me," Quinton interrupted. "I am the one who is taking you to the game. Please don't forget that you'll be sitting next to your date."

"Oh no, honey! I won't forget about you. But if Allen looks my way, act like you're with the people sitting on the other side of you." She laughed. "I'm just playing. I would never trade you for him."

They arrived at the Wachovia Center just in time to hear the starting lineup for Philadelphia. The Sixers were playing the Pistons and the arena was packed with fans.

"Wow, it looks a whole lot different down here than it does in the nosebleed seats," she screamed.

Music blared from the speakers and the Seventy-Sixers dance team ran onto the court dressed in red and black biker shorts with pom-poms in their hands. The head cheerleader directed the girls to different positions, and they followed her lead.

"That girl looks familiar," Tressie said, referring to the head cheerleader. "Do we know her?"

"She doesn't look familiar to me," Quinton said.

When the girl turned around, Tressie looked closely at her face. "It's Mariah. She's our church conference treasurer. I didn't know she was a dancer," Tressie said.

Mariah led the girls through two dance routines before the buzzer sounded and the girls dashed off the court.

For the entire game, Tressie yelled and cheered Allen Iverson on. AI rebounded, blocked shots, stole the ball, and scored four three-pointers all in one quarter. Quinton was sure Tressie would lose her voice by the end of the game.

The Sixers were down by one and the game clock didn't have much time left. Seconds ticked away. Iverson had the ball. He ran full speed toward the basket. To make the shot before the buzzer sounded, he threw the ball from half court. The fans rose to their feet and watched as the ball swished gracefully through the net just before the buzzer sounded. Iverson had done it again—a last second shot that was the deciding factor in whether this game would go into the win or loss column.

"That was great!" Tressie exclaimed.

"Yeah, that was a good game," Quinton agreed. "I'm glad we came."

"Mariah! Mariah!" Tressie called out to her friend.

Mariah rushed over to the sidelines.

"Hey girl," she said breathlessly. "I saw you over here. I'm surprised to see you here."

"This was a surprise from my boyfriend," Tressie said.

Mariah smiled at Quinton and wondered where Payce was.

"Quinton, this is a friend of mine, Mariah."

They shook hands and greeted one another.

"You are a really talented dancer," he said, complimenting her. "Have you been dancing for long?"

"I've been a part of the basketball dance team for the past three years. I started at the bottom and worked my way up."

"Mariah, why didn't you ever tell me you were a dancer?"

"Because I'm not a dancer. I'm an aspiring dancer, still looking to land my big break. I go on auditions just about every day praying that this will be my chance."

"Girl, keep praying. Your dreams will come true."

"Man, the Sixers killed Detroit." Payce grabbed his coat from his seat. "Detroit lost their defense; both Rasheed and Ben were hurt, allowing the Sixers to walk all over them."

Darshon looked down at the court from the balcony. "Yo, man, isn't that Tressie down there talking to that fine cheerleader?"

Payce turned and saw Tressie holding hands with another guy. He thought his eyes were deceiving him. He stared down at the girl that Darshon pointed to. It really was Tressie.

"Who's the guy she's with?" Darshon asked.

Payce knew that Tressie was mad at him, but he didn't think she would go out with somebody else.

"I didn't know you two had broken up," Darshon said.

"We didn't."

"Well, I think someone oughta tell her that, 'cause it looks like she's on a date with some other dude."

"Come on, man." Payce raced toward the stairs.

"Man, don't start no fight. You can't afford to go back to jail," Darshon yelled.

Payce searched the entire lower level for Tressie and the guy she was with, but saw no sign of them anywhere.

"Payce, look at all these people. You're never

going to find her," Darshon screamed above the spectators trying to go home. People pushed past them. "Why don't you just wait until you get home and call her?"

"No, she won't take any of my calls. I just want to talk to her. Wait a minute." He thought for a second. "Mariah. She would know where Tressie went." He ran toward the cheerleaders' locker room and waited outside for Mariah to come out.

Minutes passed before Mariah walked out carrying her gym bag. "Mariah!" Payce screamed.

She jumped at the sound of her name being screamed so loudly. "Payce, what are you doing here?" She was surprised to see him.

"I saw you talking to Tressie," he exclaimed. "Where is she?"

"She was here, but she's probably left by now," Mariah lied.

"Who was that she was with?" Payce asked.

Mariah wasn't going to give Payce any information about Quinton. He would have to ask Tressie about that. "I'm not sure," she replied.

"She didn't introduce you to the guy?"

"She introduced us, but she just said he was a friend of hers." Mariah quickly pretended to look for something in her bag, hoping to hide her dishonesty.

Mariah's body language told Payce she was lying. He wondered what secret she was hiding from him.

"I thought you two broke up," she said.

"Did she say that?" he asked.

"No, I just assumed. Look, Payce, I have to go. The girls from the dance team are waiting on me."

"Payce, come on, let's go," Darshon urged. "She doesn't know anything. You can call Tressie in the morning."

Payce realized he wasn't getting anywhere with Mariah. "Mariah, can you do me a favor? Tell her that I love her," he said sadly.

Mariah felt bad for lying to him. She wished she could tell him that Tressie was waiting in front of the Wachovia Center for her, but she knew it would be best if he left and talked with her later. She watched him walk away with his head down. Once Payce was out of sight, Mariah ran to the side entrance and around to the front of the building. She hoped Payce wouldn't see them on his way out, but once she turned the corner, she saw Payce marching in Quinton and Tressie's direction.

Damn, she thought. *I did everything I could.*

Tressie hugged Quinton tightly. "Thanks for bringing me to the game," she whispered in his ear.

"No problem. You know I would do anything for you."

Tressie blushed. She looked over Quinton's shoulder just in time to see Payce coming their way with Darshon not too far behind him. "Oh no," she softly mumbled.

Quinton saw the worried look on her face and turned to see what had her so concerned.

"Tressie, can I speak to you for a moment?" Payce asked.

"We don't have anything to talk about," she replied.

Payce stared at Quinton as Mariah ran up to the four of them.

"Tressie, I just want to talk to you," Payce said again.

"Talk to me about what?" she screamed.

"I've been trying to apologize, but you won't let me."

"Apologize? Apologize for what? Apologize for conceiving two children outside of our relationship? Apologize for cheating on me? Or apologize for me finding out the truth from someone else?"

Payce tried to move closer to her, but Quinton stepped between them. "Man, she said she doesn't want to talk," Quinton firmly addressed Payce.

Tressie could feel the tension in the air. She didn't want the scene to turn into a fight. "Payce, we're over. I have a new boyfriend." She grabbed Quinton's hand firmly.

"New boyfriend? How could you have a new boyfriend? We haven't broken up," he yelled. Payce slammed his fist into his hand. "Last week we were a couple and this week you're in a new re- lationship? There is no way you could have found a new man that quick unless . . ." The reality of what was going on suddenly dawned on him. "You were going out with him while I was locked up. You played me."

Tressie was silent.

"You told me you would wait for me." He pointed his finger at her. "You cried about how I lied to you when you were lying to me, too."

"Payce, it wasn't like that," Tressie tried to explain.

"Sure it was. You were spending time with this buster while I was away."

"Man, you don't know me like that," Quinton spoke up.

Darshon pushed in front of Payce. "Player, I suggest you step back. What's going on between my man and his girl is between them. It doesn't concern you."

"Everyone calm down!" Mariah screamed. "If everyone doesn't calm down, the police will be over here. We don't want to give them a reason to drag us down to the precinct."

"Tressie, you betrayed me," Payce said in her face. "You were the one person I thought I could count on."

He turned to walk away, but before he did she jumped in his face.

"Don't you dare try to turn this on me. Betrayal is what you're made of. You have broken my heart over and over again. You've taken my trust in you as a weakness. You think you can do whatever you want to do and I will always take you back because I love you. Not this time."

He knew the words she spit at him were the truth. He turned and stormed away.

After dropping Mariah off, Quinton and Tressie rode in silence, neither sure of what to say.

"Are you all right?" he asked. "I know that was hard for you."

A tear fell from her eye. The pressure of confronting Payce was wearing down on her. She was so mad at Payce for being angry with her that it made her upset.

"I know that you're still in love with Payce. I

could see it in your eyes, and I'm sure he could see it, too. That's why it bothered him so much to see you with me."

"I feel so bad. He trusted me and I deceived him. I'm no better than him."

"You shouldn't feel that way. You two are no longer together because of problems he created in your relationship—not you."

"Quinton, I think it was wrong for me to start seeing you so soon after Payce. I'm still unsure about my feelings for him. Seeing him tonight made me think that maybe I was wrong. When I found out about his children, I never gave him a chance to explain. I need to sit down and talk things over with him. If I don't, I will always wonder what the truth was behind our split."

"Sweetheart, I think you're in shock over having to face him so soon after your break up. Once people start seeing us together more often they will begin to accept our relationship, and it will be easier for you to accept us."

"This has nothing to do with me and you. It has to do with Payce and me not ending our relationship the right way," she explained. "You said you wanted my mind, body, heart, and soul, but right now I can only offer you my mind and body. My heart and soul are still with Payce. You deserve to be with someone who can give themselves to you entirely."

Quinton listened to her heart-wrenching words.

"Would you mind if we took a break from seeing each other for a while?"

He didn't want to admit it, but she was right. He did want all of her. He wanted her to look at him the same way she looked at Payce. "I guess I don't have any choice."

"Can I have a kiss to last me until we meet again?" she asked.

He leaned over and kissed her lightly. Tressie cared for Quinton, but the feelings she held for Payce were so much stronger.

CHAPTER 19

"Tressie, what's up?"

Tressie heard Darshon's voice and hoped he was calling her for Payce. She had tried calling Payce every night since the basketball game, but he wouldn't return any of her calls. "Hey Darshon, what's up?"

"I'm sorry for just getting back to you. I know you called me a few weeks ago, but I had forgotten that you called and I just remembered. So what's up?"

She sat for a moment trying to remember why she had called Darshon, "Oh yeah. I did call you. I called because I had planned on throwing a surprise birthday party for Payce, but since he won't speak to me, I'm going to cancel the party."

"Tressie, he was really upset about seeing you with that guy."

"Did he say he was upset?"

"No, but you know how guys are. They never

want to show their true feelings. He's my best friend. I know when something is bothering him, but if it helps you to know, I think he misses you."

Tressie was glad to hear that he missed her. That meant he still had feelings for her. "Darshon, let me ask you a question. Do you think if I go ahead and throw this surprise party for Payce that he'll forgive me?"

"I don't know, Tressie. He was really mad. I don't know if a party will make him forget what he saw."

"I know, but I've already reserved the Borgata Ballroom. I spent all my money to put this party together, so I really don't have anything to lose. I'm going to go ahead and still throw the party."

"Wow, this is going to be a nice party. You must have put out a lot of loot to reserve the Borgata Ballroom. How are you planning on getting him to Atlantic City?" Darshon asked.

"I'm going to leave that to you. He trusts you. Tell him you're taking him to Atlantic City to gamble. I'll need for you to get him there no later than eleven o'clock. That will allow the guests enough time to get there before him," she instructed.

"No problem."

"Darshon, are you sure you can get him there?" she asked a second time.

"Trust me," Darshon replied. "I've already thought of a plan."

"Payce, would you come on? Man, you take longer than a woman," Darshon yelled up the stairs. He impatiently sat on the couch next to Payne and made small talk. "So Payne, what do you have planned for your birthday?" Darshon asked.

"I have something special planned for my brother and me."

"Cake and ice cream at the church?" Darshon joked.

"No, imbecile," Payne replied. "It's a surprise."

Payce raced down the stairs dressed to the nines. He posed for an imaginary camera in a fancy pair of black dress pants and a solid burgundy button-up dress shirt. This was the only time Payne and Payce had ever dressed alike. The only noticeable difference between the two of them was Payne's pants stopped way above his ankles. Payce walked over to Darshon and gave him a pound. "What's up, man?"

"Man, I hear you're going out with your brother tonight. You two celebrating your birthdays to-gether?"

"Yeah, man. This is the first time since we were kids," Payce responded. "He keeps bragging about how he has something special planned. I can't wait to see what it is."

"I bet it's something out of this world," Darshon snickered. "Can I holla at you outside for a sec-ond?" Darshon asked Payce.

"Sure."

They walked toward the front door when Payne jumped in front of them and blocked the exit, pre-venting them from leaving.

"No!" he shouted. "If you go outside with him, you'll leave, and I'll never see you again."

Darshon laughed. He walked over and put his arm around Payne. "Relax, man. I think you had too much sugar today. I'm not going to kidnap your brother. I just wanna speak with him."

Payne looked at the two of them suspiciously. "All right, but I'll be watching you two."

They moved him out the way and laughed at his attempt to prevent them from leaving the house.

Once they were outside Darshon spoke quietly. He could see Payne peeping at them through the living room blinds. "Man, I don't know what your brother has planned for tonight, but the fellows and I had something we wanted to do for your birthday."

"It doesn't have anything to do with The Dollhouse, does it?"

"No, it's legit."

"Darshon, I would love to hang with you guys, but I promised my brother that I'd go out with him."

"I understand, but can't you just come out with us for an hour? You can meet up with him later. Payne is probably going to take you to the church for his annual birthday celebration."

"I don't know, man. You saw how he was just acting. He's not going to let me out of his sight."

"Leave it to me," Darshon replied.

"Payne!" Darshon yelled.

Payne hurried outside.

"Payce and I were going to hit the liquor store in Camden. Do you want to ride?"

"Do you really want to go to Camden at this time of night? It is dark outside," he replied. Payce and Darshon both knew that Payne was scared of the small, but edgy city of Camden, New Jersey. Camden was listed as one of the most dangerous cities in the country. Old wives tales circulated through-out Philadelphia about how visitors entered Camden, but never left.

"We're going to pick up some liquor. That's the only place that sells alcohol this time of night. Are you coming or what?" he urged.

Payne was hesitant to accompany them.

"Forget it, Payne. We'll see you when we get back," Darshon told him. He looked at his watch. Tressie had said to be there no later than eleven o'clock. His watch said a little past nine.

"No, wait. I'll ride with you. Let me go grab my jacket," Payne said.

On their way out of the city, Darshon stopped to pick up T.J. and John. The five of them took the Atlantic City Expressway east.

"We passed Camden thirty minutes ago," Payne yelled out.

"Payne, relax," Darshon told him. "You are the one who said you wanted to come."

"I thought we were going to Camden. Darshon has kidnapped us and now we're going to miss my surprise."

"Payne, you really are a pain," Darshon stressed. "Just to let you know, I have my own surprise for Payce."

"What about what I had planned?" Payne whined.

"Payne, forget about the shindig you put together for Payce. You will have a lot more fun with us. What was it you were going to do?"

Payne didn't want to spoil his surprise, but he knew that what he had arranged for the evening was already ruined. "I planned on cake and ice cream."

The car exploded with laughter.

"I told you," Darshon giggled. "Payne, you do the same thing every year, cake and ice cream at the church."

"No, no. This year it wasn't going to be at the church. Reverend Kane offered to hold the festivities at her house."

The car got quiet. Payce had told T.J and John about Reverend Kane. The only person who didn't know about Reverend Kane's double life was Payne.

"Why did everyone get so quiet?" he asked.

"No reason," Payce responded. "No offense, man, but I'm glad we didn't go to Reverend Kane's."

"Why? She told me she likes you."

Payce would never tell his brother Reverend Kane's secret. "You know what?" He put his arm around Payne. "It doesn't matter where we spend our birthday. As long as we're together."

An hour later they pulled up in front of the Borgata Hotel and Casino. They walked in and gazed at a vastly colored sculpture that hung in the front lobby.

"Darshon, you brought us to Satan's den. I'm going to Hell. God is going to punish us all!" Payne exclaimed with his hand in the air.

"Thanks, this is cool," Payce said to Darshon and walked toward the casino entrance.

"Sorry fellas. The casino is not the surprise. Payce's birthday surprise is in the ballroom," Darshon announced.

"I knew this was too good to be true," Payce exclaimed. "Darshon never plans anything without any women."

They followed Darshon down a winding corridor. "Payce, you're right, I wouldn't plan anything without women being involved." The archway opened up to a landing that was immersed in music. "But I didn't plan this."

They approached the balcony and Payce looked down. Dancing away on the dance floor were dozens of couples, young and old, doing the two-step. A banner hung along the wall that said "Happy Birthday, Payce!"

Payce turned to Darshon. "This party is for me?" he asked.

Darshon nodded his head yes.

"Thanks, man. I would have never guessed," Payce said, smiling.

"Don't thank me. Thank Tressie. Tressie is the one who planned it." He pointed down to Tressie who stood among a crowd of people. A wide smile appeared on Payce's face as he rushed to her.

"Happy birthday," she said to him. "You look very debonair." She pulled a single white rose from behind her back. "This white rose represents you, because you stand out from all the rest." He smiled at her choice of words.

"Can I have this dance?" she asked.

"I can't dance," he replied.

"That's all right. I'll teach you."

Payce followed Tressie's lead and matched every step she took. While they danced, a lot of Payce's friends stopped to wish the guest of honor happy birthday. Payce saw T.J., John, and Darshon each trying to step on the dance floor. Even Payne had found himself a dance partner.

Tressie and Payce danced for more than an hour before Payce started sweating. His steps got sluggish and he moved slower and slower.

"Do you want to stop?" she asked him.

"No, no. I'm all right."

Tressie grabbed his hand and led him to a nearby table. "We should stop. I don't want the birthday boy to pass out on me."

"I really appreciate you throwing me this party," Payce said to her.

"I had to do something. You wouldn't return my calls."

"I was mad," he replied.

"So was I. At least I tried to straighten things out."

"How does your boyfriend feel about you throwing me this party?"

"He's not my boyfriend anymore. I asked him if we could take a break until I was able to get over you."

"That's what you want to do? Get over me?" he asked.

"No, I would like for things to work out between the two of us, but I'm not sure if it will ever be the same."

"I wasn't really mad when I found you with that guy. I think I was more surprised. After all the things I've done to you, I had no reason to get upset when you started seeing someone else. I'm the one who messed things up between us."

"Payce, I have to take my share of the responsibility. I knew exactly what I was doing every time I accepted Quinton's invitation to spend time together. I should have kept my promise and waited for you to be released from jail."

"If I would have been a man and been honest and truthful with you from the beginning, none of this would have happened, so I'll take the blame."

Tressie looked at him and smiled. "Okay, if you insist. You can take all the blame."

He laughed. She was definitely the girl he fell in love with.

She laid her head on his shoulder. "You have no idea how disappointed I was to hear you had two children without me. I wanted to be the one to give you your first child. Now you've given that gift to two women you don't even love."

"Tressie, I promise that you and I will have a family of our own. Although I already have two children, I welcome the day when you and I can have our own."

"I love you."

And they sealed their love with a kiss.

CHAPTER 20

Payce kissed Tressie on the shoulder. "I'm going to miss you."

"I'm going to miss you more," she replied.

They lay in her bed wrapped in nothing but a sheet. They took advantage of Tressie's parents' long weekend getaway by having their own private getaway. This was their last night together before he reported to court the following day. His lawyer forewarned him that his parole would be revoked and he would have to serve out the final three years of his prison sentence.

The hardest thing for him to accept wasn't going back to jail, but leaving Tressie behind. She was the most valuable thing in the world to him. He had never opened up his heart to anyone until he met her. A lot of the girls he met in the past he used as toys, but Tressie was different. She was the kind of woman he dreamed of spending his life with, a woman who would stand by his side no matter the circumstance.

He pulled his arms around her tighter. Their eyes locked and silence seized the moment as their spirits took a hold of one another and wouldn't let go. It seemed as if God had taken the blinders off their eyes and they could see for the first time their destiny as soul mates.

"I need to talk to you about something." Payce broke away from their shared moment. "I'm going to be away for three years and a lot can happen during that time."

"Three years won't stop me from loving you."

"You're familiar with that old saying 'out of sight, out of mind?' The last time I was only away for six days and someone managed to steal you away from me. This time I'll be away for years."

Tressie was embarrassed at how she had allowed a moment of weakness to overcome her.

"If you meet someone, don't hold yourself back because of me. We can use this time as a test. If we were really meant to be, then no one you go out with will be able to come between us. Of course we'll write and I'll call you, but if it is really meant for us to be together, we'll weather this storm. Do you understand?"

She nodded.

"Promise me one thing?"

"Anything," she replied.

"Don't go out with Quinton."

"What's wrong with Quinton?" she asked.

"I don't like him. He's not someone I'd like to see you with."

"Don't be jealous," she responded.

"I'm not jealous. I think that when you two got together he took advantage of the situation. He knew I was locked up and went after you. I don't trust him. Let's change the subject. I don't want to spend my last night with you talking about him. Where is the shoe box of money that I gave to you?" he asked.

"I put it in the bottom of my closet."

"I need you to hold on to that money until I come home."

"That's a lot of money. You trust me with ten thousand dollars in cash?"

"I trust you with my life," he replied.

It warmed her heart to hear him say those words.

"Before I forget, can you leave me your Social Security Number before you leave in the morning?" she asked.

"What do you need that for?"

"I have to check your credit report just in case we ever get married. My mother believes that a man is only as good as his credit. She has always told me that a man who pays his bills on time will always take care of you."

"Well, what does she say about a man who doesn't have any credit because I don't believe I've ever applied for anything before?"

"I don't know what she says about that. I'll have to ask her."

She laid her head against his chest and drifted off to sleep.

At sunrise, Payce got up and dressed. He sat on the side of the bed for a second and watched Tressie sleep. *She is so beautiful,* he thought. He knew he was a really lucky guy to have her by his side. He had put her through hell and she still loved him.

"God," he whispered softly, "watch out for her. She's a good girl who deserves the best. I'm not going to be around, so can you send a few angels to look out for her until I come home? Thanks."

He got up, grabbed his bag, and left a single white rose lying next to her. He kissed her lips. "I love you," he told her one last time and left.

A few hours later Tressie woke up to the sound of her alarm. She turned over, hit the off button, and opened her eyes. She felt around for Payce. He was gone and in his place was a white rose. She held the flower up to her nose to get a whiff of its faint fragrance. *He left without saying good-bye,* she thought. A tear rolled down her cheek. She had hoped to touch his face one more time before he went to jail. The next time she laid eyes on him would be through a glass partition.

She understood why he left the way he did. Neither of them could bear the thought of saying good-bye. She trembled at the thought of what was going to happen later that day in court. She suppressed the urge to throw on her clothes and run down to the courthouse. She envisioned throwing herself at the mercy of the court and begging them to release the only man she'd ever loved. But she knew deep down inside it didn't matter what she did, Payce was still going to have to do the time. She missed him already—his smile, his corny jokes.

She sat up, threw her legs off the side of her bed, and looked out the window. Dark storm clouds lingered above her house. Her first morning class started in forty-five minutes, but she couldn't concentrate on school. All she could think about was Payce. She lay back down in bed and wrapped the blankets around herself.

After watching an afternoon full of talk shows, Tressie got bored and turned on her computer. "I might as well get some school work done," she mumbled. She shook the mouse connected to her computer and knocked over a small piece of scrap paper. She picked it up from off the floor. Written inside was Payce's Social Security number. *He remembered.* In no time, she logged onto the Equifax Web site, entered Payce's Social Security number, and answered a few questions. Within minutes a copy of his credit report appeared on the screen.

She scanned the report carefully. The only debt he owed was to a cellular wireless company. The outstanding balance was a little over two hundred dollars.

"That's not bad. We can handle that," she said.

She scrolled down. Listed at the bottom were two judgments against him for child support. The balance exceeded thirty-five thousand dollars.

"Thirty-five thousand dollars!" she screamed. "For two children under the age of one he owes thirty-five thousand dollars?" She studied the report more carefully. "How in the world did he accumulate a debt this large?"

She remembered her friend Hope who had gotten married last year. Her husband had three children from a previous marriage. He was also behind in his child support payments. Once they got married, anything they tried to get on credit was denied.

Hope told her that there was no way of escaping child support. They couldn't get a house, a car, or a credit card. They couldn't even get approved for an apartment. Currently they were living in a garage apartment atop his momma's house.

Tressie figured that by the time Payce was released, his debt would have tripled. *Another obstacle*, she thought. Every time she and Payce got closer, something was there to tear them apart. Anxiety filled her stomach.

"What am I supposed to do?" she yelled.

The phone rang loudly in her ear. She stared at it for a moment. Not wanting to talk with anyone, she reluctantly answered it. "Hello."

"Hello," a woman called out from the other end. "I have a collect call from Payce. Will you accept the charges?"

"Yes, I will," Tressie replied.

"Hello," Payce screamed into the phone. Tressie could hear cars driving by in the distance.

"Payce, where are you?" she asked suspiciously.

"Tressie, I can't talk right now. I need you to listen. I jumped bail."

"You did what?"

"I couldn't go back to jail. I got scared and ran."

"Honey, we need to sit down and talk this through rationally. If you go down to the courthouse now, things won't be that bad."

"I can't, Tressie. You don't how it is to be locked up. Those cells are cages and the inmates are the animals. Being confined plays with your mind. You're not just physically locked up, but also mentally."

"Payce, I understand what you're saying, but

running is not going to solve the problem. Tell me where you are and I'll come and get you."

"Remember when I told you about the safe house that the fellows and I bought out of state for emergencies?"

"Yes, I remember."

"Well that's where I am."

"Okay, just tell me how to get there and I'll be on my way."

"I don't want to say too much over the phone. I have already talked to Darshon. He's on his way to bring you the directions on how to get here. When you get here I want us to get married. I don't want to wait any longer. I want you to be my wife."

"What about my family?" she asked. "My mother will be devastated if she isn't there to see me get married."

"Tressie, we don't have to have a big wedding right now. We can go to the justice of peace. I promise you we will have a big wedding later. All right?"

"I suppose," she replied.

"I'm going to hang up. I'll talk to you later tonight." Before she hung up, he called out her name.

"Yes?" She replied. She thought he had remembered at the last minute to tell her he loved her.

"Don't forget to bring that shoe box full of money," he told her.

"I won't," she replied, disappointed.

She hung up the phone and began to pack her things. She pulled out sneakers, jeans, and sweaters. If Payce needed her, she was going to be there for him. She glanced over at her computer. Payce's credit report was still displayed on the screen. *What am I going to do? Payce wants to get married now. Does it really matter that he owes thirty-five thousand dollars in child support? Will he think I'm being selfish if I tell him I don't want to get married because of his children and the money he owes?*

She sat on the side of the bed for a moment to think. *What about all the things that Payce has done to me?* She loved him, but she questioned his love for her. Would anyone else have gone through the things she did to make their love last? He was arrested for prostitution, cheated on her twice, had two children outside of their relationship, and endangered her freedom. Now he had a child support balance of over thirty-five thousand dollars. Elise's words echoed in her mind. *Things happen for a reason. Some things weren't meant to be.*

"God, what am I supposed to do?" she cried out. She needed someone to talk to. She picked up the phone and called the only person she knew who would be honest with her.

An hour later Danyelle sat in Tressie's room.

"What do you think I should do?" Tressie asked.

"Did you pray on it?" Danyelle asked.

"No," Tressie replied.

"Did you look to the Bible for answers?"

"Yes, and I couldn't find anything in there that pertained to Payce and me," Tressie told her.

"That's hard for me to believe. Hand me that Bible please."

Danyelle held a blunt in one hand as she reached for the Bible in the other. She began searching through the Bible.

"What about this—Ephesians 5:25: 'Husbands must love their wives with the same love Christ showed the church. He gave up his life for her.'"

"Payce loves me," Tressie said, defending herself and Payce.

"I didn't say he didn't love you, but to what extent does he love you? Does he love you enough to always put your interests before his? Did he put your interests before his when he picked up that bag full of cocaine in Harrisburg?"

"That was an isolated incident. Danyelle, watch what you're doing. You're burning up the Bible."

Danyelle looked down. She had dropped a few ashes on the pages she was reading from.

"My fault," she wiped away the ashes. "Listen to this. I Corinthians 13:4-5: 'Love is patient and kind. Love is not jealous or boastful or proud or rude. Love does not demand its own way. Love is not irritable, and it keeps no record of when it has been wronged.' Does that describe you and Payce?"

"I think so," Tressie replied.

"Tressie, you can't think, you have got to *know*. We are talking about your future. Do you trust Payce with your future? You know I'm not going to tell you not to be with Payce, because I like him. But if you're thinking about marrying him, you have to be sure he's the one for you. Let's be honest, he has put you through a lot."

"I can't blame him for all the problems we've been having. I did cheat on him with Quinton."

"I wouldn't consider Quinton cheating. Quinton was a test to see if you really loved Payce, and you failed."

"You can't tell me that I don't love Payce just because I made one mistake."

"You have to ask yourself, was Quinton a mistake or were you drawn to him because there was something not quite right in your relationship with Payce? The only reason you and Quinton aren't together right now is because *you* chose to go back to Payce."

Danyelle closed the Bible. "Did Darshon bring over the directions on how to get there?"

"Yeah, they're sitting over there on the desk." She pointed to a sheet of paper. Danyelle went over and glanced at the directions, then placed them back on the desk.

"Take a day or two to sit and pray on it, and if you still feel the need to go to him, go ahead and go. Just call me first and let me know."

Tressie nodded her head okay. Danyelle grabbed her things and left. Once she got into her car, she pulled out her cell phone and made a call.

"Hello, Philadelphia Police Department," a woman answered.

"Yes, I'd like to report the whereabouts of a fugitive on the run," Danyelle informed her.

"Hold, please. I'll connect you to a detective."

Tressie, if you won't remove Payce from your life, then I'll have to do it for you. I just hope that you'll forgive me, Danyelle thought.

Julian watched his plasma flat screen television in the den. Station after station reported the results of his latest drug test. He had tested positive for steroid use.

The NBA was known to perform random drug testing on their players, but this came as a complete surprise to him. On Monday afternoon, the team had just finished practice for the day when the general manager called him into the office. It was then that he learned he had been randomly selected to take an on-the-spot drug test.

Although the league insists they don't know who is going to be selected for drug testing until that day, players were usually warned weeks in advance. One of Julian's teammates later told him that he overheard someone say that Julian's name had been switched with another player's. Suspicion arose in Julian's mind as to why he was singled out for drug testing.

He refilled his glass with Hennessy and stood in front of the television screen. He watched as a reporter interviewed Carlos Torres.

The reporter stuck the microphone in his face and asked, "How do you feel about Julian Pennington's current drug test results?"

"Whatever Julian is going through right now I'm sure he would appreciate the media's cooperation by respecting his privacy," Carlos responded and walked away.

Julian shook his head at the screen. He was glad he had friends like Carlos who didn't judge him.

"Julian?"

He turned around and saw Caitlyn standing in the doorway with a suitcase in her hand.

"Where are you going?" he asked.

"I'm moving back home," she said. "I'm going to go stay with my parents for a few weeks."

"What brought this on?" he brazenly inquired.

"My uncle thought it would be best if I put some distance between us. Not permanently, just until the suspicion of your drug use is straightened out."

He turned his attention back to the television. "You're walking out on me?"

"No!" She ran to him and wrapped her arms around his waist. "I would never walk out on you. We're still going to see each other and if you need me, all you have to do is call." She exhaled. "My uncle is scared that if the press suspects that we're a couple and living together, that they may try to connect your steroid use to the team. He said that the press could say that management coerced your drug use by pressuring you to dominate the court because you were dating the owner's niece. Any negative publicity could affect the entire Sonics organization."

"Caitlyn!" Julian grabbed her hands. "I need you here. Everyone is abandoning me. My family won't return any of my phone calls, I'm suspended from the league, and now you're leaving me!" he shouted. He fell back down on the couch and placed his head in his hands.

"I'm just trying to do what's best for everyone," Caitlyn cried.

"Go!" Julian mumbled. "Go! Leave! I don't want you here. A few nights ago you told me you loved me. Now, at a time in my life when I need you the most, you're going to bail out on me. You never loved me. You loved what I represented. I was a black man with lots of money who could buy you whatever you wanted. That's what you loved."

"That's not true!" she protested. "The only reason I'm leaving is because my family is concerned about me. They thought it would be best if I stayed with them for a while."

"Oh! Now I understand. Your parents are scared that your black boyfriend might lose it from all the drugs he's been using, and hurt their little girl."

"They would never say that."

"They didn't have to say it, because that's what they were thinking. I wonder how they would react if they found out that their baby girl forged a doctor's signature to get me that prescription for steroids."

"Julian, I'm scared!" Caitlyn screamed. "I'm sorry I ever convinced you to take those pills. I was just trying to help. You put so much importance on being named rookie of the year. I knew how badly you wanted to prove yourself to be the best. I thought maybe the steroids would help, but now I realize that I've made things worse, and I may have ruined your career."

Julian stared at her as she cried. He knew it was over between the two of them. She never loved him. She was in love with what he represented, not who he was as a person.

"Good-bye, Caitlyn."

She looked at him and knew that his good-bye was forever. She slowly rose to her feet and grabbed her suitcase.

After she left, silence filled the room. He was completely alone. Never in his entire life had he ever been alone—his mother, his stepfather, Valencia, someone was always around supporting him. Memories of crowds cheering him on, applause from fans in the stands, the sound of his mother's voice giving him praise, classmates holding banners with his name on them, and Valencia sitting in the bleachers beaming with pride filled his mind. Except now there were no fans, no cheers, and no Valencia. He got up and threw the glass he was holding into the fireplace.

CHAPTER 21

Val, Olivia, Danyelle, and Tressie gathered together at the church for their weekly Bible Study meeting.

Val watched Bryce sleep soundly in her arms. "Look at him. He has no idea of the drama that has surrounded his little life. I still can't believe that Bryant was going to sell his own son."

"And he would have been successful if Mr. Murray hadn't found him in time," Olivia said. "I feel sorry for Taima, though. She still doesn't know where her little girl is. The police are trying to help her locate the couple who adopted her daughter, but it's going to take a while. I'm sure the uncertainty of whether her child is being well cared for is driving her insane." She picked up Bryce's hand and kissed his fingers.

"Do you know how much prison time Bryant could get?" Val asked.

"I'm not sure, but I hope he gets life without parole. The prosecutor's office contacted me and asked if I would testify against Bryant. They let me know that the Greensboro Police did a background check into Bryant's past. This isn't the first time he's done this. They have a list of girls he has pulled this scam on. He not only faces charges here, but also in New Orleans, Phoenix, Minneapolis, and Boston."

"Thank the Lord Bryce was returned safely," Tressie added. "Has anyone heard from Elise? It's getting late. She should have been here by now."

"Oh! I forgot to mention that I heard from her earlier in the week," Olivia replied. "She called to tell me that she wouldn't be able to make it to Bible Study for the next few weeks."

"Did she say why?" Danyelle asked.

"No. The only thing she said was that Miles had been in an accident and was hospitalized."

"Is he all right?" Val asked.

"I'm not sure. She was rather vague over the telephone. She wouldn't answer any of my questions and was in a hurry to hang up with me. She said she'd call me next week. I'm worried about her." Olivia turned to Tressie, "Did you ever find out who tipped the police off to Payce's whereabouts?"

"Livie, maybe you should ask Danyelle that question." Tressie's bitter words shot across the church. "Danyelle, is there something you want to share with the rest of us?" Tressie asked.

Everyone stared at Danyelle, waiting for her to respond to Tressie's question.

"Tressie, I'm sorry," she finally confessed. "I tried to keep quiet, but I could see the pain Payce was causing you. I thought if he went away it would be best for everyone."

"Best for whom? Not me!" she screamed. "Do I look like I'm okay?" Tressie leaned across the church pews and pointed her finger in Danyelle's face, "You had no right to call the cops."

Val leaned over to Olivia, "Aren't you going to do something? It looks like Tressie is going to jump on her at any minute."

"No, they're fine. I think they just need to vent," Olivia said.

"Tressie, you were about to make one of the biggest mistakes of your life. Think about it. You would have not only been married to a fugitive, but you would have been one yourself. You were going to sacrifice your friends, family, and freedom. For what? Payce? Would he have done the same for you?"

"How dare you make decisions about my life? What I do is my business. You had no right to interfere," Tressie roared.

"I said I was sorry," Danyelle replied.

"Sorry is not going to change anything. Payce is locked away for three whole years. He won't speak to me because he thinks I'm the one who sold him out. What am I supposed to do now?" Tressie grabbed her things to leave. "Stay out of my way and out of my life."

The church door slammed shut after Tressie's abrupt exit.

At a loss for words, Olivia spoke up, "Why don't we start the meeting off with prayer? I'll begin."

"Jesus, I praise you and thank you for always acknowledging and answering prayers. When we call out your name, you listen. Lord, touch both Tressie and Danyelle. Touch their hearts that they may listen for your voice in everything they do. Jesus, once again I thank you for bringing my son safely home. Amen."

Danyelle prayed next. "Heavenly Father, I messed up, again. Instead of putting my trust in you, knowing that you are in control of all things, I took matters into my own hands. Now, one of my best friends is angry with me. I ask that you heal her heart from the pain I've caused and that one day she'll be able to forgive me. Amen."

Val was the last person to pray. "Lord, I thank you for providing me with a place to call home. Friends and family are people I have always taken for granted, but not everyone has a family to call their own. I want to thank you for Julian." She paused. "Although we didn't work out the way I had hoped, I know everything was according to your plans. I thank you for carrying me through one of the worst times in my life. I thank you for the memories, the love, and the strength to move on."

Before everyone could say amen in unison, a male's voice spoke up.

"Lord, I want to thank you for placing a woman in my life who loved me unconditionally. She loved me when I had nothing and I took that for granted."

Val lifted her head at the sound of Julian's voice. He stared back at her. She was shocked to see him there.

"Lord, I ask that you forgive me for the way I treated her. I was blinded by your blessings of money and prestige. I mistreated your gifts, and now I realize what really matters. Amen."

"Amen," everyone said in unison.

A surprised Olivia stood up to give him a hug. "Welcome home, stranger. We weren't aware that you were flying in. When did you get here?"

"I flew in yesterday." He spoke to Olivia, but his eyes never left Val. "I needed to see your cousin. I knew she'd be here. I've been calling you at home," he said to Val.

"I got the messages. We said all we needed to say to each other in Seattle."

"Can you just hear me out?" he pleaded. "I traveled all the way across the country to apologize to you. I've admitted that I was wrong in front of all these people. What more do you want from me?" he cried.

"How about the truth? Don't act like the only reason you came home is because of me." She snapped her neck and raised her voice. "Everyone here knows what's going on. It's all over the news. You tested positive for steroids. You've been suspended from the league for the rest of the season. Julian, how could you do something so stupid?"

"It was the pressure. Everyone expected me to excel, so I had to do something to help me compete." He tried to justify his actions.

"Were you taking steroids when I was out there?" she asked.

He nodded.

"And you never said anything to me? We used to tell each other everything. What happened?"

"I don't know," he replied solemnly. "My whole

world just started spinning out of control. I was scared."

"So you chose Caitlyn's arms to run to? Was I not there for you?"

"No, this is entirely my fault. That's why I'm here. I want us to try again," he begged.

Torn between her love for Julian and his betrayal, she didn't know what to do. "Where's Caitlyn?" she asked.

"She left me as soon as the media got word of my steroid use. She said her uncle didn't think it would look good for his niece to be dating a ball player who uses drugs."

Hostility drove her words, "So that's why you're here. She left you, so I'm supposed to take you back."

"Valencia, I love you. You know you are the only person I've ever loved." Remorse filled his words.

"Where was the love in Seattle?" she screamed. Calming herself down, she chose her next words carefully. "I'm sorry, but everyone has choices to make in life and you chose Caitlyn. You allowed another woman and sex to come between what we shared." She pulled her engagement ring off her finger and handed it back to him. "I don't want it and I don't want you."

Silence filled the room and a defeated Julian hung his head down low. Tears welled up in his eyes. He stuck the ring in his pocket and turned to leave.

"Julian, wait a minute." Olivia stopped him. "Val, can I speak to you for a moment outside?" She grabbed Val's hand and pulled her out into the church vestibule.

Once they were alone, Olivia motioned for Val to sit down on a nearby bench. "Val, I'm not trying to get in your business like Danyelle did with Tressie, but maybe you should think about what you're doing?"

"What I'm doing?" she screamed. "What about what he did to me?"

"I'm aware of everything that happened between the two of you, but did you ever think he could really be sorry?"

"Olivia, I don't believe you're going to defend him."

"What he did was wrong, but he deserves a second chance. We all make mistakes; none of us are perfect. You can see he's been beating himself up over what happened. The man apologized."

"His apology is not enough," Val replied.

"Val, the boy is being punished. He's lost basketball, the respect of his friends, family and fans, and now you. Don't you think he's suffered enough?"

Val knew Olivia was right, but she didn't want to admit it.

"You think I should forgive him?" Val asked.

Olivia nodded her head. "Val, think about it. We do things that are unpleasing to God everyday, and after we've fallen on our faces and realized that we were wrong, we drop to our knees and ask for repentance. God readily accepts us back into his loving arms each and every time. So if God can forgive, why can't you? Julian is only human; he is prone to make mistakes. The good thing is that he's realized his mistakes."

"Livie, I'm scared."

"I know, honey, but that's a part of life. Don't

think you won't have to endure heartaches just because you found true love."

"When did you get so wise?" Val asked. "I used to be the one who gave advice. This is a switch, you telling me what's best."

"I guess my experience with Bryant and Bryce made me a stronger person spiritually," she replied. "Are you ready to go back inside?" Olivia asked.

They entered back into the church just as Danyelle was wrapping up the saga involving Payce and Tressie. ". . . now Payce is in jail and Tressie is mad at me."

"I sure have missed a lot." Julian replied.

Val sat down next to Julian and turned toward him. "Julian, you hurt me a lot. The trust I had in you is gone, but I'm willing to try again." A smile spread across his face. "Don't think it's going to be easy. It's going to be a long time before I totally trust you again."

"I'll do whatever I have to."

"I should let you know. I'm not going back to Seattle. I'm staying right here and finishing out my education, so if you want to be with me, you have to move back to Philly."

He nodded his head in agreement. "What about the ring?" he asked.

"You keep it. When the time is right, you can slip it back on my finger."

Tressie was pleasantly surprised as she walked into the prison gymnasium. The brightly colored walls and friendly atmosphere was not what she was expecting.

For a few hours every day the prison's gymnasium was turned into visiting hall. Here is where inmates got a chance to spend an hour or two with loved ones.

Tressie sat and patiently waited for Payce. She watched as other visitors—mostly women—entered the prison with their children. Women carrying babies and toddlers seated themselves around her, and it wasn't long before the visiting hall was full of people. She noticed a bunch of guys being escorted into the visiting hall by an armed guard.

Out of nowhere, Payce came and sat down in front of her. Her eyes danced with joy; it had been weeks since she had last seen him.

"Hello, beautiful! Did you miss me?" He leaned forward and kissed her on the cheek.

"Missed you I have," she replied. "I thought you were still mad at me."

He moved over to the chair next to hers and grabbed her hand. "At first I was mad, but after I spoke with Darshon, he told me what happened."

"I'm sorry. I should have never trusted Danyelle."

"It wasn't your fault. Danyelle was only trying to look out for you."

"That's no excuse. I'm still not speaking to her."

"Don't be angry with her. Perhaps what she did was for the best."

Tressie was surprised to hear him say that. She was sure he would have been just as mad as she was.

"When I called and asked you to run away with me I was being selfish and thinking of only myself. What kind of life would that have been for you? You deserve better than that. Being here has

helped me to realize I was wrong. Last night, I recognized that this was all God's plan and it worked
out just the way he planned. God has been trying
to get my attention for a long time, and I would
never stop to answer his call. Now that I'm here I
have to acknowledge him. I'm here for a reason."
He continued, "Tressie, I'm finally getting my life
together, and there is nothing here to stop me. I
have no distractions. I've enrolled in college, and
by the time I'm released I'll be ready to be a pro-
ductive part of society." He beamed with pride.

Tressie flashed a phony smile.

"What's wrong?" He knew her well enough to
know that her smile was not genuine.

"What about us?" Her heart pounded in her
chest, scared of what his answer would be.

He knew when Darshon told him Tressie was
coming to visit she was going to ask about their future together. He loved this girl more than he
loved himself. Despite the many times he'd hurt
her in the past, her happiness was important to
him.

He was up half the night trying to decide if they
should continue their relationship with him being
behind bars or go their separate ways. His heart
told him to hold on tight and never let her go, but
his conscience told him that it wouldn't be fair to
her. She was far too beautiful to ask to wait for
him.

He softly touched her face. "I want to tell you to
wait for me, but I can't. I love you too much to ask
you to put your life on hold. I wasn't lying when I
told you that I want what's best for you. You are
beautiful, smart, and deserve the best. I'm not

going to hold you back. As much as it hurt me the last time we were together and I told you to move on, I'm going to tell you again. Go ahead and live your life. As you can see," he looked around. "I'm not going anywhere. Our paths will cross again."

Her heart ached; she didn't want to go on without him. She wished he wasn't locked up so they could be together. "Three years is a long time." Tressie sniffled.

"I know, but it isn't forever."

"I love you," she told him and hugged him tightly.

An hour later, Payce stood at the far end of the gymnasium where a group of inmates were in line waiting for a prison guard to escort them back to their cells. Payce turned around one last time and waved good-bye to Tressie.

An inmate standing behind Payce looked up and recognized Tressie. He couldn't believe his eyes. She was here. He had been thinking about her for years. He wondered what she was doing here. He saw her waving to Payce. He didn't know who Payce was, but he did know that Payce was the new kid on the block. He had to find out what his relationship was to Tressie.

The stranger walked up to Payce to introduce himself. "Hey man, what's up? I don't believe we've met. My name is Jabril."

Tressie, Val, Danyelle, Olivia, and the baby all sat in church and listened to the choir finish their first hymn.

Mrs. Simms stood up before the congregation. "The time has come for us to bring our burdens to the Lord. If there is anyone here who has committed a sin that has put a burden on his or her heart, I encourage you to come forward. Maybe you said something nasty or mean to a coworker or even someone in your household. Perhaps you did something that you now regret. It could have been something you did last year and the Holy Spirit has laid it on your heart to ask for forgiveness. Now is the time to repent."

Everyone remained seated. "Come on, church. It's hard for me to believe that no one has sinned, for the Bible says, 'For all have sinned and come short of the glory of God.'"

Everyone in the congregation still remained seated until Elise walked in through the church doors and up to the front of the church.

Danyelle leaned over to Olivia and whispered. "I have a feeling there's going to be some drama in the church this morning."

"Bless you, Sister Elise. Tell us what is plaguing your heart," Mrs. Simms encouraged her.

"I came up here not to confess my sins to the church and not to ask the church for their forgiveness. I'm here because I love the Lord."

"Amen," the congregation replied.

"I am a sinner, but Jesus saved me from sin. That's why he died on the cross. So the things that I did wrong in the past, present, or future will be forgiven and not held against me." She took a deep breath. "I made excuses for the church when it wanted to exploit other people's sins and not confess its own. The church is composed of sinners. There is not one without sin!" she yelled into the congregation. "We have no right to label others as sinners and not look at our own flaws." She looked over toward Olivia. "Livie, I'm sorry. I'm sorry if we hurt you in any way." Olivia nodded her head.

Mrs. Simms walked up to Elise and whispered in her ear, "Elise, maybe you should sit down now."

"No, I'm not finished," Elise replied. "I need to repent. I'm not going to disclose the details of what has been going on in my life, but I will tell you that the consequences from my sins will last a lifetime."

The church fell silent.

"I'm leaving the church. From now on anything I do will not be judged by you, but by God." Elise walked out the church doors and didn't turn back.

A buzz filled the church. Whispers ran rampant throughout the sanctuary. Reverend Kane called for the church's attention.

"Can I have everyone's attention? I also have an announcement to make. Elise was right; we should acknowledge our own sins before we ask anyone else to acknowledge theirs. I have a sin of my own that I'd like to confess. I don't think I would have ever been able to face who I really am without the help of a good friend who isn't here right now, but he's here in spirit."

"I told you there was going to be drama up in here today," Danyelle whispered to Olivia again.

Reverend Kane continued, "I'd like to confess before God and the church that I am a lesbian."

There were no amens shouted through the church. No one caught the Holy Spirit. The only sound came from baby Bryce, trying to make his presence known. A few of the older members looked at the reverend strangely.

"I am sexually attracted to women," she clarified so everyone understood. "I realize that the church sees this as a sin, but that hasn't stopped the Lord from loving me."

She held out her left hand. Mrs. Simms walked over and gripped her hand tightly. "And this is my lover. Mrs. Simms and I have been in a relationship for months."

Reverend Simms ran over to them. "Is this true?" he asked his wife.

Mrs. Simms held her head high. "Yes, it is."

"Shall we?" Reverend Kane asked Mrs. Simms and the two quietly walked around Reverend Simms and out the church doors.